TH̶ ̶ᴜRATOR

SUITCASE GIRL TRILOGY BOOK TWO (ABBY KANE FBI THRILLER #8)

TY HUTCHINSON

For my Doppelgänger

CHAPTER ONE

A MAN STOOD SLIGHTLY HUNCHED over and leaning against the trunk of a pine tree, uncertain of his next step. With each exhale, his breaths billowed in smoky plumes across his chattering teeth. His eyes shifted erratically from side to side.

Where am I?

He had just taken two steps away from the security of the tree, his bare feet sinking into mossy dirt, when the crack of a branch jerked his head to the left.

What was that?

He squinted and scanned the misty woods, carefully moving forward and nearly tripping over his own feet at the sudden appearance of a mountain bike flying right past him. It landed a few feet away, its back wheel kicking up dirt.

"The crazies are out early today," the rider spouted off as he pedaled hard, disappearing into the maze of trees as quickly as he had appeared.

The man looked down at himself. A tattered hospital gown hung from his bony frame. He gripped it and tugged. A rip formed near the shoulder. He grabbed the thin fabric with his other hand and yanked. The gown fell away from him, exposing his pale nakedness.

Aside from his breathing, the woods were eerily quiet. There were no birds singing or breezes rustling the tree branches. He walked in the direction the mountain biker had disappeared.

Am I dreaming? Maybe I am. God, I hope so.

The situation was surreal; it had to be. He hoped it was, for the last thing he remembered was puffing on a cigar and sipping scotch. There was a warm glow of a fireplace, and he wasn't alone. Others were gathered around him. It felt like he knew them, but he couldn't be sure. His memory was nothing more than spotty imagery.

He struggled to find clarity, something that could begin to explain the oddness of his predicament. The harder he tried to recall, the more confused he became. Random people and places popped into his head, but they meant nothing. He couldn't remember his name or what he did for a living.

Do I even work?

He continued down the side of the mountain, his body warming from the physical movement. Perspiration appeared, creating a slickness across his skin.

Picking up speed, he tripped over an exposed tree root, nearly falling flat on his face. In fact, his balance seemed off kilter ever since... well, he couldn't remember. A filmy substance in his eyes marred his vision, which he couldn't clear no matter how much he blinked or wiped at them. But he remained focused as best he could and pushed forward. All he wanted was to go home, wherever that was, and climb into bed.

A clearing in the trees up ahead revealed the tops of buildings—a skyline with a large bay behind it.

I hope this is where I live.

It seemed slightly familiar to his gut. But if he did live in this city, he had no clue as to where.

I'll just ask for help. Someone will offer it.

He kept his pace, skirting trees and bushes along the way. The sounds of urbanization began to fill the quiet void: a blaring horn, a barking dog, the engine of a large vehicle shifting gears. With each step, the city revealed more and more of itself.

Almost there, keep going.

Just as he'd walked out of the woods and onto a sidewalk, a loud shriek filled his ears.

He looked in that direction and spotted a woman pulling her child close to her as she backed away, while a couple carrying coffees stopped in their tracks. They all had horrified expressions on their faces.

Wait—what's wrong?

Vehicles slowed as drivers and passengers pointed and stared.

Why won't anyone help me? Can't they see that I'm not well?

A man walking his dog shouted at him. "Back off, buddy!"

What's wrong with these people? I'm just asking for help.

A siren could be heard, coming closer.

Finally, someone heard me.

A police vehicle screeched to a stop along the curb. The doors flew open, and two officers exited with weapons drawn. "Stop right there."

Is that really necessary? I just need help.

One of them advanced on him. "Get down on your knees now, or I'm tasing you."

Tase me?

"I'm not telling you again. Get down now!"

Before the man could comprehend the situation, an intense

explosion of pain ripped throughout his body, causing him to collapse onto the sidewalk. His body clenched into a withering ball, and his eyes rolled back into his head as he struggled to breathe.

I just need help.

CHAPTER TWO

EVER SINCE WALTER CHAN had been shot dead at the front door of my home, I had to endure being poked, prodded, and interrogated while recovering from a gunshot wound. It wasn't life threatening; Walter's gun had discharged, and the bullet had clipped my neck. A bloody mess was really what it turned out to be. The stitches fell out at the start of week three with the help of my scratching.

My stay at the government facility, the purpose of which I still don't fully understand, had me feeling sequestered. They kept me locked up and under observation for three weeks.

In the beginning, the doctors, as they referred to themselves, were the only human contact I had. Eventually, monitored phone calls with my family were allowed, but other than that, communication with the outside world was nonexistent. The room they kept me in didn't have a television or a radio. Thankfully they did furnish me with a selection of magazines: *Good Housekeeping, Reader's Digest*, and *National Geographic*. It was dismal, but after a few days of reading the back of the shampoo bottle, anything else was a warm welcome.

I spent most of my time in my room sleeping, which probably made up for every early rise or bad night's sleep I'd experienced that year. I actually didn't mind that part.

At some point during almost every day, I had to debrief another person I didn't know. Either no one got the memos, or they didn't believe me and wanted to see if my story would change. It never did.

The conversations were always the same.

I spoke.

They listened.

I asked questions.

They ignored them.

They always wanted a full account of everything that had happened from the moment we discovered Xiaolian, formerly known as the Suitcase Girl, outside our offices, to the fatal shooting of Walter Chan. There was no reason for me to withhold information. They never spoke of their intentions, nor did they ever talk about Xiaolian. I had absolutely no idea where she was or what had happened to her.

It was hard to talk about the shooting of Walter and not knowing what had happened to my son, Ryan, afterward. I had to assume the Bureau, the facility, and God only knew who else, had questioned him extensively as well—probably my entire family had endured it too. *That's me, sucking as a mom.*

After a week without answers and me running my mouth, they allowed a phone call from my partner, Kyle Kang. He assured me that Ryan, my daughter Lucy, and my mother-in-law Po Po were okay and that he was staying at the house. "Don't worry. I have everything covered here," he assured me. The following day I was allowed a phone call with the family.

Kang also clued me in on Xiaolian. She was being held at the same facility. He had seen her when he visited with Agents Reilly and House. The doctor monitoring her would not specify how long she would remain there.

Two weeks into my experience of being a detainee, the family surprised me with a visit for two whole hours. Kang had brought them. I felt certain my increasing lack of cooperation had prompted the goodwill gesture. Seeing them in person made all the difference. It provided me with renewed strength.

Freedom. It's hard to appreciate it until it's taken away.

At the end of three-weeks, I was discharged, free to go home.

That first morning back home, Ryan decided to join me on my run. This surprised me, since he had only once before gone running with me and, that one time, I'd forced him.

Ryan and I stood at the end of the Aquatic Park Pier, staring out over the calm waters of the bay. Scattered clouds marked the skies, but the sun still had a firm presence. The pier was a concrete pathway that jutted outward, forming a half loop around the aquatic park, popular for open-water swimming. It was part of the city's Maritime National Park.

I breathed deeply, filling my lungs with that familiar crisp air. I held it for a moment, my eyes closed and my ears listening to the seagulls squawking, before exhaling slowly.

"How are you feeling?" I asked him.

"I like this. It's fun. Where to next?"

"We'll head back up toward Ghirardelli Square and make our way to Columbus and then straight home from there. Sound okay?"

"Yup."

I was happy to have the company. The incident at the house seemed to have brought us closer, if I had to find something positive to say about it. Don't get me wrong; I wish it hadn't happened at all.

Both Ryan and Lucy had been talking to a psychiatrist. So far, the incident didn't seem to have had any long-term negative impacts on either of them. The doctor said Ryan was mature for his age. Sure, he'd had nightmares the first few nights but none since. I'd told him at least a dozen times that he could talk to me about anything. I wanted him to know I was there for him.

I also felt extremely thankful that, after all his pestering about wanting to learn more about my service weapon, I'd relented. His education had started with learning how to disassemble and assemble the handgun, as well as clean it. Once he could do all of that without looking, or hesitating, and in a timely manner, I took him to a small gun range in Alameda and taught him how to shoot. Of course, I had a strict rule in relation to all of this—he was not to touch the firearm unless I asked him to. He'd ignored the rule that day, thankfully.

As for Lucy, she had apparently blocked out the incident from her memory. She didn't remember a thing. She might later in life, but currently it was too early to tell.

To be honest, I worried more about her than I did her brother. Ryan had always been levelheaded and responsible. He was pragmatic, like his father. A realist. Lucy, on the other hand, was the complete opposite. She was the daydreaming, freethinking, trusting, open-minded spark of our family. And I loved that about her.

Ryan and I ran the rest of the way home with just one stop— a detour to Fanelli's Deli. It had been a while since I'd eaten their cannolis. I planned to pick up two boxes—one for the house and one for the office. When we arrived, Salametti, Finocchiona, and Sopressata—Sala, Fino, and Sata, for short—greeted us. They were the three homeless dogs that lived outside the deli and were cared for by the residents of the neighborhood. I loved Fino's crooked tail.

Back at the house Po Po had just finished making breakfast

—silver dollar pancakes.

"Just in time," Ryan said. "I'll shower really quick and be back down, okay, Po Po?"

"I got cannolis," I said, placing the box on the dining room table. Even Po Po couldn't resist them; a slight smile appeared on her face.

On the way up to my room, I bumped into Lucy on the stairs and gave her a kiss on her head.

"Eww, you're sweaty," she said, backing away.

"Good morning to you too."

Once inside my bedroom, I stripped off my clothes and then gently peeled the gauze off of my neck. I moved in front of the mirror above the bathroom sink and tilted my head to the side for a better look. *I'll end up with another scar.* I grabbed my hair and pulled it around my neck, hiding the wound. *I guess I have a reason to keep my hair long.* I shrugged off the thought and stepped into the shower.

As warm water poured over my body from a rain shower-head, I couldn't help but think if I was taking all this too lightly. I had a tendency to do that. Deflecting was definitely a coping mechanism for me. I'd convince myself that it was part of the job, or that it was an anomaly, or my favorite, "I've had worse happen to me."

The truth of the matter was, this really was the worst thing that had happened to me as a result of my job. And it didn't affect just me; it affected everyone I cared about. An experience like that shouldn't be taken lightly. Perhaps the universe was tapping me on the shoulder to remind me that I wasn't invincible, that I could lose my turn in the game of life. Or worse, cause someone I cared about deeply to lose their spin.

But anytime something similar had happened in the past, I would just swear to be more careful or change my ways, but I never did. And I hated that about myself.

CHAPTER THREE

When I returned downstairs, I found Kang and the family sitting at the table enjoying a healthy helping of breakfast. When he spotted me, he had just taken a bite from his cannoli, so he bounced his eyebrows twice.

"How much weight have you gained while living here?" I asked as I sat in the empty chair next to him.

He shrugged. "You know me. I'm like you. Nothing sticks. I'll miss staying here for sure." He ate another mouthful. "How was your run?"

"Invigorating."

"How's the neck?"

"It's fine. The run didn't seem to bother it."

He stared at the fresh bandaging for a moment and then continued eating. "Are you heading into the office today?"

"I think so."

"Kang and Kane, back in action," Ryan said as he chewed on a slice of bacon.

Kang pointed his fork at Ryan. "Now that's the positive talk we need to hear."

"I'm positive 'Kane' comes before 'Kang,' alphabetically," I chimed in.

"I know that," Ryan said, "but Uncle Kyle said you two agreed it sounded better to say 'Kang and Kane.'" The kids called my partner "Uncle Kyle," though there was no relation there.

"Oh, is that what he told you?" I looked at my partner in crime. "How about we lop off the last two letters of each name and call that suggestion exactly what it is. Ka-ka."

Lucy erupted in laughter. "You said ka-ka."

After we gave Ryan and Lucy a lift to school, Kang drove us to the office. On the way I got a call from my supervisor, Special Agent in Charge Scott Reilly. Our presence was requested back at the facility.

"What? Why? I just left that place."

"Apparently, they want you to meet with Xiaolian."

"Oh, *now* they think of it. The entire time they kept me there, it didn't dawn on them? Idiots. I told them I had a rapport with her. I even asked them nicely, but did they listen? Nooooooo. In fact they wouldn't even admit they were detaining her there."

"Yeah, Abby, I'm sure your request to help was convincing."

"What's that supposed to mean?"

"It means they're accepting your help now."

This visit would mark my first time seeing Xiaolian since before she had gone missing from my home.

For reasons that weren't explained, no one would tell me anything about Xiaolian. They kept me completely in the dark. Even Reilly couldn't give me an answer. Not because he didn't want to, but because he had also been cut off.

"They know we're coming, right?" I asked Reilly.

"I just got off the phone with Gerald Watkins, the director

there. He's the one who called with the request. Did you meet him while you were there?"

"No. Did he elaborate on why he suddenly needs me to speak with Xiaolian?"

"Maybe they're not getting anywhere. Seems like you're the only one who might be able to break through."

"I must have told them that a million times." I could feel my cheeks becoming flushed. I didn't need to be taking it out on Reilly. I knew we were on the same side, but I had to vent.

"I'm aware they didn't treat you with the respect you deserve, but I'm asking that you play nice when you get there."

Sometimes the government can be the most asinine person in the room. During the drive, I stared out the window at the passing scenery. Most of my thoughts were about Xiaolian. I had to assume she was scared and had retreated back into her shell.

When we reached the facility, there was a mix-up with security at the entrance gates. Apparently we hadn't been cleared to enter. *Watkins, you idiot.* A couple of calls later and we were allowed onto the property.

"What's so secretive about this place that the FBI can't even access it?" I asked Kang.

"Beats me."

"It's days like this I feel like shooting someone."

Kang parked the SUV in one of the guest parking stalls outside the main building, and we headed inside.

A uniformed guard manned a reception desk just inside the doors. Unbelievably, we encountered the same clearance problem. A few calls later and we were told to have a seat.

The waiting room was comprised of a few chairs lined up against a wall. There was nothing to read, but there was a water dispenser. The walls were painted beige and decorated with a photo of the president and California's governor. The area was clean; it just looked drab and depressing.

"This place is like a ghost town," I whispered to Kang. We hadn't seen a single soul walk through the waiting area, nor had anyone entered or left the building.

"I don't think they get a lot of visitors here. In fact, I didn't notice a lot of people aside from the posted guards. What about you?"

"The only people I saw were the 'doctors,'" I said as I made air quotes. "Besides nursing certain individuals back to health and keeping others under observation, I wonder what else they do here."

"My guess is anything the government wants to keep under wraps."

"You think this is a black site?"

Kang shrugged. "What else could it be?"

Before I could respond, the double doors near the reception desk opened, and a man wearing a navy-blue suit appeared.

"Come on," he said, with a wave of his hand as he held the doors open.

As I approached, he extended his hand. "Agent Kane, I'm Gerald Watkins, the director here. I believe this is our first meeting. Agent Kang and I met earlier."

I took his hand and gave it a firm shake. "Pleasure."

That was the extent of his welcome. He led us down a white-walled corridor dotted with a number of gray doors equipped with security-card access panels. Other than a double-digit number followed by a letter on a plaque, nothing indicated what might be on the other side of the doors. Watkins acted as if they didn't exist.

Our shoes click-clacked on the floor as we followed him. He kept quiet. Kang and I didn't bother with questions. We passed through a number of double doors that required a swipe of his key card until we reached a corridor lined with observation rooms, an area I recognized. We entered the very first door, which was simply an office. Inside, Dr. Julian Yates, who'd treated me during my stay there, sat behind his desk.

"Agent Kane. I'm glad to see you up and moving," he said as he made his way around his desk. He offered his hand, and I shook it. "Agent Kang, always a pleasure."

Watkins exited the room and closed the door behind him without saying a word.

"What's his problem?" I asked.

"Don't let him bother you. Sit, sit," he said, pointing at the two chairs in front of his desk. "Before I take you to meet with Xiaolian, I wanted to talk to you both about what's happening here."

Finally some transparency. I crossed a leg over the other. "We appreciate that."

"First off, let me say she's nothing like I've seen before. And I mean that literally. I'm aware of three-parent babies... are you two familiar with it?"

We nodded. "More or less," I said.

"Let me just review quickly. Three-parent babies are the result of a procedure that incorporates DNA from three individuals. Why would the parents want their baby to have DNA from another person? Say one parent has a genetic mutation for a particular disease; introducing the third gene as a dominant gene will prevent the genetic mutation from presenting itself in the child."

"I can see how people, at least the parents in this situation, could see this as a positive," I said.

"Yes, that's what's exciting about it. Unfortunately, continuing to develop this technique will, as it always does with science, lead to other discoveries and uses. Such as in Xiaolian's case. She is the first of her kind, apparently. During the last three weeks, I've done extensive research, and no one has published documentation suggesting that they've achieved a result like Xiaolian's. It's unprecedented. It's like the parents were used as hosts. I don't know how it was achieved exactly, but I'm hoping to find out with more research. Whoever is behind this managed to tinker with the process so that they could control how much of each parent existed in the nucleus before it started dividing into an early-stage embryo."

"So whoever did this purposely chose to make this baby seventy-five percent me, or whatever the percentage is, and the rest divided between the other two people?"

Yates nodded. "And that's why this research is banned in many countries. The scientific community is smart enough to see the potential of a process, even if it has not yet been realized. However, not every country or doctor will recognize this ban and adhere to it."

"What are your theories on why someone would do this—I'm talking specifically about Xiaolian's case—use my DNA without my knowledge?"

"I can't be one hundred percent sure of this, but if I had to theorize, I would say the reasoning is that they wanted to recreate someone *like* you without exactly creating *you*. I'm guessing the parents weren't really parents but most likely paid volunteers who acted as hosts. At least I'd like to think they volunteered. Of course, you, apparently, did not have that option—to volunteer."

Kang and I sat in silence for a few seconds, until Yates asked if there were any more questions on the three-parent technique. My questions weren't about the science, or the how. They were more about the motive behind all of this, which I knew Yates would not have the answer to.

"Shall I move on?"

I nodded.

"A lot of the tests we administered with you, we also did with Xiaolian. We wanted to see how many of your personal traits had really translated over to her. We were surprised to find that the similarities between you two were closer than we'd imagined. The IQ test you took placed you in the 130–140 range."

"Wow, look at you, Miss Brains," Kang said.

"Xiaolian tested in the same range as well. You tested off the charts when it came to problem solving—primarily, deductive reasoning. So did Xiaolian. She's also quick witted and possesses keen observational skills—a little Sherlock Holmes, I'd say. Her ability to pick apart something, step back, question it, and find the obvious answers that others never see is incredible."

"Are you sure?" I pursed my lips as I paused. "It's just that I didn't really notice any of these traits in the time I spent with her. She came across as the complete opposite of what you've said. Shy, meek, quiet—that's what I saw."

"Abby, she also couldn't recall a lot because of the propofol," Kang reminded me.

"That could be it," Yates said. "I'm aware of how she arrived in the States. That's a very traumatic experience for a twelve-year-old, especially being locked up in a suitcase. This most likely affected her personality during the time she spent with you. I think you'll be surprised when you meet Xiaolian today. She has... how shall I say this? She has come out of her shell."

Kang and I glanced at each other, eyebrows raised.

"I'm fully aware that all of what I'm saying can come across as very sci-fi, but I assure you it's not. Science is what's behind Xiaolian. Nothing more. Nothing less. With that said, I suspect she's had training specifically to enhance these natural traits of hers. It's the only way I can explain her abilities at this age."

"Are you saying someone wanted Xiaolian to not only look like Abby but to act like her too?" Kang asked.

I followed up Kang's question with one of my own. "Why on earth would someone want that?"

"Excellent questions. I hope we can answer them one day. Agent Kane, would you consider yourself athletic?"

Kang jumped in, "I can answer that question for her with a resounding 'Yes.'"

"Tell me you're not making this comparison as well," I said, "because I definitely didn't see Xiaolian as athletic."

"Oh? Very interesting." Yates tapped a finger on a pad of paper he had been using to take notes. He stood up. "Follow me. It's time you met with her."

We followed him to the very end of the hall, where he pointed at a closed door. "Agent Kane, Xiaolian is just through that door. Agent Kang, I'd like for you to join me in the observation room."

CHAPTER FOUR

I PUSHED DOWN on the metal handle and slowly opened the door. Before I saw her, a familiar drumming sound filled my ears, telling me exactly what she was up to. Dressed in workout clothes, Xiaolian stood flat-footed in front of a speed bag. Her tiny fists were wrapped with athletic tape, and they alternated in pummeling the hanging bag. Perspiration flew off her arms as she drilled the leather pouch, telling me she had been at it for quite some time.

"Abby, is that you?" she called out without looking back.

They must have told her I was coming.

"It is," I answered. "How are you, Xiaolian?" I closed the door behind me.

She said nothing as she continued her workout.

Lined up along the wall were a treadmill, an elliptical machine, a rack containing free weights, and a heavy bag. In the center of the room was a large, rectangular floor mat. Off to the side of where I stood was a small table with bottled waters neatly lined on top. There were no mirrors on the walls, except for the reflective glass that I assumed had an observation room on the other side of it. I spied a camera in one of the corners of the ceiling.

I took a few steps forward. She still hadn't turned around, not even a glance.

The leather bag hung from an adjustable platform, allowing it to be at the right height for her, in line with her eyes. She stood square in front of it with her feet at equal distance. Both fists were held up in front of her, close to the bag, and moved in a tiny circle.

Right, right, left, left, she attacked. Each hit sent the bag swinging back and forth, creating a cadence of accented and unaccented beats. Her rhythm was spot-on.

"I had no idea you were a boxer."

"There's much you don't know about me."

"Enlighten me."

By then I was standing to the side of her. She looked at me and continued to hit the bag, never missing a beat. She returned her eyes to the bag and gave it a knockout finish. Her chest rose and fell with her rapid breathing. Her face and neck were slick. She grabbed a bottle of water off the floor and gulped. As she did, she signaled with her eyes to the bag.

I was a little taken aback by the new Xiaolian. This wasn't the meek little girl I had known. *Where did this attitude come from?* With that said, I wasn't about to let some little girl show me up.

I stepped up to the bag and adjusted its height. I raised both fists and went to work.

One, two, three.

One, two, three.

One, two, three.

The same cadence that Xiaolian had created earlier rang out.

She shrugged. So I stepped it up and switched to a double punch.

One, one, two, three.

One, one, two, three.

One, one, two, three.

I then switched to a double bounce punch, where my fist hit the bag not only from the front but also from the back. I started with a single fist. Once I had a nice cadence, I added my second fist. This particular drill created a sound much like that of a snare drum roll.

Even though I was focused on the bag, I could sense Xiaolian watching me intensely. A quick glance showed me her wide eyes and slack jaw.

There's more, little grasshopper.

I then alternated between one-fist strikes and two-fists strikes. And finally, to up the ante even more and to make sure that cocky attitude of hers was properly adjusted, I allowed my eyes to settle on her while my fists perfectly connected with the bag.

Yeah, I can do the whole no-look thing too. "It's been a long time since I worked with the speed bag. I forgot how fun and easy it is."

Xiaolian quickly composed herself and shrugged. I delivered a final crushing blow to the bag. Back and forth it swung until the squeaking of the hinge finally stopped.

"There's water on the table if you're thirsty," she said, pointing.

"I need a much tougher workout to build up a thirst," I answered. "But you help yourself to another bottle."

Xiaolian walked over to the mat. On the floor next to it were two sets of boxing gloves. She picked up a pair and slipped them on. Then she kicked the other set over to me.

Dumb move.

I removed my jacket, my Chuck Taylors, and my socks, leaving me in just my jeans and a T-shirt. I slipped on the gloves before stepping on the mat. We circled, neither one of us smiling. Even with my short stature, I still had a height advantage over her, and my reach was longer.

Xiaolian struck first with a jab, looking to define the distance. My head swiveled away with each strike. She moved in closer and continued with the jabs, her confidence building, probably because I had yet to throw a punch.

She delivered a combination, and her left hand caught my chin just as I jerked my head back. A slight smile formed on her face.

———

Kang and Yates stood silently watching from behind the glass partition. The room was mic'd, so they could hear everything that Abby and Xiaolian were saying, which wasn't much. The action spoke louder than words anyway.

"Perhaps I should step in and put a stop to this," Yates said.

Kang grabbed his arm. "Nah, let them go. I know Abby; she'll go easy on the girl."

"I was actually worried about Agent Kane," Yates countered. "I've seen Xiaolian hit the heavy bag. She's had training. I'd hate to see Agent Kane get hurt."

Kang looked at the doctor. "You don't know Abby."

They both watched as Abby and Xiaolian exchanged blows, neither one fully connecting.

"I hope you're right."

No sooner had Yates uttered those words than Xiaolian was lying flat on her back. Abby had connected with a solid left.

"My God, she hit her. She knocked her down. I thought they were playing around."

"I told you—you don't know Abby very well," Kang said. "This has got to stop."

"Xiaolian asked for it. Let them be."

They watched Xiaolian jump back to her feet. A look of determination fell over her face. A few seconds later, she went down again. She knelt on the mat for a moment, shaking the cobwebs from her head. Then she stood back up with raised fists.

Abby proceeded to pick her defenses apart, snapping Xiaolian's head back with stinging jabs.

"Agent Kane looks like she's enjoying this."

"Yup," Kang said cheerfully. He had his hands buried in the pockets of his slacks as he rocked back and forth, heel to toe.

Yates turned to Kang, his brow crinkled. "Don't tell me you are as well. This is absurd."

A high-pitched squeal yanked Yates's attention back to the action inside the room. Xiaolian was down on both knees, holding her gloves up to her face while Abby stood over her.

***

I slipped my gloves off one at time as I looked down at Xiaolian. I could hear her sniffling behind her gloves. Did I feel bad? A little, but I think I hurt her ego more than I did her face.

She parted her gloves enough to look at me. Tears streamed down the sides of her face. "I'm sorry," she said between stuttered breaths. "It's this place." She glanced to the glass partition. "I didn't mean to."

I knelt down, and Xiaolian fell into my arms.

"I know you didn't, sweetie."

I held her tightly until her cries softened. She pulled her head back. Her eyes were a little swollen.

"Are you mad at me?" she asked.

"No, I'm not." I wiped a tear from her face. "But I am concerned about you."

I proceeded to slip her gloves off of her hands. "I've never seen this side of you before."

"I know. I'm lonely here. I want to come home with you. Can I?"

"I'm afraid that's a decision that isn't entirely up to me."

Her eyes fell to the side in disappointment.

"But I will come and visit you as often as I can."

She looked back up at me. "Do you promise?"

"I do. And you should know that I always keep my promises, but I want you to promise me one thing as well."

"What's that?"

"That you will behave yourself while you're here. No more challenging people to boxing matches, okay?"

She giggled. "Okay, deal."

I stood up and grabbed hold of her hand. "I think I will have some water."

She laughed out loud. "I knew you were pretending not to be thirsty earlier."

"You got me."

Over at the table, I unscrewed a bottle for Xiaolian and then did the same for myself.

"What's going to happen to me?" she asked before taking a sip.

I looked her straight in the eyes. "I don't know, but I'm working on finding out. Trust me."

———

The man sat in the front seat of the black sedan as he peered through an SLR camera with a telescopic lens. The shutter let out a percussion of clicks as he snapped pictures of Abby and

Kang exiting the government facility in their vehicle and then driving away. Once they were out of view, he lowered the camera and placed a call on his cell phone.

"They've just left. Still no sign of the girl. Yes, I agree. Start the protocol."

CHAPTER FIVE

Once we were safely in our vehicle and out of range of prying ears and eyes, I asked Kang what he thought.

"It didn't play out exactly as I had imagined it would," he said as he put the vehicle in reverse and backed out of the parking stall.

"You talking about the boxing bit or the attitude change?"

"The attitude."

"It caught me off guard as well."

"You never saw this side of her while she lived with you? Not even a tiny bit?"

"Not in the least. I'm just as dumbfounded as you. Maybe the trauma was worse than we thought."

"Maybe. What did you two discuss after you knocked her to her knees? The mic didn't pick it up."

"She apologized and said the place made her that way. I'm guessing what she really meant is that it made her aggressive, which I understand. I hated being there. Did Yates say anything?"

"He seemed oblivious to her attitude, as if it were normal. I will say one thing: That new personality of hers... I see some of you in there."

"What? Shut up." I batted his comment away.

"I'm not kidding."

"Okay." I folded my arms across my chest. "How so?"

Kang waited to answer, as he had to lower his window and return the car pass to the guard at the entrance. Once we cleared the entrance gate, he spoke. "The way she talks. It just reminds me of you."

"Care to elaborate?"

"You know," he glanced at me, "your mouth. Your attitude. I know this isn't helping, but I can't quite find the right words to convey what I'm thinking right now."

"You're saying I'm cocky?"

A big smile formed on Kang's face. "You saying you're not?"

"Oh, come on. I'm not that bad."

"Don't take this the wrong way, Abby. It's her mannerisms; they resemble yours. She's definitely an alpha like you. Plus the testing, her deductive reasoning. Yates said she's witty and highly observant."

Kang was right. I had also seen the similarity, but I didn't want to admit it to myself. Knowing someone looked exactly like me was plenty enough. Having them think and act the same... well, it was a little creepy.

"She's scared," I said.

"I would be too if I were in her shoes. Did you have a chance to ask the obvious question?"

"You mean whether she can explain why we look exactly alike? No, I didn't. The boxing thing threw me. I think I can dive deeper during our next meeting. We all know the science behind how she's able to look and act like me. What we're missing is the motive. Why would someone create her with my DNA?"

"I actually pressed Yates on that subject. He said he never asked her why she thought she looked like you."

"When she stayed at the house, she mentioned a doctor in her dreams."

"I'm guessing she's talking about Dr. Jian Lee, the guy who took her from your home and then ended up dead at the motel, killed by Walter Chan." Kang briefly looked my way.

"Probably, but I'm wondering if there's more than one. Most likely there's a team of doctors behind this medical miracle." My last words were thick with sarcasm.

"Makes sense. I imagine there's a lot Xiaolian knows that she's not telling us."

"And I bet she's willing to give up that information only if she sees a benefit for herself. I mean, that's what I would do. And given that she's me..."

"She's a smart kid. Hey, you hungry? There's this deli I know of near here with mile-high sandwiches. And they're fantastic."

Kang wasn't kidding about the deli. The place made their own corned beef and pastrami, and it was the real deal. I went for pastrami and corned beef on rye while Kang kept it pure and ordered only pastrami.

We sat at one of the four small tables and ate as we watched the local newscast on a flat-screen television hanging on the wall. The news channel was airing cell-phone footage captured earlier that morning of a naked man handcuffed and being escorted to a police vehicle. He shouted a bunch of stuff that I wasn't really paying attention to, as I was trying to unhinge my jaw, like a python, so I could eat my sandwich.

"San Francisco crazies. They're a dime a dozen," Kang said as he watched the telecast. "Wait a minute... I've heard of this guy. He's a tech genius from Silicon Valley."

"Really?" I mumbled.

"Yeah, he's a known party boy. The work-hard, play-hard type. Supposedly made millions from selling his first company."

The cell-phone footage played on a loop while the newscaster talked. Finally the newscaster stopped talking for a moment, and I could hear the cuffed man say something like, "They did this to me. I'm not responsible for my actions."

"Typical rich. They think they can get away with any type of behavior," Kang said. "And he probably will. His hotshot lawyer will have him home by dinner, and his PR people will spin this so that it's over in a day or so."

We both shook our heads and returned to the really important task at hand. Kang took a massive bite of his sandwich that caused both of his cheeks to pop out like a chipmunk. I squirted more mustard inside my sandwich and then did the same.

CHAPTER SIX

CONNIE SHI STOOD QUIETLY in the frozen-food section of the grocery store, her gaze trained on the selection of frozen waffles. She wore jeans and a floral blouse and had her black hair pulled back into a ponytail. Eyeliner and nude lipstick completed her look.

Blueberry... strawberry... original?

She mulled her frozen waffle options for a bit longer before pulling open the door to the freezer case and grabbing a box of each flavor. One by one she gently tossed them into her shopping cart. She stopped at an open freezer case housing a selection of frozen pizzas on sale. She grabbed two pepperoni and two sausage pizzas and added them to her cart.

"Connie, is that you?" a voice shrilled out.

She spun around to find a woman dressed in yoga attire and sporting bleached-blond hair approaching her.

"I knew it was you," the woman said, pushing her cart alongside Connie's and looking her up and down. "Recognized that fab figure of yours."

"I haven't been to the gym in weeks. I barely fit these jeans," Connie replied with a dismissive gesture. She glanced into the woman's cart and saw a dozen single-serving yogurts. "And what have you been up to?"

"I signed up for these yoga classes at a small studio in Pacific Heights. It's right on Fillmore, near Pine. It opened just two weeks ago. You should come. The ladies there are super nice, and the woman who teaches the classes... she's a doll. Totally helpful and not pushy at all."

Connie nodded, but her eyes were drawn to the woman's chest. "Is that new?" she asked.

"Oh, this?" the woman said, placing her hand on the diamond pendant sitting just above her revealing cleavage. "Just a little something to treat myself. I had a rough two weeks. I swear—my kids are signed up for so many after-school activities, I can barely deal with it all."

"Looks like you spared no expense."

"It's two carats in a platinum setting. I almost did three, but I do have some self-control," she said with a laugh.

"What did your husband say?"

She waved her hand and rolled her eyes. "Roger's so easy. The second he starts to protest, I start blowing him. All is forgotten. Listen, I've got to meet the contractor at the house—we're having the kitchen cabinets redone. Call me about yoga. I promise you'll love it."

She spun her cart around and disappeared into the cereal aisle.

Connie removed her phone from her back pocket and checked the grocery list she made. *Just need a bag of rice, and that should do it.* With her cart piled nearly to the brim with food, she gave it a hard push and headed toward the grain aisle.

After paying for her groceries, the bag boy offered to escort her to her vehicle, a silver Range Rover. He loaded the bags into the back, and she tipped him with a crisp five-dollar bill.

Connie drove out of the parking lot of the grocery store and west on North Point Street. She lived five minutes away, on Alhambra Street. While she was waiting to make a left onto Fillmore Street, her phone chimed, indicating a text message.

She read the text and then returned her phone to her purse. She made her left onto Fillmore but instead of turning right on Alhambra, she continued straight on Fillmore all the way until she reached California. She headed east until she reached Grace Cathedral on Nob Hill. She found parking on the street and then exited her vehicle, leaving her groceries inside.

Connie walked over to Huntington Park, a small park directly in front of the cathedral. She searched for a bench and took a seat. The park wasn't particularly crowded—it was a weekday. There were a few people walking their dogs and a few tourists who had just visited the church. Other than that, Connie had the place to herself.

About ten minutes later, an elderly man dressed in chinos and a checkered button-down approached and sat next to her on the bench with a poodle at the end of the leash he held. She smiled at the man. The dog circled once before lying on the grass, its tongue hanging from the side of its mouth.

The man wore oversized sunglasses and a light-gray beanie. A toothpick poked out from between his lips. He chewed on the sliver of wood, occasionally picking at his teeth while looking at a newspaper.

Connie stared ahead, ignoring his hygiene theatrics. After about fifteen minutes or so, the man stood up and left, with his dog trailing behind him.

Connie waited a few minutes and then glanced over to where he had been sitting; she saw that he had left his newspaper behind. Without hesitation, she picked it up and promptly walked back to her vehicle.

Once inside and sitting in the driver's seat, she peeked between the pages and spotted a manila envelope; she tucked the paper into her purse and turned the key in the ignition. The pleasant smile she'd had on her face all day disappeared. Her jawline tensed, and her eyes narrowed. She shifted into gear and stepped on the gas pedal. The wheels of the vehicle chirped as the car lurched out of its space, nearly clipping the rear bumper of the sedan parked in front of it.

Connie hooked the wheel to the left, and the SUV gripped the asphalt and executed a U-turn. The force sent most of the grocery bags in the back onto their sides. A number of items tumbled out, including a tub of ice cream. It rolled to the rear of the vehicle and settled against the tailgate. Melted ice cream leaked out and pooled onto the carpeting as Connie sped down the street.

CHAPTER SEVEN

We reached the Phillip Burton Federal Building around three in the afternoon—northbound traffic on the 101 Highway had been worse than usual. I had thought of heading straight home, but I figured Reilly deserved an update on our meeting with Xiaolian that day instead of the following morning. There wasn't much to report, as Yates had limited my time with her.

Kang had to visit the restroom, so I took a seat at my desk and waited. From where I sat, I could see Agent Hansen's empty desk; it was still assigned to him, even though he had yet to recover from the shooting incident with Alonzo Chan. He was on medical leave and had not been cleared by the psychiatrist treating him to return to duty. Whether he would ever be cleared was still up in the air. Reilly had made it clear that, until Hansen told him he was done, he would hold that desk for him. We all hoped he'd come back.

Kang had mentioned that he'd visited with Hansen while he recuperated. Hansen's parents were retirees and had flown out from Maryland to look after him. He was an only child, and his closest friend in the Bay Area had been his partner, Agent Pratt, who was killed by Alonzo. It made me happy to hear he had family with him and that his recovery was going well. Kang said he would regain full use of his arm with rehab. He also said they discussed everything but the job, and he never got a read either way on what Hansen's thoughts were about returning to the Bureau if he were cleared.

I couldn't call or visit while on lockdown at the facility, but now that I was out, it was something I wanted to do.

"Hey, you ready?" Kang asked, shaking me out of my thoughts.

We made the walk down the corridor to Reilly's office. He was reading a report and making notes. His office was a familiar sight: a desk piled with folders and papers. His money-tree plant was still alive. It was comforting to me.

"Come in, guys. Have a seat."

We sat.

"How's Xiaolian? Did the fellas down there crack the mystery surrounding her?"

"They did a lot of testing. She's intelligent. She's athletic— someone trained her to box."

"Really?" Reilly sat up and placed the file on his desk. "What's their assessment?"

"I'm not sure they have one yet. They're busy discovering all the things she's capable of. Someone obviously put a lot of effort into her. Why? Well that's still to be determined."

"Kang, what's your take?"

"I'd have to agree with Abby. How she was educated, where she received her training, and why are still unknowns, though we did see another side of her personality-wise."

Reilly raised his eyebrows.

"The Xiaolian we saw today was aggressive and cocky," I said. "She wanted to spar with me."

"Are you serious?"

"I am. Dr. Yates had an early thought. He thinks whoever created her had knowledge of my past and set about developing specific traits that would come naturally to her. Apparently she's a wiz at solving puzzles and riddles."

"Yates called her 'a little Sherlock Holmes,'" Kang added.

"Maybe I should recruit her when she's of age," Reilly said as he shifted in his chair. "Do you think you can rekindle your relationship with her?"

"I think the personality change we saw today was a defensive measure resulting from the poking and prodding and questioning that she's had to undergo. If given time, I'm sure I can penetrate her wall."

Reilly nodded. "I'm glad to hear that. Because it seems whatever took place today was promising enough for them to want you guys to continue engaging with her. Tomorrow morning, you're both to report to Camp Parks. You'll receive a briefing on your roles from here on out."

"Camp Parks?" Kang said. "Isn't that a military installation?"

"It's a training center for the US Army Reserve and other things."

"Why do we need to meet on a military base?" I asked.

"I don't know. I think this is just where the meet-and-greet is scheduled. These orders came down from up top. I'm just here to pass them on. The meeting is at ten o'clock sharp. Don't be late."

"Wait. Who are we meeting with?" I pressed.

"I don't know exactly," Reilly said with a shrug. "I've been informed that the guards at the security gate are expecting both of you and will take it from there."

I'd never left Reilly's office more confused than I was that day. He seemed indifferent regarding the meet at Camp Parks. Was he under strict orders not to say anything? He had to know more than he was letting on—after all, he was the Special Agent in Charge of the San Francisco FBI office. Surely, his ranking offered him the privilege of knowing what was going on.

Or not.

CHAPTER EIGHT

I T WAS NEARLY seven in the evening when the silver Mercedes sedan pulled into the driveway of the two-story Queen Anne Victorian. The lights were on inside, and the sounds of children laughing could be heard. Albert Shi exited his vehicle with a leather shoulder bag in one hand and walked to the front door.

Inside he found his two boys, Colin and Merrick, ages twelve and ten, horsing around in the living room. Colin had his younger brother pinned on his back. He had hooked an arm under Merrick's legs and pulled them up so that his thighs were pressed against his chest.

"Okay, I give. I give. You win," Merrick shouted in between forceful breaths.

"And what else?"

"You're the king of all kings, and I bow to you for all eternity."

"And what else?"

"I pale in comparison to your awesomeness."

Colin was about to ask for more praise when he noticed his dad standing in the doorway. "Hey, Dad, did you just get home?" He released Merrick.

"I did. Now that you guys have established who is king of all kings and who is more awesome, I want you both to wash up for dinner."

Albert watched them as they hurried up the stairs before heading into the kitchen. His wife, Connie, stood in front of the stove, using a wooden spoon to stir something inside a large pot. He placed his bag on the countertop of the kitchen island before wrapping his arms around her midriff. He pressed his lips gently on the side of her neck.

"That feels nice," she said softly.

"And you taste delicious."

He peered over her shoulder and into the pot. "That sauce smells wonderful."

"The boys were craving spaghetti and meatballs."

He slid a hand up, cupped a breast, and squeezed gently.

"The kids," she protested.

"Don't worry, they're upstairs." He continued to fondle her. "Any chance I can have a little sugar before dinner?"

"You'll have to wait." Connie removed his hand from her chest.

"Where's Hailey?" he asked as he placed his hand back on her breast. Hailey, at age eight, was their youngest.

"She's in her room."

Connie turned around and drove a finger in Albert's chest, backing him up just as the three kids appeared. He spun around, clasping his hands and rubbing them vigorously. "Who's hungry?"

Over dinner, Albert drilled all three children about their studies and asked about the homework they were given that day. Anything less than straight A's across the board was unacceptable to him. After they had finished dinner, the children were allowed one hour of playtime, which they could use watching television, playing video games, or whatever else they wanted to do. If they hadn't finished their homework by dinner, then that would take priority.

By nine o'clock, the last of their children, Colin, had gone to his bedroom. He had the latest bedtime. Hailey went to bed first at eight o'clock, followed by Merrick at eight-thirty.

With the kids asleep, Albert retired to his home office. He was sitting at a desk made from reclaimed wood and tapping away on his laptop when Connie appeared. His eyes dropped to the manila envelope she held in her hand.

She closed the door behind her and sat in the chair on the other side of his desk. She placed the sealed envelope on the desk. Albert leaned back in his black leather chair and let out a breath, staring at it for a moment or so before leaning over the side of his executive leather chair and removing a similar envelope from his briefcase. He placed it next to the other envelope. They looked at each other, neither saying a single word.

Albert nodded. "Might as well get on with it."

They opened the envelopes simultaneously.

Connie removed a standard sheet of paper from her envelope. Chinese characters written in pencil covered every square inch of it. She set it down on the desk.

Albert removed a thin piece of plastic from his envelope; it was exactly the same size as Connie's sheet of paper. Holes had been punched through the plastic in no particular order, but they were all of the same size, as if a hole-puncher had been used. He turned the paper around so it faced him and then placed the plastic piece on top of it. The holes revealed only a small number of Chinese characters—an answer key.

He took a moment or so to study them before looking up at his wife, his eyes meeting hers. He watched her chest expand as she drew a breath and held it.

"The time has come," he said softly. "We've been activated."

CHAPTER NINE

THE FOLLOWING MORNING, when walking the kids to school, I noticed Ryan remained a few steps ahead of us, and as we neared the school, he increased the distance. He didn't need an escort, but seeing that Lucy did, it just made sense that the three of us walked together. But I knew what was going on; he didn't want the other kids to think he needed me to walk him to school. I got it. He was older now. It was uncool to have his mom around him all the time. Still, it sucked a little. *They grow up so fast.*

By the time I returned to the house, Kang had already arrived. He was sitting at the dining table, eating and talking with Po Po in Chinese.

"What's got you two so chatty?" I asked as I sat, snagging a piece of bacon off of his plate.

"We were talking about the various types of porcelain fired during the Ming dynasty and how it differs from those fired in the Yuan dynasty," he said dryly. I glanced over at Po Po, and she nodded.

One of Kang's unique traits is his vast knowledge of all things Chinese. Ever since he was a kid, he'd been fascinated with Chinese history and its culture. So when he told me he was discussing pottery with Po Po, I had no real reason to doubt that wasn't the case.

"Really? Sounds fascinating," I said with the same enthusiasm.

"Sure is," Kang said. "There seems to be a disagreement between a few historians on whether some designs in 1368 AD are representative of the Ming dynasty or really holdovers from the Yuan dynasty."

Po Po again nodded in agreement. Both had had a look of seriousness on their face. I had apparently interrupted a weighty conversation.

A beat later, Kang let out a huge belly laugh. "We got you," he said pointing at me. "We got her, didn't we, Po Po?"

I looked over at her, and she had a grin on her face, her shoulders bouncing.

Son of a bitch. "I'll admit it. You had me. I really thought I'd interrupted your chat about pottery."

"Whoo-wee." Kang was still enjoying his laughing fit as tears welled in his eyes.

"All right, Confucius. Calm down. It was funny but not that funny."

But the two continued to enjoy the fruits of their labor for another five minutes. Even after Kang and I climbed into his SUV, he was still chuckling quietly to himself.

"Sheesh, you make it seem like you killed it on the *Tonight Show*."

"It's funny, that's all."

"Only you and my mother-in-law would find something like that hilarious."

Morning traffic had died by the time we hit the road, so our drive to Camp Parks took us only a little more than an hour. Kang slowed the SUV to a stop at the entrance to the base. An

MP dressed in combat fatigues and carrying an M4 carbine rifle exited the small office manning the security gate. He asked for our identification. We handed him our badges, and he went back inside the small booth. A few minutes later he returned with a printed map. He had circled a building on it.

"You're to report here. Just follow the signs," he said. He raised the arm of the barrier gate. The iron gate behind it slid to the side.

Ten minutes later, we exited our vehicle and headed into a beige, non-descript building like the many others we'd passed.

Inside, another man dressed in combat fatigues met us and led us to a small seating area, where he told us to wait. Then he disappeared.

"Any thoughts on what the hell is going on here?" I whispered to Kang.

"Not a clue."

I thought the whole secrecy thing was a bit ridiculous, but I behaved myself. For fifteen minutes, we sat quietly. I stared at the picture of the sitting president hanging on the wall while Kang slouched in his chair and bounced his left leg. The wait felt like a lifetime.

We were both expecting the guard who had escorted us to the seating area to return, but a man neither of us recognized appeared from behind a closed, unmarked door directly across from where we sat. He wasn't wearing a military uniform. He wore gray slacks and a white dress shirt with a blue-and-yellow-striped tie.

"Agent Kane. Agent Kang. Would you please step inside here?"

Kang and I glanced at each other before standing up and walking through the door.

Inside the room were three more men we didn't know. They were sitting spread out around a large, oblong conference table.

There were various file folders and paperwork on the table, along with a few coffee mugs. *No one asked us if we wanted coffee or tea.*

Two of the men were dressed casually, one in khakis and a white polo shirt, the other in gray cargo pants and an untucked blue button-down. The third man was dressed similarly to the one who had called us in. None of them looked military, so I assumed they worked for the Department of Justice in some sort of capacity.

We weren't asked to sit, so we just stood. One of the men— the other one who wore a shirt and tie and was sitting the farthest away—hadn't looked up yet, as he was reading from a file. After a few more minutes of silence, he stopped reading and peered over the top of his reading glasses at us.

"Agent Kane," he said. "You worked your way up to Inspector of Organized Crime and Triad at the Hong Kong Police before moving Stateside and joining the Bureau. In the short time you've been in the federal government's employ, you've risen to the rank of Assistant Special Agent in Charge of the San Francisco FBI office." He paused briefly, clearing his throat. "Agent Kang. You held a decorated career as a homicide detective with SFPD before joining the Bureau a year ago. I've been informed you have considerable knowledge of Chinese history and culture." He shut the file folder and put it down on the table.

No one else said anything. They all just stared at us like we were the main attraction at a carnival freak show. Did he expect a cookie or applause for reading our resume out loud? I kept my mouth shut.

One of the men, the one wearing cargo pants, sipped on a smoothie. After each suck on the straw, he smacked his lips. I wanted to smack that damn cup straight out of his hand.

"Is there a reason why we were asked to drive all the way out here?" I finally asked.

The man sipping on the smoothie smiled. His eyes locked on to mine and never shifted away. He placed the cup on the table, smacking his lips one last time. "Agent Kane, I understand you've developed a unique relationship with a little girl being held in our Mountain View facility."

"You could say that. Her name is Xiaolian, by the way."

The man continued to eyeball me, as if we were the only two in the room. Not once did I see him look at Kang.

"You have two children, Ryan and Lucy."

"Yes. I'm sorry—who are you?"

"I'm the man heading up a special task force."

"Are the other people in this room part of this task force?" I asked.

"Pretend they aren't here."

"Excuse me?"

"Think of our conversation like an email, and I've bcc'd these other people. They're clued in, but you aren't aware of it."

Just then the door to the conference room opened, and a young man, late twenties, entered. The first thing I noticed about him was that he was chewing gum. *Who comes to a meeting chewing gum?* He wore a gray hoodie and jeans and kept his hair cropped tight against his head. He removed the black Oakley shades from his eyes and took a seat. No one said anything or addressed him.

"He's been bcc'd too," Cargo Pants said. "I'd like for both you and Agent Kang to be a part of my special task force. What do you say? Care to have some fun?" He picked up his smoothie and started sucking and smacking again.

I glanced briefly at Kang. "What exactly do you want us to do?" I asked Cargo Pants.

"I need you to keep talking to the girl. Continue to earn her trust."

"That's it?"

He nodded his head as he looked around the table. "Anybody care to add anything?"

No one said a word. *Because, you know... bcc'd.*

"And what do you want me to do with the information I obtain from Xiaolian?"

"Pass it along. Can you do that for us?"

"Pass it to whom?"

Cargo Pants looked at the gum-chewing guy and flashed his plastic smile before addressing my question. "This is Archer. He'll be in contact with you."

I swept my gaze across the room as I let out a breath. "Sure. Anything for the team."

"I knew we could count on you."

The person who'd invited us into the room opened the door and said. "Please step outside."

And just like that, our meeting ended. We didn't know it at the time, so we sat outside for fifteen minutes like a couple of dummies thinking someone would come and brief us on our next steps or escort us out or *something*. Nope.

Once back inside our vehicle and out of earshot of anyone but each other, we let loose.

"What the hell just happened?" I blurted out.

"Strangest meeting I've ever had. Some secret crap taking place in there, if you ask me," Kang said. "I don't think they're with the DOJ. Most likely the State Department."

"Why the secrecy though? And the guy wearing a hoodie—what was his deal?"

"I think he was a spook," Kang said as he started the engine.

"CIA? Really? I thought they weren't allowed to operate inside the United States."

"They aren't. But I'm guessing there's one good reason why the CIA would be involved."

I raised my eyebrows. "Oh? What's that?"

"They probably think Xiaolian is a spy."

Ryan stood next to the boy and gave him instructions on how to defend a throw-down. He moved slowly through the motions as he spoke. The other boy nodded his head as he listened.

"Okay, let's try it," Ryan said.

Ryan grabbed the other boy's judogi, slipped his left leg in front of the boy, and pulled forward, but the boy countered with the defensive move Ryan had just taught him.

"You got it!" Ryan shouted. "Good job. Just keep practicing so you can do the move instinctively."

"Thanks for the help, Ryan."

"Colin, your father is here," Master Wen called out from the front of the dojo.

Ryan helped Colin gather his gear. "Tomorrow we can work on another favorite move of mine."

"Cool. I can't wait."

"How was your first day?" Colin's father asked.

"It was awesome. I like this place."

"Who's your friend?"

"This is Ryan. He's teaching me a few defensive moves."

The man stuck his hand out and smiled. "Nice to meet you, Ryan. My name is Albert Shi."

CHAPTER TEN

THAT NIGHT AT DINNER, conversation started from the get-go
—an unusual thing in our family. We tend to hold our tongues
and focus on satisfying our bellies first, at least for a few
minutes. But Ryan had a lot to talk about, as he was really
enjoying helping Master Wen with the other kids.

"And today we had a new kid sign up, and Master Wen
assigned him to me."

"'Assigned'?" I asked.

"Yeah. There are four of us who help newbies at the dojo.
We show them where things are and how things work. We also
mentor them a little until they are comfortable."

"Well, that sounds like a big responsibility."

"Yeah, and it's cool too. I was assigned to Colin Shi. He's
one-year older but not as advanced. I also met his Dad. He's a
dentist."

"Ewww, I hate dentists," Lucy whined. "They only exist to
cause me pain."

"Well, if you brushed and flossed your teeth like I keep
telling you to, maybe your visits would be much more enjoy-
able," I said.

"Impossible. I could have a mouthful of perfection, and the dentist would still find something wrong," she said before shoving a forkful of noodles into her mouth.

"Speaking of dentists," I said, "that reminds me: I need to schedule cleanings for both of you."

"I'll take a pass this time," Lucy said. "We can save the money for something else, like another family vacation."

"Nice try."

"Speaking of saving money for something else, have you given my proposal any thought?" Lucy lowered her fork. "My birthday is coming up real fast"

"What proposal?" Ryan asked.

"Mommy is considering giving me pierced earrings for my birthday—isn't that right?"

With all that had happened in recent weeks, I had totally forgotten about that discussion. Her birthday had slipped my mind, but that was exactly why I had an alarm on my calendar set to go off ten days beforehand. *I'm not the only mother who needs to set reminders for her kids' birthdays, right?*

"I'm still considering," I said.

"Well, don't be shy to ask me for a consolation," she said.

"It's *consultation*," I corrected her.

Ryan jumped in with, "Aren't you a little too young to get your ears pierced?"

"I'm a lot older than you think."

"Uh, no you're not. You're eight. And that's how old I think you are."

"Well, it's not your decision. And anyway, aren't you a little young to be shooting a gun?"

Yeah, she went there. The one topic I was hoping to keep off the list of approved family discussions.

"Hey, I've been trained, and I take it very seriously," Ryan replied quickly. "And if you haven't noticed, I—"

"Ryan, that's enough. We all know what you did. And I'm glad you are trained and serious about it. But let's leave the past behind us, okay?"

"I was just answering her question," he said somberly.

"I know. We all know. Look there is no right or wrong age for anything. It's all about mindset, whether the individual is mentally ready. Lucy, when it comes to the idea of pierced ears, it's about your level of maturity. It's about whether I think you're ready for the responsibility."

"Oh, Mommy, I promise I'll be the most responsible person you've ever seen."

"I'm sure you will."

The conversation never did veer back to the shooting. Still, I sat there at the dinner table realizing how close we had all come to having a really horrible thing happen to our family. I almost lost Lucy. Who knew if that madman would have stopped there? Would I have been next? The rest of my family? If it hadn't been for Ryan following his training... well, I don't even want to think about it.

I glanced over at Po Po. As usual, she was a rock. Never allowing her emotions to show. I had talked to her about that day and even suggested she talk to a psychiatrist as well. She declined, of course. "I'm fine," I recalled her saying. The funny thing? I believed her completely. I had learned a lot about my mother-in-law during our family trip to Hong Kong. Let's just say she's experienced, and might even have been personally involved in, situations that were probably, most likely... eh, let's call it what it is: illegal. I don't bring it up. She doesn't either. We pretend. And that's fine by me.

I never did mention my visit with Xiaolian to the family. I wasn't sure if it was a good idea, especially after my meeting at Camp Parks. I was still perplexed by what Kang had said—that the government thought Xiaolian was a spy. Hearing this also got me thinking about my own stay at the facility. Were they suspicious of my allegiance as well?

The lights were off in the room; just a sliver of light shone through the square viewing window in the door.

On the floor next to the bed, Xiaolian lay on her back with her fingers interlaced behind her head. She sat up and twisted her torso from side to side.

"Forty-six."

Perspiration bubbled on her face and cheeks.

"Forty-seven."

Her hair was pasted to her cheeks, and a determined look graced her face as she counted breathlessly.

"Forty-eight. Forty-nine. Fifty."

She fell onto her back, her chest rising and falling with every breath. She rested for a few moments longer before flipping over onto her belly. She placed the palms of her hands flat against the floor and began counting off push-ups.

CHAPTER ELEVEN

THE NEXT MORNING, as I drove to the office, my thoughts returned to the meeting at Camp Parks—a room full of men treating me like an instrument in their precious task force. *How could Reilly not have known what was going down?* It just made no sense to me. He had to have known. Besides, I was the Assistant Special Agent in Charge at the San Francisco FBI office, not some eager beaver out of Quantico, trying to make a name for myself.

"You don't need to know their names. Pretend they aren't here," I singsonged, mimicking Cargo Pants.

He's lucky I didn't slap that smirk off his damn face. The more I thought about the way those men had treated me, the more pissed off I became. Plus, they had treated Kang just as badly, like a complete nonentity.

I managed to cool down somewhat as I took the elevator to our floor. I walked over to my desk, dropped off my things, and then headed straight toward Reilly's office.

"Hey, what's the rush?" Kang called out.

I stopped and turned around. "You should be in on this meeting. Come on."

Reilly was typing on his laptop when I stepped into his doorway. "You got a minute?"

"Sure." He closed the laptop and pushed it off to the side. "You're here about the meeting, aren't you?" He motioned for us to sit, but Kang and I stayed standing.

"You knew who would be in that meeting, didn't you?"

"If I told you, you wouldn't have gone into it with an open mind."

"I'm an investigator. When I signed up with the Bureau, it was for the sole purpose of investigating crimes."

"You *are* helping in an investigation... theirs."

"It's not the same. This secret, clandestine bullcrap? It doesn't fly with me. Those spooks over in the CIA can play all the secret games they want, but I'm not interested."

"My understanding is that you agreed to join the task force."

"I changed my mind," I said with a shrug. "You do know what they're asking, right?"

"Why don't you fill me in?"

"They want me to buddy up to Xiaolian because they think she's a spy." Of course, that wasn't what they'd actually said, but Kang and I were pretty sure that was their motive.

"Is she?"

"What?"

"You housed her, Abby. You know her better than anyone else. In your honest assessment, is there a chance they might be right on this?"

I held my tongue and took a moment to really consider what Reilly had asked. Did the CIA have reason to be concerned? Had Xiaolian fooled me... fooled everyone? Was the whole point of her being dropped off outside our offices in a suitcase so that I would find her? Was I really her mark?

"This is preposterous—you know that, right?"

"Answer the question, Abby."

I glanced at Kang and then back at Reilly. "It could explain why she was left outside our offices. I'll give them that. Most of the reasons we came up with didn't quite fit the puzzle."

"And this one does, doesn't it?" Reilly pushed.

"So you also think she's a spy? What exactly could she possibly want with me? What State secrets do I possess knowledge of or have access to? I can't be the end-all. Or better yet, why don't I just come out and address the bigger elephant in the room? Does the government think *I'm* a spy?"

"What?" Reilly and Kang said it at the same time.

Reilly leaned forward over his desk. "Why would you think that?"

"I was kept in that same facility and interrogated. Sure, they passed it off as trying to understand what I knew about Xiaolian, and our DNA connection, but come on… it makes total sense now. And treating my gunshot wound? That could have been handled at any hospital."

"Abby—" Reilly started.

"No, wait. Let me finish. I've thought about this. It's all I did last night, thinking about this. It's clear to me now that part of the reason the government kept me there is to find out if I was a spy. I get it. I'm originally a Chinese national. Maybe I'm really a sleeper spy inserted into the FBI, and Xiaolian, the twelve-year-old girl, is my handler who activated me. Better watch out —I've been spilling secrets left and right." I flicked my thumbs out to the left and to the right.

"Enough, Abby," Reilly snapped. "Both of you take a seat and calm down. The three of us are on the same side. Let's not forget that. Now, for the record, I do not believe you are a spy. Never did, never will. Even if they came to me and told me so, which no one has, it would be hard to convince me, and I'd probably laugh in their faces."

"I second that," Kang said and then turned to me. "But we

know you, Abby. Those guys don't, and with a lot of unanswered questions circling around Xiaolian, I can see how they might think you could be a spy. But they did let you go, so it's obvious they've seen the errors of their ways."

"Or maybe they're still watching me."

The room fell silent for a few moments before Reilly spoke. He drew a deep breath. "My advice is to continue doing your job. Do what they ask of you."

"Abby, I'm sure they looked at me too, to some degree," Kang said. "I'm Chinese, and I know a lot about Chinese history and culture, but you brought Xiaolian into your home to help the investigation, which it did. I'm guessing that's what made them take a harder look."

Reilly cleared his throat. "Whatever their reason for holding you for so long in that facility, they've now released you and asked you to resume your relationship with Xiaolian. If they think she's a spy, you need to let them finish their investigation. And if she is, she may not have been after you. You very well could have been a stepping stone."

I shifted in my chair and let loose a drawn-out breath. "Okay, look. Let's assume Xiaolian's a spy. She's not a very good one if she is, because she basically got herself caught from the very start."

"Did she? Or was that the intent?" Reilly countered.

I let out a breath of disbelief and looked away. I simply couldn't believe that little girl was recruited... wait, strike that, was *created* for the sole purpose of infiltrating the FBI through me.

Or was she? Dammit, now I'm second-guessing myself. Listen to your gut, Abby.

I looked at Kang. "What do you think?"

"I think you need to do what you do best, Abby. Investigate every lead. Cozy up to her. Be her best friend. Get her to confide in you like you did for our earlier investigation. And if it turns out the spooks were all wrong, fine. No harm. But if they're right, you'll be in the perfect position to flip her."

I buried my face in my palms and rubbed while groaning.

Reilly added, "Kang's right. This really is no different than what you did earlier."

I looked up. "The intent is different."

"Who cares what the reasoning is behind the questioning? We're trying to find out if Xiaolian is guilty of espionage."

I shook my head. "I get what you two are saying. And I'm trying not to get caught up in the details, but still, I mean, let's not forget about the three-parent thing. Did the Chinese really go through all this trouble twelve years ago to create a girl who looks like me so that I would be interested in her and bring her into my home?"

"Someone did. Xiaolian's proof of that. And you did take an interest in her, and you did bring her into your home."

I wasn't sure why I was being stubborn. I was usually the one with an open mind to all theories. Maybe it was because I had treated Xiaolian like family. If she really was a spy, then the hard truth was that she had played me. Was that it? My ego? Was I too embarrassed to admit I'd been hoodwinked by a twelve-year-old?

"I know exactly what you're thinking, Abby," Reilly said. "I know you all too well. There's a possibility that we were all fooled. Come up with evidence that supports either claim. It's all we can do."

Reilly and Kang were right. Whether I liked it or not, I'd have to join in on the mind games.

CHAPTER TWELVE

AFTER OUR MORNING meeting with Reilly, Kang and I made the drive to the government facility where Xiaolian was being held. It wasn't the same drive, filled with nonsensical conversation through mouthfuls of food. This time, we strategized while eating.

"Aside from you continuing to take the lead, any other thoughts on our approach to questioning?" Kang asked before taking a sip of coffee from his travel mug.

I swallowed the remaining bite of my muffin. "We need to keep reinforcing that we're on her side. She's unhappy there. There's no hiding that she's being kept beyond the whole treatment/recovery excuse. She asked to come home with me the last time."

"What did you say?"

"I told her that decision wasn't mine to make." I brushed a few crumbs off my jacket. "Really, I think we have to play this according to which Xiaolian we encounter. She's already demonstrated she has two sides."

"But didn't you say it was because she was unhappy there?"

"She said it was all an act. It felt genuine when she said it. I had no reason to question her words, but with what we now know, I can't be sure."

"Assuming she still thinks you're on her side, you really need to keep playing that angle. Don't let on about anything. If she's been trained to handle advanced interrogation techniques, there's a good chance she'll pick up on any type of shift in your body behavior or tone of voice."

"I agree, but knowing what we know certainly makes it harder."

"Forget what you know for now. Treat her exactly the same way you did when she was staying with you. Think back to those moments, and let that lead you."

At the facility, Yates met us in reception instead of Watkins. He remained pleasant and positive about us being there. Kang and I weren't sure if anyone at the facility had been clued in about our meeting at Camp Parks or even if they were aware that the CIA thought Xiaolian was a spy.

As we followed Yates, I whispered to Kang, "I wonder if the whole spy angle was developed here."

"You think the doctor is the one behind the accusation?"

"It's a likely way to come to that conclusion."

At the next security door, while Yates swiped his key card, I asked him, "Any new developments with Xiaolian we should know about?"

"Not really. She still continues to exhibit exceptional intelligence and physical prowess."

"Will you be implementing any other type of tests besides those? I imagine that, after a while, it'll become pointless."

"It's never pointless."

"Let me be a bit clearer," I said. "Right now it seems like

most of your time has been spent discovering what she can do. At some point, wouldn't the focus turn to why she has been trained to do them?"

"I believe that's where you come in. You can help to answer that question by finding out what Xiaolian isn't telling us."

Yates led us down the hall to the same room where I'd met with Xiaolian during my last visit. Kang followed Yates into the observation room, and I entered the recreation room.

A change in Xiaolian's personality was immediately visible. She was curled up on a beanbag, reading a book.

"Hi, Abby," she said, closing the book and rising to her feet. She hurried over to me and gave me a hug.

Now this is the Xiaolian I remember. "It's good to see you again, sweetie." I planted a kiss on the top of her forehead. "I see you have some new additions here."

The room no longer looked like a gym. The equipment was still there, but added to that was a bookcase lined with books and a couple of beanbags on an area rug.

"Yes, it's much more comfortable now," she said, grabbing hold of my hand and leading me over to the beanbags.

We plopped down on one together. "What are you reading?"

She sheepishly lifted the book so I could see the cover.

"*The Hunger Games.*" I gave her an approving nod.

She set the book on the floor and grinned. "Katniss kicks butt."

"Yes, she does. Is that how you see yourself?"

She threw her head back as she laughed. "Noooo, I can't shoot a bow and arrow."

But I bet you're just as tough as she is. I glanced over at the bookshelf and saw there was a variety of books that would suit any girl her age. "I'm happy to see you have other ways to fill your time."

"Do you want to play a card game?" she asked.

Before I could answer, she fetched a deck of cards from the top of the bookshelf.

"We can play Go Fish." She sat cross-legged in front of me and began dealing the cards.

We played quietly for a bit. I didn't see the point in questioning her right away when it was so clear she was enjoying her time with me. She was lonely.

"Abby..." she said, allowing her thoughts to trail off.

I moved a few cards around in my hand. "Yes?"

"Um, I was wondering... Did you have a chance to ask about me coming home with you?"

I glanced up and saw that she had her gaze focused on her cards. "I have, yes, but I don't have a definitive answer yet."

"I see." Her shoulders slumped a little.

"Ryan, Lucy, and Po Po all miss you. They asked about you and told me to tell you hi."

"Really?" She looked up from her cards with wide eyes.

"Of course."

"I miss them too. I really miss Po Po's cooking."

"They don't feed you well here?"

"It's okay, but it's not Po Po's cooking."

"I tell you what: I'll ask her to cook you something special, and I'll bring it the next time I visit."

She smacked her lips and rubbed her belly. "I can't wait. I'm hungry already." She lowered her hand and cocked her head slightly to the side. "Where's Uncle Kyle? Is it okay if I call him that? That's what Ryan and Lucy call him."

I smiled. "Yes, it's fine. I think he would like that very much." I glanced quickly at the mirrored glass partition in the wall.

Xiaolian drew a sharp breath. "Is Uncle Kyle here?" She jumped to her feet and ran over to the window. Her palms slapped against the glass, and her face squished up against it. "Uncle Kyle, are you there?"

As she continued to press her face against the glass, the door opened, and in walked Kang. In an instant, she ran over to him. Kang's face lit up from her enthusiasm.

"It's great to see you, Xiaolian," he said as he bent down to hug her.

She grabbed his hand and led him over to where I was sitting. "I'm so happy we're all here." She quickly reshuffled the cards and dealt all of us a new hand.

We spent the rest of our time there playing cards and talking about everything except what we should have been talking about.

CHAPTER THIRTEEN

By the time we left, I was convinced we needed to figure out a way to spend time with her away from the facility. While we never once discussed the constant testing she had to endure and why she was being held there, the whole process was obviously taking a toll on her. When we'd said our goodbyes and started to leave, Xiaolian had gripped my hand tightly and refused let go. For a brief moment, her eyes had watered, but she'd contained herself. Heck, I'd struggled to keep *my* composure.

"Maybe we can get clearance to take her out for the afternoon for a few hours," I said to Kang as we drove away. "You know, just someplace other than *that* place."

"Yeah, I think that's a good idea. We can grab lunch, take her to a park or something," Kang said.

"And more importantly, we can talk without prying eyes and ears. I mean if it's up to us to crack the code here, then surely we need to do it in the way we think will yield results."

"I agree, but the question is: how do we get permission?"

"You leave that up to me. I have an idea that might work. In the meantime, I need you to step on it. Lucy has a parent-teacher meeting today, and I can't be late."

Kang did his best to get us back into the city and to Lucy's school with minutes to spare before my scheduled time. Of course, when I checked in, I found out they were running about forty minutes late. *Great.*

The Girl Scouts of America were also there that afternoon, recruiting. Lucy had expressed some interest, so we went and listened to their spiel and took a bunch of pamphlets. Since Lucy was eight, she would be a Girl Scout Brownie, which she instantly fell in love with. I suspect it was more for the name than what the Brownies did.

While Lucy talked to one of the scoutmasters, another woman arrived with her daughter. The woman looked a little frazzled.

"Let me guess," I said. "You raced over here, thinking you were late only to find out the school is the one running late."

"Yes—how did you know?" she responded.

"Same thing happened to me. So now I'm killing time. Is your daughter interested in the Girl Scouts?"

"Apparently, though this is the first I've heard of her interest in it. We were at another booth earlier for the Boy Scouts."

"Well, you're at the right one now. These uniformed ladies represent the Girl Scouts."

"Oh, okay. Do you have a daughter?"

"Yes, she's eight, which would make her a Brownie."

"Mine is eight as well, so she'll also be a Brownie. She's in the bathroom. I swear she has to go once every hour. Oh, there she is."

The woman waved her hand and caught her daughter's attention. "These are the women who represent the Girl Scouts. Check them out, and I'll join you later," she told her daughter.

"I'm surprised I haven't seen you here before, considering our daughters are the same age," I said.

"Oh, it's because Hailey recently transferred here."

"That explains it."

"Has your daughter attended this school very long?" she asked.

I nodded. "She and her brother have been enrolled here since we moved to San Francisco."

"Where from?"

"Believe it or not, Hong Kong."

I watched her draw a deep breath as she placed a hand over her chest. "I love Hong Kong. My husband has family living there."

"We had a family trip there not too long ago, our first since we left a number of years ago."

"And do you miss it?"

"Yes and no. It was great being back. I have a lot of fond memories of growing up there, and a close friend of mine is still there, but it doesn't feel like home to me anymore. San Francisco is home now. Are you from the Bay Area?"

"I am. Redwood City. My husband is from Hong Kong, Sai Kung peninsula area."

"Yup, I know it."

"He was an only child, so his family scrimped and saved to send him here to attend university. That's where we met... been together ever since."

"What a nice story."

"And you?"

"My husband passed while I was still living in Hong Kong."

"I'm so sorry to hear that," she said with a frown.

"It was a tough time for all of us. The kids are both his from a previous marriage."

"I can only imagine what that was like. It must have felt overwhelming."

"That's exactly how it felt. Add in the pressures of work, and it wasn't the happiest time in my life. His death was really what prompted the move here—a fresh start. I wanted to put the past behind me and focus on building a new life."

"Has it worked?"

"It has," I said, smiling. "I'm happy here. I've made some good friends, and the kids love it. My mother-in-law still prefers Hong Kong, but she's acclimated."

"Well, I'm glad to hear that..."

I stuck my hand out. "I'm sorry, all this gabbing. The name's Abby Kane."

She shook my hand. "I'm Connie Shi. It's really nice to meet you."

CHAPTER FOURTEEN

DURING OUR WALK home from school, Lucy and I talked about the Brownies. She was surprised to discover that a large part of their program involved the girls participating in outdoorsy types of stuff. The only interaction she'd ever had with the Girl Scouts in the past involved us buying cookies from them—which is probably where her interest stemmed from.

"I don't think that's all they do," I said, as I flipped through a pamphlet. "It looks like you also take field trips in the city and perform science projects."

"But I'm not that good in science," she said with a frown.

"Well, this can be a way for you to become better. I think the purpose of the Brownies is really to contribute to society in positive ways by taking action on things you care about. Remember when we were at the beach and there were cigarette butts everywhere?"

"Yeah, it was gross. It's littering, and we aren't supposed to do that."

"It says here that Brownies are encouraged to identify problems and do something about them. So you could organize a cleanup day with your troop."

"Ohhh, I see. I like that."

"Also, you don't have to join a troop right away if you don't want to. You can just participate in events hosted by them. That could be a great way to get your feet wet and see if you like it."

When we reached home, Po Po was just beginning to prepare dinner. Lucy eagerly ran into the kitchen to help.

"Lucy, don't you have homework?"

"I do, but I can do it later."

"No, I think you need to sit down and do it now." One critical feedback I received from Lucy's teacher was that she often turned in work that looked rushed. In the past, I would let Lucy do her homework after dinner. I figured food comas were the culprit. I briefly considered that it might be due to the Walter Chan incident, but it wasn't. Her teacher said it had been going on since the beginning of the school year.

"But I always do my homework after dinner," she whined.

"We're trying something new. Now, scoot." I gave her a pat on her butt.

She stomped her feet on the stairs as she headed up to her room.

I already knew the answer, but I asked Po Po anyway. "Can I help?"

She said no, that everything was under control. I glanced at my watch and noted Ryan would be home any time. He was my workhorse—killing it in school and in his after-school activities. I really couldn't ask more of him. In fact, I didn't even have to ask. The boy just did it.

Later, as I watched my family eat like it was their last meal on Earth, I couldn't help but look at the empty chair next to Lucy, where Xiaolian used to sit. Even though there was a decent argument for her possibly being a spy, I still found it hard to believe. Of course, it seemed like I was the only one who felt that way. Kang seemed to think it was worth investigating, and Reilly wanted me to do my job, which meant he was inclined to believe it as well. Again, I found myself on the outside of an investigation—the only one who wasn't fully buying the theory that everyone else was.

It wasn't unfamiliar territory. Some of the biggest cases I'd solved were because I hadn't agreed with the rest of the gang. It was lonely being the odd man out, but my gut had never steered me wrong. *Do what you do best. Dig and dig and dig.* I would keep telling myself that whenever I started to have doubts about my instincts.

Of course, the one thing that bothered me the most about this spy angle—and I hated to admit it because it seemed petty and personal—was this: I never saw it coming.

It was an attack on my ability to read people correctly, a trait I had always prided myself on. I had allowed Xiaolian to eat, sleep, and interact with my family. If she truly was relaying information to some unknown person or entity, what was she saying? Was she reporting on what Ryan and Lucy did? Did she mention to her handlers what Po Po had cooked for dinner? Or was it just about me?

I rarely discussed work with the family, and the only time I had talked about work with Xiaolian was when I'd questioned her about who she was. It had resulted in our human-trafficking investigation, but again, I'd only questioned her. She wasn't aware of all the details of the investigation. I failed to see anything about the old investigation that would be of current interest to China. I tabled those thoughts for the remainder of dinner and focused on my family. The best I could do was to investigate the spy angle and let the facts speak for themselves.

It must have been about eleven. The kids and Po Po were already asleep, and I was watching television in bed. The late news was reporting on the tech guru found running around naked. *Why is this still news?*

It just seemed like all the station wanted was to make more out of it than what it was. Heck, someone ran around the city naked every day. Big deal. However, this guy was a known party-boy bachelor with millions in the bank—so it was newsworthy. It was about ratings.

The news station continued to air the same cell-phone footage I remembered seeing a few days ago, the one that showed him being hauled off by SFPD while he shouted about being abducted and experimented on. He sounded like another crazy person spouting off about an alien abduction.

Why on earth would an alien want to abduct you? Because you made an app and sold it for millions? Would that make an alien think, "Hey, we gotta take this guy. He's the real deal."

I picked up the remote and shut the television off. As I lay there in the dark, I couldn't help but think of the naked tech guy's claims. *Buddy, you really have no idea what it's like to be abducted. Trust me.*

CHAPTER FIFTEEN

THE FOLLOWING morning at the office, I bumped into Kang in the breakroom. He was standing patiently in front of the coffee machine watching brewed coffee drip into the glass decanter.

"Hey, partner," I said. "It's like boiling water—staring doesn't speed up the process."

"Someone finished the coffee and didn't brew a fresh pot. One of these days, I'll catch this person."

"And what, press charges?" I filled a travel mug with hot water and then added a pinch of tieguanyin tea leaves from my stash.

"I'll give him or her a piece of my mind. I'm willing to bet this person is also guilty of swiping other people's food from the fridge."

"Maybe that's the person Xiaolian is after. Ever think of that?" Kang failed to find the humor in my joke. "Come on. There's enough coffee in that pot to fill your cup. Get it to go."

Kang met me back at our desks with his personal travel mug filled. "If I'd known we were seeing Xiaolian first thing, I would have picked you up so we didn't both have to come in to the office."

"It was a joke. I'm sorry."

"It irritates me. The rule is so simple. You drain the joe, you make some mo'.'"

I looked away as I struggled to contain my laughter. Kang's comment was about the funniest thing I'd heard in a while.

"Abby, I'm serious." He looked at me deadpan.

"I know you are." The chuckling stopped, but the grin wasn't disappearing anytime soon.

As we drove out of the building, Kang made a detour from the normal route we took to the 101 Highway. "I know this great place where we can pick up a couple of breakfast burritos."

"Yay! The Kang I know and love is back," I cheered.

Kang smiled at me. "Sorry. I don't know why I got so bent out of shape earlier. And over something so trivial."

"It's not. That's probably the hundredth time you've walked into the breakroom and seen an empty pot."

"Exactly! That's totally it." He banged a palm against the steering wheel.

"But we'll have to hold off on that burrito for a bit longer."

"Why's that?"

"We have some other place we need to go. Hang another right up here. We're going to Pacific Heights."

"What's there?"

"Remember the naked tech guy?"

"Yeah?"

"Well, that's where he lives."

"I'm confused. What do we want with him?"

"While I was watching the news last night, they had yet another segment on him and played the cell-phone footage again."

"The one where he claimed he was abducted?"

"Yes, that's the one. Doesn't it seem strange to you that a

brilliant guy, albeit a partier, suddenly starts spouting off tabloid headlines?"

Kang made a face. "I don't know. I guess so."

"Humor me for ten minutes. After that, we're all over that burrito place. We should pick one up for Xiaolian too."

Geoffrey Barnes lived on Broadway in Pacific Heights, otherwise known by locals as Billionaires Row. Once an enclave for elitist old money like the Gettys, it's now overrun with high-tech moguls like Larry Ellison, founder of Oracle, Mark Pincus, founder of Zynga, and Jonathan Ive, head designer at Apple.

"I Googled the guy. Apparently, Barnes dropped out of Princeton after a year—to pursue a hunch. One that turned into a company in two years with a hot app that he then sold four-teen months later for a cool eight hundred million dollars."

"Sheesh." Kang shook his head in disbelief.

"I think this is it," I said as I pointed at a white three-story mansion at the corner of Broadway and Divisadero.

I was wrong. It was the next house over, hidden behind tall hedges. We buzzed the gate, and after introducing ourselves, we entered the property.

Barnes met us at the door dressed in a plain terry-cloth robe.

"What do you want?" he asked rather abruptly.

With a bright smile on my face, I said, "We want to talk to you about your abduction."

"You believe me? Really?" His eyes scanned the entrance gate behind us. "This isn't some prank TV show, is it?"

"May we come inside?"

Barnes waved us in. "Quickly, before anyone sees you. Last thing I need is the media seeing you here and turning this into something more than it really is."

We stood in the foyer; it was apparent that we would venture no farther into his home when Barnes crossed his arms over his chest and asked us what we wanted to know.

"Tell us your story. Everything that happened the way you saw it."

"I had some friends over. We were drinking, smoking cigars, and having a good time. Nothing crazy—no beer bongs or snorting coke off of hookers like the media wants you to believe. Anyway, I walked them out to the gate and said goodbye. They drove off, and I headed back inside."

"You remember this, or you were told this?"

"I remembered. I'm still trying to piece together that night. It's like I'm starring in my own *Hangover* movie, only it's not funny."

"So you walked them out. Was it to their cars or just to the front gate?"

"The front gate. Maybe I took a few steps outside the property, but I definitely didn't walk them to their cars. I would never do that."

"So then what?"

"Next thing I know, I'm opening my eyes, and I'm in the middle of the woods."

"Just like that. From the gate to the woods. Everything is one big blank?"

"Are you mocking me?"

"No, I'm just trying to make sure we completely understand. Okay, so you're in the woods. What were you doing?"

"Nothing. When I opened my eyes, I was sitting on the ground, leaning against a tree. I was probably passed out or something. Anyway, I get up and start walking around. I can't remember shit. I'm wracking my brain, but nothing is coming. I don't even know I'm in San Francisco or even who I am. It really freaked me out. Thinking back, I can see how people thought I was a nut."

"Well, it didn't help that you were completely naked."

"But I wasn't when I woke. I had on one of those gowns they

give you in a hospital. I tore it off... for reasons I don't really understand right now."

I glanced over at Kang.

"What? You two keep looking over at each other every time I say something."

"Mr. Barnes, are you on any medication at the moment?"

"I'm not high, if that's what you're asking. I'm telling you everything as I remember it. If you don't believe me, you can stop wasting my time and get the hell out of my house."

"Calm down, buddy," Kang said. "We're not here to waste your time. We're busy people too, believe it or not."

"Mr. Barnes, when you were being led to the squad car by the officers, you kept shouting about being abducted. Why did you think that?"

"Because by the time I got off the mountain, I'd had brief memories of people surrounding me."

"Who?"

"I don't know. A bunch of men I'd never seen before."

"Can you describe them? Anything would be helpful."

Barnes shook his head. "That's the whole problem. I saw enough of the flashback, or whatever you want to call it, to know they were standing over me but not enough to tell you what they looked like."

"When they're standing over you, are you lying down, sitting? Outdoors or indoors?"

"I'm definitely inside somewhere, and I want to say I'm lying on my back, probably a bed, and they're standing over me. Two on one side, two on the other."

I removed my card from my purse and handed it to Barnes. "If your memory starts to clear and you recall more details, please call."

He took the card from me. "Why is the FBI interested? I'm not in any sort of trouble, am I?"

"No, you're not. We have reason to believe that your allegations of being abducted might be connected to another investigation."

"What? Like this has happened to someone else?"

"I'm sorry, but we can't discuss that with you. Like I said, if your memory comes back, give me a call."

CHAPTER SIXTEEN

"You CARE to tell me why we wasted our morning with that fruit loop?" Kang asked as we walked back to our vehicle. "I mean, who cares about this guy?"

"There's something about his story that doesn't sit right with me. It's a gut thing, so I can't quite verbalize it."

Kang stopped next to the SUV and looked across the hood at me. "You know, Abby, I'm pretty easy going, and I usually don't mind seeing where your hunches lead, but this one today, I gotta say, I don't get it. Clearly, he left with his friends or, after they left, he took off. The guy was probably high as a kite and ended up in the ER of a local hospital and later walked out wearing a gown." Kang got into the vehicle. "Am I right or not?" he asked as I slid into the passenger seat.

He had a point, but I disagreed with it. And that was the end of that discussion. I said nothing more about our visit, opting to drop the subject until I could better understand my own feelings and why my gut raised a flag with this guy. With that said, the drive to the burrito place was solemn, but once we each had a hand wrapped around that oblong tasty goodness, all was good.

I'd packed a duffle bag containing workout clothes. After seeing what Xiaolian was capable of from our first meeting, I wanted to see what else she could do.

Again Yates met us in the reception area and escorted us to Xiaolian. I inquired about Watkins, and Yates said he had other obligations that morning. The procedure was the same. I was to meet Xiaolian in the recreation room, and Kang would accompany Yates into the observation booth.

I changed into my workout gear before entering the room. The minute Xiaolian saw me, her face lit up, and she ran over to me for a hug.

"I'm so happy to see you," she said, beaming from ear to ear. "Why are you wearing shorts?"

"I thought we'd train for a bit."

"What kind of training?"

I took her hand and led her over to the mat. "Do you know how to grapple?"

"You mean wrestle?"

"Yeah."

She pushed me down until I was in the referee bottom position, essentially on my hands and knees, sitting back on my heels with my toes tucked under them. Xiaolian moved into the referee top position. She dropped down behind me, placing her right knee on the mat, while keeping her left raised. Next to her knee on the mat, she grabbed hold of my arm just above the elbow and then hooked her other arm around my far side, gripping my stomach.

"On the count of three," she said. "One. Two. Three."

She pushed forward, yanking my right arm out from under me. I rolled forward with the momentum, forcing her up and over. I continued rolling until I was on top of her, where I easily pinned her shoulders.

"Come on. Let's go again," I said, as I got off of her. It was clear she'd had some training, as she did utilize a move, but my size and weight were an advantage.

I allowed her to retain the same position behind me: the offensive position. Three times in a row, she tried unsuccessfully to roll me onto my back. The weight difference between us would be problematic. I stood up, extending my hand to help her off the mat. She gripped it and popped up.

"Maybe we should try something else," I said, standing as I rested my hands on my hips.

"I know," she said.

Before I could say another word, she dropped down and executed a leg sweep, taking me off my feet. I landed flat on my side. A second later, she pounced on me, moving into a full mount position. Instinctively, I hooked both arms around her and pulled her tight against my chest.

But this time, her size gave her the advantage.

Xiaolian easily slipped out of my grasp and moved forward, sliding her left knee into my armpit. Then she brought her other leg up and planted her right foot flat on the mat. I knew exactly what she was attempting—a Kimura, a painful armlock. She'd had Brazilian jiujitsu training.

Xiaolian pushed down on my head to break my grip around her, while at the same time trapping my left arm between her right thigh and her side. If she broke my grip, she would then need only to push down on my trapped arm, and I could either give in or end up with a broken arm.

I planted my feet against the mat and pushed down, arching my torso up. Xiaolian's feet left the mat, and she lost her leverage. I bucked up once more with as much force as I could muster, and Xiaolian fell off of me.

I didn't stop there.

Neither did she.

We both scrambled for the dominant position. I was quicker

and moved into a side mount. With Xiaolian on her back, and I on top of her perpendicularly from the side, I hooked an arm under her back and coiled my other over her chest. I shoved my right knee into her rib cage, preventing her from wiggling back and forth. I then applied the Kimura armlock on her. Within seconds, she tapped the mat in defeat.

I got up off of her and leaned back on my hands. "Where did you learn to grapple?"

"Doesn't everybody know how to grapple?" she asked as she sat up.

I arched an eyebrow. "Uh, no. Is that what it's like where you're from?"

"I always thought so. I mean, the other kids my age all knew how to grapple and box."

"Interesting. Care to tell me more about these other kids?"

"What's to tell? We had a lot of fun together."

"Were you related?"

"Um, I think so. They were always around. We grew up together. Why? Am I being sent back?"

"I didn't say that."

"But it sounds like it. Why can't I just come home with you?"

"I'm working on some sort of arrangement."

"You said that last time. I don't understand why I have to stay here. I feel like a prisoner."

"You're not. It's just that... well, we need to make sure you're safe, and we want to learn more about you. The Chan brothers came after you—that doesn't happen to the average person. Does that make sense?"

She nodded, and her gaze fell to the mat.

"But I want you to know that I'm working on a solution. I promise."

"I hope so. I don't want to go back home."

At that point, Kang popped into the room holding a paper bag. "I've got a treat for you."

Xiaolian jumped to her feet and ran toward him. "What is it? Tell me."

Kang removed the burrito from the bag and handed it to her. "It's received our seal of quality goodness."

Xiaolian tore the foil off the top of the burrito. "What is it?" she asked before sniffing it.

"You've never had a burrito?" Kang asked. "Well, I won't say anything more. You need to take a bite."

She did and swooned, nearly toppling over. "Mmmmmm," she mumbled as she took another bite, even before swallowing the one already in her mouth.

She said something else, but I couldn't understand her with all that food in her mouth.

"Looks like we have another member in our food club," Kang said.

Xiaolian destroyed that burrito like a champ. For some absurd reason, I felt like a proud mama.

She plopped on the floor and leaned back, resting on her hands, with her belly bump protruding through her shirt. "That was the best thing ever. Count me in the next time."

With a load of eggs, chorizo, fried potatoes, cheese, and other good stuff inside of Xiaolian's belly, there would be no more training.

"We didn't eat like this back where I'm from," Xiaolian said. "Our meals were boring. Usually rice, some pork or fish, and vegetables, and we were never allowed big meals like this burrito."

"Welcome to America," I said. "Land of humongous portions."

Yates entered the room just then, saying he had to cut our visit short that day. When I asked him why, he essentially ignored my question. I had sort of thought the guy was on our side or at least neutral, being a doctor and all. Maybe not. Kang and I both gave Xiaolian a hug before leaving.

As usual, we kept our mouths shut until we were sealed away in our vehicle, with no one listening.

"Still think she's not a spy?" he asked as we drove away from the facility. "She exhibited other forms of training today. Almost had you with... What do they call that move?"

"It's called a Kimura."

"I'm telling you, Abby, the more I see, the more I buy into the cautionary tale the government is spinning—a twelve-year-old with her intelligence and trained in hand-to-hand combat. It wouldn't surprise me if she has also had weapons training. Probably counter-surveillance training too. She might even be toying around with the doctors, you know, giving them—"

"Okay, okay, enough already," I said. "I get your point."

"Plus there's her admission of others like her."

I didn't want to agree, but Kang was right. What twelve-year-old possessed those types of skills?

CHAPTER SEVENTEEN

LATER THAT NIGHT, after the kids were in bed, I headed up to my home office on the third floor. Something about our meeting with techie Barnes that morning continued to nag me. I couldn't place my finger on what it was, but I couldn't shake the feeling. And in my experience, that always meant there was something there.

I turned on my laptop and logged into the secure server at the Bureau. I wanted to see if the ViCap (Violent Criminal Apprehension Program) database had anything on Barnes. While its purpose was to collect information on homicides, sexual assaults, and other violent crimes, it did house information on kidnappings and missing persons.

Barnes came up empty.

Around town, Barnes was known to have a revolving door of beauties. I wasn't exactly sure if he had family nearby, so if he had indeed been abducted, would anyone have noticed and cared enough to have reported him as missing? Were his friends really his friends or just money-sucking leeches? What about his partners at his old start-up? Did they care? Whatever the

reason, I figured if a missing-persons report had been filed on
the tech titan, it most likely would be with SFPD.

I browsed aimlessly through the photos of missing persons;
some of them dated back forty years. I clicked on a picture of
two teen girls; both had last been seen on October 31, 1969.
The report said they weren't known to be friends, but it was
thought that they had skipped school together that Halloween
day.

Then I did a search for missing persons in the Bay Area over
the last six months. As I perused the information, something
caught my attention. Some of the cases had been rescinded. It
wasn't common, especially for our database; this was more likely
to happen with reports filed with the local police. In two cases,
family members had made the reports, but had rescinded them
twelve to eighteen hours later. My guess was they had found the
missing person. It happened.

So why did one, a doctor—a brain surgeon, no less—stand
out to me? Maybe it was because I could understand a known
party guy going missing for a day, but a brain surgeon with a
successful practice?

Still unsure of why I continued to look at these files, I dug
deeper on the doctor. According to the website for his practice,
he was at John Hopkins in Washington, DC before moving to
the Bay Area. He was married and had three children.

According to the report, the wife thought her husband flew
to New York for a speaking engagement, but she had the dates
on her calendar mixed. When he hadn't answered his cell
phone, she called the hotel to leave a message but was told he
wasn't staying there. Thinking something happened to him, she
panicked and filed a missing persons report with NYPD. That
he supposedly went missing in New York but lived in California
may be the reason why it was in the Bureau's database. *She
freaked. Happens all the time.*

I yawned.

It had been a long day; that nagging feeling would just have to wait. I shut my laptop, headed downstairs to my bedroom, and fell asleep the instant my head hit the pillow.

CHAPTER EIGHTEEN

"WHAT?" Kang jerked his head back as wrinkles formed on his forehead. "Are you serious?"

"I am. So start driving, because we're wasting time. Head south on Polk."

During our drive back from the facility the day before, Kang and I had discussed taking Xiaolian out for a little field trip. Nothing big, maybe lunch. We'd agreed it would go a long way toward making her feel better and more inclined to opening up to us. But I had other plans first.

"I don't get it, Abby. We did this yesterday with Barnes, and now you have another person you want to question?"

"I realize that, but are you listening to what I'm saying about this missing-persons case?"

"Abby, we already have a case. It's Xiaolian. You can't go chasing every whim that flutters your way."

"Flutter? Whim? Relax, GI Joe. We're still chasing the spy angle, but I just want to dual-path this thing."

"What thing? These missing persons are not a 'thing.'" Kang slouched a bit in his seat and pouted like a little boy not getting his way.

I turned away and stared out of my window. I couldn't understand why there was so much pushback from him. It wasn't like we were behind schedule or had a deadline. It was an hour out of our morning. No biggie.

"Okay, then help me understand your thought process," he said.

"It's simple. I think there's something funky going on, and I want to find out what it is. Just play along. If it turns out to be nothing, it'll be apparent to both of us, and if something's there, you won't need me to explain anything—because you'll get it."

"Who's this guy anyway?"

"Lyle Hammond. He's a successful brain surgeon who has been running his own practice in the city for fifteen years. Before that, he was in DC at Johns Hopkins. He's married and has three children."

Kang said nothing.

"Stop here." I pointed.

"What? The doctor's practice is on Polk?"

"No, Bob's Donut Shop is." Apple fritters always made everything better between us.

On the drive to the doctor's practice, we each wolfed down a fritter that was perfectly crisp, with generous amounts of filling.

The doctor's practice was located in the Transamerica Pyramid building, the white triangular building famously associated with San Francisco's skyline.

"Is he in the actual triangle or the other, normal-looking, building behind it?"

I checked the address once more on my phone. "Um, I think he's actually in the pyramid, twenty-sixth floor. This will be a first for me."

"Same here."

"We each get to check this off our bucket lists. You're welcome."

"There used to be an observation deck, but they shut it down after 9/11," Kang said. "I heard that only tenants and their guests are allowed beyond the lobby area."

"Good thing we've got all-access passes, courtesy of the FBI."

It was nine-thirty a.m. when we arrived at Hammond's office. There were no patients in the waiting area, and the young lady sitting behind the reception desk was engrossed with her cell phone.

"Hello. I'm Agent Kane. This is Agent Kang. We'd like to speak to Dr. Lyle Hammond."

The girl casually looked up at us. "Um, okay. What is this regarding?"

"Just tell him the FBI is here. That should be plenty enough motivation."

"Okay," she said as she placed the handset of her desk phone against her ear and relayed my words. "It'll be just a minute; please have a seat."

About a hot minute later, Hammond appeared from a hallway to the left of the reception desk. He looked better in person than in the picture on the website. He kept his wavy brown hair, with streaks of gray, parted in the middle. His groomed five o'clock shadow complemented his chiseled jawline. He dressed in black slacks and a charcoal-gray dress shirt—no tie. The outfit was more dressy than business. And he could have held back a bit on the aftershave.

"Hi, I'm Dr. Lyle Hammond. How may I be of help?" Two dimples appeared when he smiled.

"We have a few questions we'd like to ask you," I said as I stood. "Is there somewhere we can speak in private?"

"Yes, of course. My office is back this way."

Hammond's office looked as if it belonged to some slick hedge-fund manager on Wall Street rather than a doctor—at least from my experience. I expected overstuffed files, x-rays piled high on his desk, and an anatomical model of a brain sitting somewhere. Nope, it was a lot of glass and brushed steel, and everything was perfectly in place.

"Please, have a seat," he said as he pointed at the two chairs in front of his desk. He scooted around his desk and sat in an ergonomically perfect Aeron chair.

"A few months ago, you were reported missing by your wife?"

"Missing?" He chuckled. "I think you're mistaken."

"No, I'm not. She filed the report but later had it rescinded."

"Oh, that. Yes, yes, my wife..." He threw both hands up into the air. "She's a worry wart, and sometimes her imagination gets the best of her. A harmless mistake, that's all. I hope that's not the reason why you came here, because there's not much else to tell."

"Is that so?"

He shrugged.

"Why don't you tell us where you were?" I asked, even though I already knew from the notes in the report.

"I went out with some friends, and time got away from me. You know how it is," he said as he looked at Kang with questioning eyes.

"Your wife reported that you were missing for almost eighteen hours."

"What can I say? It was all a mistake. I'm sorry if she caused any problems." Hammond lazily crossed a leg over the other as he leaned back in his chair.

"Five years," I said.

"Five years?" Hammond smiled and frowned at the same time. "I don't understand."

"That's the jail time you can receive for making false statements to a federal agent."

"You're joking, right?"

I traced a circle around my face. "Does it look like I'm joking?"

Hammond's smile disappeared, and he sat up in his chair.

I said, "Let's try this again. What happened?"

"Okay, it's true. I was missing, if that's what you want to call it."

"What would you call it?"

"I don't know. Look, I was too embarrassed to say anything, so I just kept blowing off the accusation, but the truth is I left the office, and the next thing I knew I woke up inside my car at Ocean Beach. I can't remember a damn thing between the moment I left my office to when I opened my eyes and saw the beach in front of me. Complete blackout, and no, I wasn't drinking, and I don't do drugs. Even my wife and close friends don't know the truth."

I looked over at Kang and then back at Hammond.

"What? I swear, I'm telling you the truth."

"I believe you," I said.

"You do? It seems so far-fetched."

"Did you catch the news story on Geoffrey Barnes?"

"I don't know who that is."

"SFPD found him naked and wandering the streets near Mount Sutro. He claims to have been abducted."

"Wait—you guys think I was abducted?"

"At the moment, we're exploring various missing-persons cases. There could be a connection. Are you sure there's nothing else you can remember?"

"Positive. I've been struggling with this ever since it happened."

I handed Hammond my card. "If you remember anything, call."

As Kang and I walked back to our vehicle, he broke the silence.

"I gotta hand it to you, Abby; there's something fishy, and it seems like there might be a connection between the doctor and techie dude. Still, I don't know what it has to do with our current assignment."

"I don't either, but my gut is telling me not to let this slip through the cracks."

CHAPTER NINETEEN

WE SPENT NO MORE than twenty minutes speaking to Hammond that morning, not long enough to affect our scheduled meeting at the facility. As had become customary, Yates met us in reception and led us to the recreation room, where Xiaolian waited for me.

Yates had his laboratory coat unbuttoned and it flapped behind him. It reminded me of Dr. Timothy Green, the city's top medical examiner. He never buttoned up. I asked, "Is she ready?"

"Yes, of course. Just go inside. Agent Kang and I will be in the observation room."

I arched a brow. "What are you talking about? We've been given permission to take Xiaolian off site for a couple hours. Weren't you notified?"

Yates scratched the side of his head. "Uh, this is news to me. I—"

"I was told the right people signed off on it. Please don't tell me we came all this way for nothing."

"Well, you didn't come for nothing. You still have access to Xiaolian."

"You don't understand. In order for me to gain her full trust, we need to make it seem like we're working on getting her out of here."

"But that's not what's happening."

"I realize that, but she doesn't. This is perception. Look, we've been given an impossible task of earning her trust while at the same time you're keeping her locked up. You've seen her mood swings. One day she's loveable and outgoing, the next day she's cold and closed-lipped."

Yates opened his mouth, as if to say something, but changed his mind.

"It's a couple of hours," I said. "We're grabbing lunch, and that's it. We need to make progress. Remaining here and working out with her won't get us anywhere."

Yates looked at Kang.

"She's right. We can keep doing the same thing day in and day out, but the results won't change."

"It's just that I haven't received any paperwork and—"

"I'm sure your director—what's his name, Watkins—is aware of it."

Yates stood paralyzed, unable to say yes or no. I made the decision for him by walking into the recreation room and returning with Xiaolian holding my hand. Ten minutes later, the three of us were driving out of the facility.

"I can't believe you got me out of there," Xiaolian said.

She and I were sitting in the back seat of the SUV.

"Neither can we," I said with a smile.

"What do you mean?"

"We didn't really have permission. We sort of broke you out."

Her eyes grew wide. "You did?"

"We did. It's only temporary, though. We're still working on securing your release, but for now, I think lunch is a good start."

"So do I," she said, grinning.

Kang and I had known we had no say in what happened to Xiaolian, but we hoped that Yates would be the kind of doctor who's more interested in learning about his patient than follow security protocols. We'd been right. He'd folded so easily.

"Where are we going?" Xiaolian asked.

"Ever hear of a place called Great America?"

She shook her head. "What kind of food do they serve?"

"The food's nothing special, but the rides are. Just wait. You'll love this place."

When we arrived at the amusement park and saw the reaction from Xiaolian, I knew we had made the right decision. Our original plan was to take her to Chuck E. Cheese's. While that probably would have sufficed, I thought there was a small chance she might be a bit too old for a pizza joint with arcade games and an animatronic mouse as a host, even if she had never been to one before.

Once we were past the entry gates, Xiaolian's mouth fell slack, and her eyes just about popped out of her face. "What is this place?"

"This is the place where time flies by."

"Huh?" She looked up at me quizzically.

"Never mind. Ever ride a roller coaster?"

"No. Is it fun?"

"You're about to find out."

The kids and I had been to Great America a few times. Flight Deck was my favorite ride.

"Maybe we should start her off on something small," Kang suggested.

"Nah, she's a tough little girl. I say we start with the fastest, most intense ride the park has. You don't want a kiddie ride, right?"

"Nope. I want the ride you're talking about."

I looked at Kang and shrugged. "She's the boss today. If you need to start off on the kiddie rides and work your way up, you know where to find the two of us."

"Don't worry about me," he said, keeping in step with us.

Flight Deck was the park's most popular ride. Basically the rider sits suspended below the tracks in seats that hit speeds of 50 mph. It has a zero-gravity roll, basically a cool corkscrew, a couple of 270-degree turns that whip you around, and finally a huge, 360-degree loop, where instead of looping inside the circle, you loop on the outside. I peed my pants the first time I rode it.

We strapped into the first row of seating, with Xiaolian sandwiched between me and Kang. The coaster jerked, moved forward, and immediately started its steep ascent, with the loud, familiar clicking sound ringing out.

"I think I've changed my mind, Abby," Xiaolian said.

"Oh dear, I'm afraid it's too late now," I said with a mischievous grin. "You'll just have to suck it up."

Xiaolian started screaming as we reached the top. I couldn't stop laughing—not because she was screaming, but because Kang was screaming even louder than she was. The first drop whipped us down and to the left, straight into the 360-degree loop.

I glanced over at Xiaolian. Her mouth was wide open, and her eyes were closed. Kang had fainted and sat limp in his seat. I laughed even harder and peed my pants for the second time on that ride.

Immediately after finishing the ride, we hopped back into the line for a second round. Kang spent a good portion of that wait time denying that he had fainted, not once, not twice, but thrice.

We spent the rest of the day riding every ride in the park and playing the arcade games. Xiaolian won a stuffed Snoopy dog that was almost her own height, for making five basketball shots in a row. It also seemed like we ate everything the park had to offer.

The original plan was three hours—that quickly turned into six.

We exited the park at four thirty and did our best to make it back to the facility as quickly as possible. We never pressed Xiaolian for information like we'd planned; she was having too much fun being a kid, and I didn't want to spoil it for her. There would be other days.

All in all, I felt like the outing had helped. Even during the short amount of time we had spent visiting her at the facility, Kang and I could tell we weren't making progress. She was holding back. We needed to give her a reason to let go. Hopefully a day at the park would crack the foundation of her wall.

Yates met us upon our return to the facility and waited until Xiaolian was back in her room before voicing his displeasure. "You had no authority to take her." He struggled to contain his emotions as the two of us faced him in his office.

"This field trip did more to help our relationship with her than all of the time spent in that little recreation room of yours. We're after results here, are we not?"

Yates nodded, but the redness in his face signaled he was anything but calm.

I added, "We all have our methods. You need to trust ours. Remember, results are what count. Not some stupid protocol."

"You should have told me your motivations," he said in a low voice.

"So you agree, then?"

"What I'm saying is, I may not agree that this facility is all that conducive to Xiaolian opening up. Still, I have a job and a boss I need to answer to."

"We're sorry. In the future, we'll work with you."

It seemed that Yates was on our side. He spent a lot of time with her and could see that she was unhappy, probably even a little depressed. Testing a subject under those conditions wasn't ideal. In the end, Yates was a scientist. He wanted to learn as much as he could about Xiaolian.

"So, anything to report?" he asked.

"No, but I think from now on, we'll start seeing results. We'll be back tomorrow."

As Kang and I returned to our vehicle, Archer, the hoodie-dressed spook from our meeting at Camp Park, intercepted us. The guy appeared out of nowhere, slipping into the back seat of our SUV.

"Did you guys have fun?"

We looked back at him. If he was angry, he masked it well.

"Why? Did you want to join us?" Kang asked.

"Do you have any idea of the risks you took today?"

"Oh, please." I allowed that last word to drag. "She's a child. What are you afraid of? That she'll tackle us and escape back to the motherland?"

"She's not to leave the facility again unless you have permission."

"Well, why don't you do something to make it okay for her to leave? You and your band of merry men want answers, but you're not giving me the tools to do my job. She's not an animal that needs training."

"Fine. I'll see what I can do."

"See about me housing her as well."

"That's a no-go."

"It has proven to work in the past, but what do I know? I'm just the person with the inside track on Xiaolian."

"Tell me about today."

"We went to Great America. It's an amusement park in Santa Clara. It has—"

"I'm familiar with it. What did you learn?"

"She loves roller coasters and can eat more pizza than Agent Kang here," I said with a straight face.

"You think this is a game, Agent Kane? Do you? You think securing a potential threat is something to take lightly?"

"Listen, my methods may not align with yours, but I do get results."

"You need to press her harder."

"You need to back off and let me do my job."

Archer kept his gaze locked onto mine. *Here we go—the macho stare-down.*

Kang was the adult who broke the stalemate. "If I may butt in here, you guys asked us to do this because we have the relationship with Xiaolian. And there's a reason for that. It starts with treating her like she's human. You know, the whole basic human-decency thing. Also the people working there," Kang used his thumb to point back at the facility, "they suck at being friendly and hospitable. She's a child. And even if you think she's a spy—yes, we know that's the thinking here—treating her like a grown adult, or worse, will get you nowhere."

Archer continued to stare us down. Eventually he opened his door. "Remember what I said; she doesn't leave until you hear from me." He climbed out and slammed the door shut.

"If they really want me to flip her, I should be housing her. That would be the best way."

"Is that something you really want? I mean, knowing what you know now. There is the chance that these a-holes are right."

"I know, I know."

I knew exactly what he meant. Xiaolian was the reason Walter Chan had shown up at my home. Of course, at the time I had no knowledge that she was a threat to my family. It was different this time.

"I'd think long and hard about it, Abby," Kang warned. "You

know I'm saying this as a friend and as someone who cares a lot about you and your family."

I gave him a pat on the shoulder. The mom in me agreed with him one hundred percent. However, the investigator in me wanted Xiaolian in my custody.

CHAPTER TWENTY

AFTER DROPPING her kids off at school, Connie drove over to Agent Kane's home and parked under a tree, a few houses away. She sat quietly in her car, drinking kombucha she had picked up from an organic juice bar, as she kept watch on the house.

All was quiet on Pfeiffer Street; most of the neighbors were at work. Two houses down, Connie saw a woman unload what must have been at least twelve bags of groceries. A pair of women walked by with yoga mats. A cat stalked a crow on the lawn across the street.

A little while later, Connie reached into her purse, removed her cell phone, and placed a call to her husband. He picked up on the third ring.

"Hi. How is everything?" Albert asked.

"Not much to report. I saw her drop the kids off at school today. She was dressed as if she was heading into the office right after. As for the home, it's just the mother-in-law, from what I can tell. She came out once and stood on the porch for a minute or so before heading back in. About thirty minutes later, she left. She had one of those little pull carts with her. I'm assuming she went to do some shopping. I took the opportunity to snoop around at that point."

"Yeah, and...?"

"It doesn't look like they have any sort of home security system. No sign in the front yard or stickers on the window. However, there are large lamps attached to the sides of the house. I imagine they have motion sensors on them, but other than that, nothing troublesome. I peeked in a few of the windows. I'm fairly certain the mother-in-law is home by herself all day."

"Okay, let's escalate. You take the lead," Albert said.

"All right. See you later tonight."

Connie disconnected the call. Then she found Agent Kane's number in her phone's address book and called her.

"Agent Kane speaking."

"Oh, hi, Abby. It's Connie Shi calling. We met each other a few days ago."

"Yes, of course. I remember you."

"I hope I'm not calling at a bad time."

"No, it's fine. What's up?"

"Well, I think my son and your son are attending the same dojo. Colin came home yesterday and couldn't stop talking about how much fun he'd had. He mentioned another boy who's helping him acclimate. He said his name is Ryan Yee, and I remember you saying your son's name is Ryan and he also attends judo classes, but I wasn't sure because the last name didn't jibe."

"It's funny that you're telling me this because Ryan mentioned helping a new kid at his dojo named Colin. It didn't click when we met and you said your son's name was Colin. As for the name... well, I'm not sure if I mentioned it to you—both of my kids are from my late husband's first marriage."

"You did, and that explains it."

"Yes, it certainly does."

"Anyway, this coincidence is too much to ignore. I want to invite you and the kids over to the house this weekend. We can grill hamburgers, and we have a pool, so the kids can swim."

"That sounds like fun. It's nice of you to think of us."

"And bring your mother-in-law. I'd love to meet her."

"I'm positive the kids will be fine with it. Just let me collect the head nods later when I get home."

"Sounds good. Talk soon."

Connie returned her cell phone to her purse and then started her vehicle. Everything was falling into place.

CHAPTER TWENTY-ONE

For dinner that night, I picked up lasagna from Fanelli's Deli. The night before, Lucy had mentioned how we hadn't eaten it in a long time. We put it to a vote, and Italian night won. Even Po Po loved the pasta from there and didn't protest. Even though she insisted on cooking every night, I try to give her a night off by taking the family out for dinner or ordering takeout. On rarer occasions, I somehow convince her to let me cook.

We chowed down on Bolognese lasagna, antipasto, Caesar salad, and crispy garlic bread. Lucy and Ryan both loved making little lasagna sandwiches by taking the ends of the loaf, hollowing it out and then stuffing the cheesy pasta inside of it. I must admit, it was pretty tasty, and why I always bought two loaves—Po Po and I both had become fond of the idea. It was way too much bread for a family of four, but we are pigs. What can I say?

Once we had managed to fill our stomachs a little bit, I brought up Connie's invitation.

"So, what do you guys think? Hamburgers. A pool. Your friends."

"Sounds super cool," Ryan said. "I really like Colin."

"Do I know someone there?" Lucy asked.

"Sure you do. You met Connie's daughter at school, when we had your parent-teacher conference. Her name is Hailey."

"Oh, yeah. I remember her. She's nice. I think this is an excellent plan."

"Po Po, what do you think? You were invited too. I think it'll be good to get out."

"They Chinese?"

"Yeah, why?"

"Okay, I go."

The Shis had just settled into their seats at the Sundance Kabuki Cinemas off of Fillmore and Post. Connie passed out hotdogs to each of her kids and then placed a large bucket of popcorn between the three of them. "Share this. Understood?"

They all nodded as they shoved fistfuls of popcorn into their mouth. Albert had the sodas and placed one in each of the seat cup holders. "Don't drink them too fast. You won't be getting a refill."

With the kids seated and stuffing their faces, Connie and Albert took their seats, bookending their children. As they watched the movie previews, Albert's phone buzzed. He pulled his phone halfway out of his pocket and peeked at the message on the screen. A beat later, he stood up and walked out of the movie theater.

Once outside on the sidewalk, he replied to the text with a single letter: Y. A few seconds later, he received another text message with the words, *"Peace Pagoda."*

The Peace Pagoda was a five-tiered concrete stupa located about forty yards away from the theater in an open plaza next to the Japan Center shopping center. Albert walked briskly, arriving at the plaza a few minutes later. The sun had already dipped below the horizon. There were a few outdoor lamps here and there, but none near the stupa.

He walked toward it, his eyes scanning the area surrounding the structure. He saw no one, so he waited under the stupa, his back facing it. The burning ember of a cigarette caught the corner of his eye. From the shadows, the outline of a man appeared. The cigarette burned brighter as he took a long pull.

"I'm supposed to be watching a movie with my family," Albert said to the man once he was close enough.

"The security at the facility is too tight. We can't get a guy inside. We need you to put ears in Agent Kane's home ASAP."

"We're in the early stages of building a relationship."

"Continue with that, but we need ears inside. She visits the girl daily, and we want to know if she talks about it with her family."

"Is that all?"

"Yes."

Albert left the shadowy figure without saying another word and hurried back to the theater.

CHAPTER TWENTY-TWO

On our drive to the facility the next morning, Kang brought up what Archer had said to us the day before.

"You think he has a point? That we're not pressing Xiaolian hard enough?"

I took a sip from my travel mug as I mulled over his question. "Perhaps. It's not worth debating, is it? We all want the same answers."

"I agree. And I hate to admit it, but he's probably right. We've spent enough time establishing that we're more friend than foe."

"We could push harder," I said.

When we met Yates, he seemed his usual self and didn't seem to harbor any hard feelings about the stunt we pulled the other day. I was glad to see he had put it behind him.

"How is she today?" I asked as we followed him down the hall.

"She's in good spirits and still riding the high from yesterday's excursion to the amusement park."

"So you agree it was worth it."

Yates stopped and turned to face us. "We have protocols

that must be adhered to. Do I agree with every one of them? No. Must I follow them?" He paused briefly. "Luckily, not everyone is in the same position as I." A small smile appeared on his face. Kang and Yates continued on into the observation room, and I entered the recreation room.

Inside, Xiaolian was lying on her stomach on the mat, reading a book. Her hands were cupped under her chin, supporting her head. As soon as she saw me, she closed the book and jumped to her feet.

"Abby, I'm so happy to see you."

We gave each other a hug.

"I'm happy to see you too. You're so full of energy today."

"I'm still thinking about yesterday. I had so much fun. I could barely sleep last night. When can we go back? Can Ryan and Lucy come the next time?"

I laughed. Her enthusiasm was contagious. "We'll see." It was a bullshit answer, but what else could I say?

"Do you want to train today?" she asked.

"Maybe later. First I want to talk to you. Let's sit down."

We both plopped down on the mat. I sat cross-legged, and Xiaolian leaned back on her hands with her legs stretched out.

I got straight to the point. "Why don't you tell me about your name? Your real name, not the name we gave you."

"Oh." She deflated a tiny bit.

"I won't lie to you, Xiaolian. There are a lot of people who are interested in finding out why you came to America, and about you in general."

"But I've told you everything."

"I'm not one of *them*," I said in a quieter voice and with a slight tilt of my head to the observation window. "There's no need to pretend here, okay? Now, your name."

"What's to know? It's 'Abby.' It's what I've always been

called. I don't know why it's the same as yours. A lot of people have the same name."

"I would agree with you and say it's no big deal, but there's a catch. You and I look remarkably alike. You know it. I know it. Everyone who sees us together knows it. Now, let's try again. Why were you named Abby?"

"I really don't know. I didn't even know I looked like someone else."

I didn't know what I expected her to say. Maybe to confirm what we already knew—that someone had stolen my DNA and created her. Perhaps she was speaking the truth. Why would the people who created her tell her?

"Did your mother and father give you that name?"

"I don't know."

"Do you have a mother and father?"

Xiaolian's gaze fell to the mat.

"It's okay, sweetie. I'm not here to condemn you. I'm just looking for answers that can help us help you."

"No," she said softly.

"No, you don't have any, or you don't know where they are?"

She shrugged. "I didn't know I was supposed to have a mother and father until I got older."

"Who fed and clothed you? Who provided your education and trained you in martial arts?"

"The teachers did."

"Teachers? Like in a school?"

"I guess. From as long as I can remember, we were surrounded by the teachers."

"And they taught you everything you know, even to speak English."

"Yes."

I leaned in a bit closer. "Why did they teach you all of this?"

"I don't know. It's just something that they did since forever."

"Do you remember talking to Agent Scott Reilly, the man with the glasses, when you arrived at my home after escaping from the motel?"

"Yeah, he was nice to me."

"You told him that, in the place you used to live, they performed experiments. Do you remember saying that?"

She nodded.

"Could you elaborate?"

She let out a breath and quickly said, "They taught us stuff and tested us."

"So these experiments were really instructional classes."

"I guess." She shrugged and looked away, but not before I saw her roll her eyes.

"You know what I think? You're a bright girl... when you want to be. So let's stop playing verbal games here. You and I both know you're not telling me everything."

Xiaolian lifted her head. Strands of her hair fell across her face, but I could clearly see that her eyes were locked onto mine. Gone was the playful smile, replaced by a tight line across her face.

She crossed her legs and leaned forward, closing the space between us to just a foot's length. And then in a low voice, she asked, "What exactly is it you want to know, Agent Kane?"

CHAPTER TWENTY-THREE

THE PIANO CONCERTO flowed from two speakers that hung in the corners of the office, giving the room a peaceful, yet elegant ambience. An ergonomically designed chair and a small circular table fashioned out of glass and marble were positioned near the center of the large open space.

The only other furniture was a tall console table that stood against floor-to-ceiling windows, which ran the entire length of the far wall. The view outside was a wooded area.

There were two paintings, both Dali, which hung on one wall. Another wall had five glass-enclosed shadowboxes, each containing a colorful butterfly pinned to a board.

Sid Devlin sat in the chair next to the round desk. He wore a plaid suit with a fitted vest. His hair was parted on the side and neatly combed, sideburns melding seamlessly into a groomed beard that pointed downward from his chin.

With his eyes closed, his right hand followed a repeated path of up and down movements, coinciding with the time signature of the orchestra.

Devlin continued to faux-direct the symphony, even though five minutes ago an Asian gentleman had entered the office. The man stood waiting, patiently, quietly, with his hands clasped behind his back.

Another two minutes passed before the bearded man addressed the waiting man. "What is it, Min?" He lowered his hand, and his eyelids opened. His light-blue eyes popped against the chocolate-brown fur on his head and face.

"Have you made a decision yet?" Min asked.

"I suppose you want me to say yes."

"We do have a schedule to abide by."

"Yes, such a pesky little thing, that is. To rush a decision like this is to rush blindly into a dark room and then shout in anger when you crash into a wall."

"Be that as it may... may we?" Min gestured to the long table near the window.

Devlin stood and tugged gently on his vest before buttoning the jacket he wore. He was six-four and towered over Min, who was seven inches shorter.

"Are they not happy with the work we've done here?"

"They are."

The two men walked over to the table.

"Then I don't understand."

"It's cultural."

"If they want the results they desire, they must accept that it takes time."

"Of course."

Laid out neatly in a row were five folders. Each one had a single portrait picture taped to the front. They were a mix of men and women. Also on the table was a single glass loupe made of polished brass and ivory.

"Min, this operation exists because of me. It's possible because of me. Who are they to tell me how to do my job?"

"Well, with all due respect, they have some say, as they do fund this entire operation."

Devlin dismissed Min's answer with a quick flick of his wrist.

The two men allowed their gaze to move from picture to picture. The bearded man picked up the last file folder. "She fits all the requirements." He handed the folder to Min.

"Of course... they all fit the requirements, but we need to choose based not only on what they can do for the program but also whether now is the right time to induct them. Need I remind you that if our work is to continue, it's imperative we draw no attention. We've already made a few costly mistakes. Any more and... I don't want to think about it."

Min returned the file to the table, ensuring that he put it in the exact same position as it was in before he picked it up. "Perhaps another male this time? Or since they all meet the requirements, how about the lowest-hanging fruit?"

"Min, the final decision is not a two-man task."

"Yes, of course. I was merely serving as a sounding board... so she's the one?"

Devlin hemmed and hawed.

"I see you still need time to decide. Please let me know when you've made a decision."

Min exited the office, leaving Devlin with the task of selecting the next specimen.

CHAPTER TWENTY-FOUR

XIAOLIAN'S RESPONSE had caught me off guard, and my natural reflex was to pull back. She quickly reached out, placed a hand on my arm, and stopped me.

"Don't," she said. "Stay close and they won't hear us. Smile, Agent Kane." She giggled. "Pretend we're just having a fun conversation." Her words slipped through a false smile.

I smiled back at her. "Am I speaking to Xiaolian or someone else?"

"Don't be silly. I'm not crazy."

"Forgive me for jumping to that conclusion, but your personality... well, it has changed. It's as if I'm speaking to another person."

"I'm locked up. Every day I'm questioned about my past, who I am, and why I'm here. And I wish I could provide all the answers, but I can't."

"Are you still having trouble remembering?"

"It's not that. I just don't have all the answers." Xiaolian threw her head back and laughed out loud.

"Is that so?"

"I sense doubt."

I nodded approvingly, my smile still stretched across my face. "You are so correct."

"Why don't you believe me?"

"Because I think you know more than you're telling me or Dr. Yates. You're a very intelligent young lady. You've received hand-to-hand combat training. The average twelve-year-old girl doesn't possess these qualities."

She batted at my arm playfully. I returned the bat.

"Earlier you asked me what is it I want to know, as if you had the answers."

"Maybe, but what will I get out of it? I'm stuck here. My only connection to my home was Dr. Lee, and he's dead. Your family is the only family I know here, and I'm being kept away from them. I'm even beginning to think you don't like me anymore."

"That's not true. We took you out for a day. We didn't have permission, and we got in trouble for it. I'm trying to get you out of here."

Xiaolian pulled away from me, sitting up straight. She twisted her torso, stretching it out in both directions. "You still haven't given me an answer to my original question."

I straightened up and did the same stretching exercise. "It's simple. I want to know why you were sent to me."

CHAPTER TWENTY-FIVE

It was BBQ day, and the kids were eager to hurry over to the Shis' residence. Even Po Po seemed enthusiastic. I was the only one feeling a little apprehensive. Not because I thought it was a bad idea, but because I always got cold feet when I was about to put myself in a social situation with the potential for new friends.

I didn't know why I felt that way, especially since I had already spent time with Connie. Maybe it was because our meeting at Lucy's school was an impromptu moment—there was no need, or opportunity, to impress. But this BBQ was a planned event. Our families would be coming together. Would we all get along? Would Connie have second thoughts later? Would we say "Let's get together again," but neither one would make an effort to contact the other because it wasn't genuine? The scenarios that formed in my head were ridiculous. I was creating drama where there shouldn't be any.

Come on, Abby. Pull it together. It's just a BBQ.

"Lucy, Ryan, let's go," I called out from the bottom of the stairs. The two of them had been talking about this get-together all morning, and how they couldn't wait to go swimming. Now that it was time to leave, suddenly everyone was moving like a snail. I headed up the stairs.

I peeked into Ryan's room. "What's the holdup?"

He was standing in front of his bed, staring at two pairs of swimming trunks he had laid out. "I was trying to decide what swim shorts to wear."

"Go with the pair that you're already wearing."

I walked over to Lucy's room. "What's slowing you down?"

Lucy was still dressed in her pajamas. "I'm getting ready."

"What on earth have you been doing for the last hour?"

She shrugged. "I dunno."

"You have five minutes to change and get downstairs. I'm not playing."

I headed back downstairs. Po Po was ready and sitting patiently in the living room.

"The kids will be down soon," I said.

Five minutes turned into ten, which turned into fifteen, but eventually we were all in the car. I had broken a sweat mobilizing the clan, but at least we were on our way.

From the cover of his car, Albert Shi watched the black Charger back out of the driveway and drive off. As soon as it was out of sight, he slipped a ball cap on his head that touted a fumigation service. He exited his vehicle, slung a satchel over his shoulder, and then removed a plastic garden pressure sprayer from the trunk. He walked over to Agent Kane's home and started spraying along the hedges and bushes in the front yard. Then he moved around to the side of the house, continuing his ruse until he was in the backyard.

Once there, he put the pressure sprayer down and entered the screened-in porch, quickly picking the lock on the door leading into the house. He stepped inside the hallway and checked the two bedrooms. One was a guestroom, and the other belonged to the mother-in-law. He walked past the kitchen and into the dining room and looked for a place to plant a listening device. The ceiling light would do.

He climbed up onto the table, unscrewed the cover, and placed it on the table. Then he removed a plastic container from his bag. Inside were four small GSM listening devices. Each was about an inch long and three quarters of an inch wide and contained a SIM card. All Albert would need to do was dial the SIM card from his cell phone to activate the device so he could monitor conversations in the room. He tested the device. Satisfied that it worked, he taped it to the side of the light bulb base and screwed the cover back on.

Where else?

He headed upstairs, checked the bedrooms, and decided to place a bug behind the headboard in Kane's bedroom. On the third floor, he hid one in the entertainment room, behind a large sofa against the wall. He also put one in Abby's office, behind her desk. No sooner had he finished pushing the desk back against the wall and checked to see that not a single item had been moved out of place, he heard the rumble of a car's engine. He looked out the window and saw Kane's vehicle pull into the driveway.

Crap!

Albert Shi spun around. His mind raced. He didn't have a chance in hell of making it down the stairs and out of the house. He glanced out the window. The boy and girl exited the car, but Kane remained seated behind the wheel.

This relaxed him a bit. *They probably just forgot something. I'll wait it out.*

"Mommy, I forgot my floaties! I need them."

Just when I thought I was home free. I wanted to ask if she really needed them, or suggest that the Shis might have some she could borrow, but I knew that wouldn't work. Lucy wasn't a strong swimmer, and she would naturally be more comfortable with her own things. It also reminded me that I needed to sign her up for swim lessons. I made a right as soon as I could and headed back to the house.

We pulled into the driveway. I shut off the ignition and handed her the house keys. "Hurry, okay?"

She hopped out and ran up the stairs of the front porch. Before I knew it, Ryan was also getting out of the car.

"Where are you going?"

"I want to get a book on Bruce Lee. I told Colin I would let him borrow it, but I keep forgetting to bring it with me to school."

Next thing I knew, Po Po had exited the car.

"Bathroom," she said.

For crying out loud.

As I sat there, I remembered telling Connie about a camp I had sent Ryan to a few years ago. I told her I still had the brochure somewhere in my office and would give it to her.

Well, I might as well get it, seeing that everyone else has gotten out of the car.

I headed inside. Up the stairs I went. When I hit the second floor, I called out for Ryan and Lucy to hurry. *How long does it take to grab one item?* I continued up one more flight to the third floor and hurried down the hall to my office.

The door was closed. I never close it. *Hmmm. Well, whatever.* I reached for the knob and pushed it open.

I shuffled through the stacks of paper on my desk. *Where is it? I swore I saw it not too long ago.* I had even thought to throw it out, but I hadn't. I opened the top drawer and did a brief search through the pile of junk. *Nope. Not here.* I glanced over to the corkboard mounted on the wall and scanned it. *Not there either.* I rested my hands on my hips as I spun around, my eyes taking in the entire office before settling on the door. There was a small closet space behind it. *Maybe in there?*

I wanted to dismiss the thought, but the investigator in me would only question my actions for the rest of the day; and Connie would remind me of the camp brochure and I would have to lie and tell her I couldn't find it, when the truth was I hadn't looked hard enough.

Ugh. I pulled the door away from the wall, revealing another smaller door. *This is so stupid. I know it's not here. I never go in here. It's just junk, mostly old Christmas wrapping paper.*

I reached for the tiny knob and pulled. The door remained stuck. *See? It won't even open. That's how long it's been since I last used this storage space.*

I tugged a little harder, and the wood against wood released a tiny squeak as the door moved a few centimeters. *Sheesh. Of course, it's not in here.* I gripped the small brass knob with both hands and jerked back hard. The door flew open, revealing a dark space about five feet in height and about six feet in depth. It was narrow, probably no more than three feet across.

Just inside was a stack of banker boxes that blocked half of my view to the back of the space. Leaning against them were the rolls of old wrapping paper, a small broom, and a dustpan. I didn't see the brochure. *I could step inside and look around the boxes just to be thorough, but why on earth would I put the brochure behind the boxes? Jesus, Abby, you already have the door open; just go in there and look around.*

I stepped inside, turning my body sideways so I could slip by the boxes and peer behind them. Nothing but a dark, empty space, and probably cobwebs. I exited the closet, shut the door, and gave my office another once-over.

Hmmm... I walked over to the small plastic rubbish bin near my desk and dug inside of it. Near the bottom, under a bunch of crumpled papers, I found the brochure. I had tossed it after all.

———

Albert Shi exited the entertainment room on the third floor and tucked his handgun into the waistband of his pants as he returned to Kane's office.

He peeked out the window and watched her and her family pile back into the car and drive off. Then he placed a call on his cell phone to Connie. "Everything is in place. I'll pick up salad dressing. See you in a bit, dear."

CHAPTER TWENTY-SIX

I ARRIVED in the office Monday morning with a bounce in my step, leftover goodwill from the BBQ at the Shis' place. Needless to say, we'd all had fun. No drama. No awkward moments. It had been a while since the family had done something like that. And truthfully, it was nice talking to someone who didn't work in law enforcement, someone who didn't care to know the details of the investigations I worked on.

Don't get me wrong. Agent Tracey House was still the best female friend I had, but there was something about Connie that complemented me in ways that House didn't. Probably because she was a mother. I loved listening to her talk about how she had lost her two boys at Disneyland, and how she'd totally flaked and forgotten her husband's birthday and their anniversary all in the same year. It made me feel better about my own shortcomings.

She told me I wasn't a bad mother. "No one's perfect. Everyone screws up. All we can do is try to minimize the damage," she said.

"Good morning," Kang said. He was leaning back in his chair and sipping coffee from a mug.

"Good morning to you too." I dropped my purse next to my desk and sat.

"You look chipper."

"I am. The whole family went to a BBQ this weekend, the parents of two boys and a girl who attend the same school as Ryan and Lucy."

"Look at you, mingling with other moms and dads."

"Hey, I *can* talk about something other than solving cases. I'm interesting."

"Didn't say you weren't." Kang placed the mug on his desk. "So, these parents. What are they like?"

"The wife, Connie, is a stay-at-home mom. Her husband, Albert, is a dentist."

"Let me guess: they're Chinese?"

"What makes you say that?"

"Come on, Abby." Kang crinkled his brow.

"Okay, okay. So they're Chinese. Maybe that's why we got along. Her husband is from Hong Kong, and she's local, from Redwood City. They both attended the same university. That's where they met. Anyway, their oldest son also trains at the same dojo as Ryan. Their youngest, the girl, is considering signing up to be a Brownie, as is Lucy."

"Brownie? That's news. Never pegged her as being interested in the Girl Scouts."

"She's enamored by the idea of wearing a uniform. We'll know if she's serious if she maintains interest after thirty days. What did you do this weekend?"

"I had two cousins, my mother's side, visit. We went fishing for perch at Half Moon Bay and ended up catching a bucketful. I even reeled in a couple of Dungeness crabs."

"How does that work?"

"They're pretty stubborn creatures. Once they lock onto the bait, they don't let go, even if it means being reeled right out of the ocean. What time do you want to head down to the facility?"

"I thought we would visit Barnes first."

"The tech guy? Why?"

"Hear me out. Barnes and Hammond, the brain surgeon, are both accomplished in their fields and have money."

"Barnes has stupid amounts of money. There's no comparison."

"Yes, I know, but ride along with me here. Both have wealth. Both go missing for less than a day. Both have trouble recalling what happened. I'm thinking the same person might have abducted them."

"What's the motive? Money?"

"Could be. Maybe it's blackmail. Someone discovers information about these people. He abducts them and confronts them with it. The victims don't want this information getting out, so they agree to pay the guy off. They don't take it any further, like going to the police, for fear that questions will be asked that might uncover what they're trying to keep a secret."

Kang popped his lips as he stared at the ceiling. "You know, you always have a way of making the tiniest of threads appear plausible and fully connected."

"Yeah, and so?"

"What are you after here?"

"The truth. I want to know exactly what's going on. I also think there's more to their stories that even they might not know."

"You're serious?"

"I am."

"So on top of the blackmail, you also think there's stuff they're not telling us because they themselves aren't even aware of it?"

"Even if they weren't trying to cover up some embarrassing

or incriminating information, they both have a spotty memory of what took place. It reminded me of how little Xiaolian could remember when we first met her."

Kang sat up straight in his chair and rested his forearms on his desk. "Sooner or later, you were bound to bring this back to her."

"I was the one questioning her, so maybe it's only something that I can recognize."

Kang nodded his head.

"They could have been drugged during the abduction and—"

"Tell me you aren't trying to strengthen a tie between Xiaolian and these two guys?"

"I'm not purposely trying to do anything. I'm just following the path."

Kang rubbed the side of his face. "So another conversation with Barnes?"

"That's right. Just a conversation."

CHAPTER TWENTY-SEVEN

Barnes was surprised to see us. He even hesitated and asked if he needed to have his lawyer present. I quickly assured him that all we wanted was to ask a few more questions. He paused for a moment before letting us through the front gate.

"Sometimes multiple conversations can help the investigation," I said as we trailed behind him. "Also we've received new information since our last discussion."

"Is that so?"

We passed through the foyer and into an open space with a large, round wooden table in the center. The décor was rustic villa. Barnes stopped next to the table and eyed the large centerpiece on top of it—a mini lemon tree, complete with hanging fruit.

"And this is all we're trying to do here. We appreciate you taking the time to talk to us. We understand you're a busy man."

Barnes continued to ogle the arrangement, even picked a few dead leaves off of the tree. I glanced around the room. There were numerous accent tables with various pieces of art decorating their tabletops. They looked expensive. Wood replaced the marble flooring that had graced the foyer.

Barnes turned his attention back to us. "I can't really see how this will help. I've told you everything I know, but if you have the time to spare, I guess I can do the same."

He walked toward a pair of French doors and slid them open. "It's a beautiful day. Let's continue our talk outside."

No sooner had I set foot on the stone veranda than I became distracted. The view from inside was deceiving. Barnes had unobstructed views across the entire bay: from the Golden Gate Bridge to Alcatraz Island to the Bay Bridge.

"So this new information you've received, can you share it with me?" he asked.

"We discovered another victim with circumstances similar to yours."

A smile grew on Barnes's face as he wagged a finger at us. "You see? I'm not crazy. I told you someone kidnapped me. The same thing happened to this other person, right?"

"There are comparisons between the two of you that we find interesting. Our other victim remembers leaving his office, and the next thing he knew, he woke up sitting in the driver's seat of his car parked at Ocean Beach."

"He can't remember anything in between?"

"It's spotty. He was released unharmed. His money and jewelry were still intact, so we know whoever took him wasn't after his personal effects."

Barnes tugged repeatedly on his chin. "This is interesting. So you're thinking the same person took both of us?"

"That's a possibility we're exploring. Let's go over the part where you woke up in the woods."

"Like I said before, my memory starts with me leaning against a tree and then walking and..."

Barnes's eyes suddenly glazed over, as he seemed to be looking beyond us, out over the bay. I snapped my finger.

"Mr. Barnes, do you remember something?"

"Yes, a guy on a mountain bike rode past me. He shouted something at me. I think he called me crazy."

"Could you describe this guy well enough for a composite drawing?" Kang asked. "We could comb the area and see if anyone recognizes him. He might be a regular rider."

Barnes shook his head. "It's like flashes of him on the bike, and just when I try to lock on him, the image disappears. Damn!"

"Perhaps more time will make it clearer," I said. "This is good, though. You're remembering more. So you wake up in the woods, against a tree. You take a few steps, and a mountain biker rides by and shouts something at you... and then what?"

"He disappears from my view. But I remember knowing enough to follow him, thinking he was riding down the mountain. The rest of the way, I see flashes of the woods until the tops of buildings and the bay appear through a clearing in the trees. Then I'm standing on the sidewalk, naked and scaring the crap out of people. I've seen the footage, you know. I realize I looked like a homeless madman shouting nonsense at people. But the thing is, that's not what it felt like in my head. In my head, I was calm, speaking rationally. Every time I opened my mouth, I believed I was simply asking for help. And then I got tased."

"But there's no recollection before you were standing near the tree?"

Barnes shut his eyes, and his jawline tightened. He remained that way for a moment or so before drawing a deep breath and opening his eyes.

"I've got nothing for you."

I puckered my lips and swished them side to side.

"Sorry." He shrugged.

"Do you think you can take us to the location where you saw the mountain biker?"

Barnes glanced at his watch. "What? Like now?"

"Uh, yeah. Unless you've got other pressing matters."

"Well, if you go to the place where the police tased me, you'll see the trail. Just follow it up. I'm sure the hospital gown is still up there."

"Mr. Barnes, were you looked over by a physician after you were arrested?"

He laughed. "I got booked and thrown into a cell until they felt I had calmed down enough. Only then was I allowed to phone my lawyer. It took the rest of the day for me to be released. I went to my doctor the following day. He said I'd experienced some trauma, but there was nothing physically wrong with me."

"He didn't by chance have bloodwork done, did he?"

"He didn't draw blood, so I'm guessing the answer is no. Why?"

"Well, it could tell us if someone drugged you." I looked at Kang. "It's been about a week. What do you think?"

"I think it couldn't hurt," he replied.

"Could we stop talking in police code?" Barnes asked, clearly annoyed.

"We'd like one of our guys to give you a thorough physical. They'll know exactly what to look for."

"You think I still have drugs in my system?"

"You might. Is finding out worth an hour or two of your time?"

CHAPTER TWENTY-EIGHT

AFTER OUR TALK WITH BARNES, we made a decision to check out the woods, and he agreed to head down to our offices to have his bloodwork done. It was a long shot, but I had a hunch building in my stomach.

"I'm pretty sure propofol exits the body within twenty-four hours," Kang said as we drove away from Barnes's residence.

"I realize that, but I want to cover all our bases," I said. "Maybe it was used initially, and something else was used after."

"Perhaps."

Mount Sutro is an eighty-acre forest protected by the city and the University of California, San Francisco, which controls a vast majority of the area. There are dozens of trails winding around the mountain, showing off the two-hundred-year-old growth of the forest. The drive there didn't take us very long.

Barnes had been apprehended by SFPD on Edgewood Road. Edgewood Trail begins where the road dead-ends. Kang parked, and we exited our vehicle. I slipped my jacket off and left it in the car. Kang did the same. We were both wearing flat shoes but wished we had hiking shoes or at least athletic shoes.

A small board with a map of the various trails was posted at the trailhead. There were a number of trails that funneled into Edgewood Trail, which led directly to our location.

"I wonder if he was even on a trail," Kang said.

"I had the same thought. He could have just been roaming around and hit a trail as he reached the bottom of the hill."

"Probably makes sense to follow Edgewood Trail, and then when it begins to branch off into the other trails, to play it by ear from there."

"Sounds reasonable to me."

Kang snapped a picture of the map with his cell phone. "Don't want to get lost."

We started following Edgewood Trail. It was neatly groomed but steep. We continued at a slow pace, our eyes searching the woods. The area was quiet, save for the chirping of the birds. The hike was physically challenging, but the canopy of trees helped keep us cool.

Barnes estimated that the time between when he had removed the gown and when he had hit the street was about forty minutes. So we knew we had a ways to go before we would have an opportunity to recover the gown, if we got lucky.

Eventually, Edgewood Trail came to a T intersection. Kang removed his phone and pulled up the picture he'd taken earlier.

"According to this map, this is where Historic Trail turns into Stanyan Trail. If we follow Historic, it'll take us north but down around the lower part of the slope. If we follow Stanyan, we'll head south and eventually down the hill, but Stanyan connects to the North Ridge Trail, which takes us farther up the mountain."

"I think that's the route we take," I said.

With a decision made, we followed Stanyan until we reached the juncture with North Ridge, which was a trail that shifted back and forth up the hill with multiple switchbacks.

Eventually, we intersected with another trail, Fairy Gates, but decided to stick it out on North Ridge since it literally would take us to the top of the mountain.

Interestingly enough, we discovered that North Ridge Trail intersected with a road: Medical Center Way.

"Hmmm. Barnes didn't mention anything about crossing a road," I said.

Kang pulled up the map on his phone. "Looks like there are two roads that cut across the mountain. I say we stick with the trail, since it continues to the top. We can pick it up on the other side of the road."

The entire North Ridge Trail loop wasn't very long, just two miles total. I did find myself enjoying the scenery—the entire woods had a magical, fairy-like appearance to it, and the wonderful scent of the eucalyptus trees was intoxicating. As we neared the top, fog had begun to roll in. Smoky-gray mist drifted slowly between the trees. I half expected a tiny hobbit to appear, asking for directions.

"If this hike gets any more magical, I'll have to backtrack and check to see if we accidentally passed through a wardrobe."

"I hear you," Kang said. "This is my first time up here. I had no idea how beautiful it is."

"Isn't it always like that? The places where we live, we explore the least."

As we continued through a section of steep switchbacks, I noticed a few tire treads.

I pointed at them. "Looks like mountain bikers utilize this trail."

"Over here," Kang said as he gestured toward a small trail that cut through low bushes and funneled into the main trail. "I guess the bikers go off trail. This isn't a maintained footpath. Let's follow it for a bit."

The trail was barely visible, maybe a little more than a foot wide—enough for a bike. It weaved around trees and larger bushes. In some instances, it widened to about three feet, and in other parts, it almost disappeared. We stopped in an area where it widened and disappeared into a small clearing of brush. That was when I spotted footprints.

I smacked my forehead. "Tell me we can't be this lucky."

Kang stood next to me, staring at the footprints in the hardened mud. "I think we are."

We followed the prints through the low-lying brush for another twenty yards or so before I spotted what looked like a piece of cloth caked with mud.

"Kyle, over here. I think I found Barnes's hospital gown."

I grabbed a small branch off the ground and used it to lift the material up into the air.

"Certainly looks like one." He removed a plastic bag from his back pocket. He held it open, and I used the stick to shove the gown inside.

"I think we need to buy lottery tickets once we're off the mountain," he said as he closed the zip seal.

"You got that right. Splitsies if either of us wins, okay? Now that we're in the area where Barnes's memory starts, we should comb the area more carefully. Maybe we can figure out how he ended up here."

We split up again, looking to pick up Barnes's trail. Kang found it a few feet away, on the makeshift bike path we had originally followed.

"Looks like he was right about following the biker down the hill," I said.

We followed Barnes's tracks, and eventually the path intersected with the North Ridge Trail, albeit higher up the mountain.

"So, up or down?" Kang asked, looking in both directions of the trail.

"I say we head up. I imagine we're near the top."

Kang pulled up Google Maps to find our location. "You're right."

The trail began leveling out as we neared the top of the hill. My neck was slick, but my breathing wasn't taxed. The hike, while beautiful, was actually very invigorating. Kang was a few steps ahead of me when he stopped.

"What's up?" I asked as I caught up with him.

"Look over there, through the small clearing in the trees."

I looked over to where Kang was pointing and spied what looked like a small field of some sort. As we made our way over to it, we could see that it was anything but a field. A large section of the area was concrete pavement, as if it were the foundation for an old building that had been completely demolished and its remnants removed. Old fencing, barely propped up by a few rusty poles, surrounded part of the area.

"Strange seeing this in fairyland. It's like a cruel reminder of the urbanization surrounding Mount Sutro," I said.

We made our way across the pavement. Graffiti covered parts of it. There were a few old soda cans and other unidentifiable garbage. We neared the fence and viewed the rectangular concrete pad. Directly in the middle were two narrow steel plates, which were now rusted an orangey-brown.

"What do you suppose this is?" I asked.

"You know, I think this might be the remnants of an old missile site."

I looked at Kang. "Are you serious?"

"I remember once when I was a detective with SFPD, my partner and I were having a conversation about the days of the Cold War and how both governments were sticking missile silos just about everywhere. While he was living in Novosibirsk, the military installed one in the park that he used to play at. He mentioned there were silos hidden in San Francisco."

"You think this is one of them?"

"Abby, these aren't just large sheets of metal. These look like blast doors. Look, there's a split down the middle. That's where it opens up."

Now that he had mentioned it, they did look like large, metal doors. We walked around the blast doors. They looked as if they hadn't been opened in years.

"Why would the government just abandon it and leave it here? Makes no sense," I said as I studied them.

Kang had made his way to the far end of the doors and knelt.

"What are you looking at?" I walked over to him.

"These two smaller metal slabs look like doors to an entranceway."

"Yeah, and...?"

"It's just that the larger blast doors look like they've been sealed shut, but not these."

"Maybe the person who abducted Barnes kept him here," I said. "Come on. Let's pull them open."

Kang reached down and gripped one of the handles. I gripped the other, and we both pulled. The doors opened with surprising ease. They weren't as heavy as they looked.

Inside, a metal ladder descended maybe ten feet or so. I removed my flashlight from the holder hooked to my waistband, and shone the light inside. I saw broken beer bottles, some empty spray cans, and what looked like an old beach towel.

"Teenagers might have used the space to party a while ago," Kang said, as he, too, shone the beam from his flashlight inside.

"Only one way to be certain." I climbed down the ladder. Kang followed.

The concrete floor was wet in some areas, and the space had a musty smell. Along one of the walls were lighting fixtures, but they were empty, no bulbs.

"Man, I can think of a trillion other places to drink beer with my friends."

"Watch your step; there might be needles," Kang said.

The space continued to the right and into a short corridor, about five feet in length, where it ended with a metal door secured by a large padlock—one that was brand new.

CHAPTER TWENTY-NINE

THERE WASN'T MUCH MORE to look at after we hit the secured door. We took another look around the silo but found nothing strange. The anomaly was the brand-new padlock. Everything else looked as if it hadn't been touched in years. Did the government provide periodic maintenance and had it found that the lock needed replacing? Had someone else replace it? Someone who had no business being there? Those weren't questions we would find the answers to while on the mountain.

We made good speed down the mountain and stopped at a nearby deli, where we hurriedly munched on roast beef sandwiches and washed them down with cold pressed juice. It was a little after one o'clock when we started our drive to the facility.

Kang said, "We should find out who is responsible for maintenance in or around that silo. City or the military?"

"That's very proactive of you," I said.

"Just so you know," Kang glanced at me, "I haven't quite bought into a connection between Xiaolian and our two abductees, but I do think there might be a connection between Barnes and Hammond. I'm curious to know what's behind that door."

"Likewise."

When we arrived at the facility, we spotted Yates walking toward the entrance of Building D. He seemed to be in a hurry. Kang honked the horn, and Yates nearly jumped out of his shoes. I waved at the doctor as we pulled into a parking stall. He looked irritated.

"Agent Kane. Agent Kang. How good of you two to make it here today." He shielded the sun from his eyes as he squinted at us.

"We got held up with another investigation," I said as I closed my door.

He nodded. "Multitasking. It's good to see our tax dollars hard at work."

Yates held the door to the building open for us. Once we had passed through the waiting area and through the security doors, he spoke again. "She's been agitated all morning."

"Why's that?" I asked.

"It's not something new. I've seen this side of her before. You have too—on your first visit. It's just that these mood swings have progressed. There have been outbursts."

"What do you mean?"

"I think it's better that I show you."

We entered Yates's office. Kang and I each took a seat in the chairs in front of the doctor's desk.

"I have some footage I'd like to show you."

He tapped at his laptop and then turned it around so we could see the screen. Video footage of the recreation room filled the screen. It looked empty, but a few seconds later, an object flew across the screen.

"Was that a pair of boxing gloves?" I asked.

A chair followed next. That elicited a "Whoa!" from both me and Kang.

A short beat later, Xiaolian appeared in the frame. Her fists were balled tightly, and her feet stomped the floor with each step. She had a determined look on her face. And, if I wasn't mistaken, she was talking to herself.

"This is what's become of her lately," Yates said. "There's more."

He fast-forwarded the video footage until we saw Xiaolian in her bedroom. The lights were off, so the footage had the green-colored effect, but we could clearly see Xiaolian's glowing eyes as she stood next to her bed, staring at the camera.

"That happened this morning at approximately three forty-five a.m. It's not the first time she's done this."

"What's she looking at, besides the camera?"

Yates looked at me. "Nothing's there but the camera. She stood staring at it for twenty minutes before returning to bed."

He tapped at the keyboard. "This took place earlier in the night, at eleven p.m. She started this routine shortly after we stopped strapping her to the bed."

Xiaolian was on the floor next to her bed, doing twisting sit-ups.

"If my count is accurate, I believe she does fifty crunches before switching to fifty push-ups."

"Why weren't we informed of this earlier?"

"I had orders not to mention this to anyone."

"So why the sudden change of heart?"

Yates closed the laptop and then leaned back in his chair. "I'll be frank. I'm not making the progress that I'd hoped I would. I can continue showing you what she's capable of, but what I can't figure out is why she's this way. Why does she have mood swings? I don't know. Why does she stare at the camera late at night? I don't know. Why is she trained in hand-to-hand combat? I don't know. I can continue to discover unique things about Xiaolian, but it won't answer the bigger question, the motive or reasoning behind everything about her. Those answers, unfortunately, are not something science can answer, but she might be able to. However, as much as I try, I can't get her to open up. You are the only person I know of who has shown some ability to break through her wall. With that said, I also think you too are being hampered."

"I would agree. There are times I feel she's shutting me out."

"It's this place," Kang said as he gestured around us.

"Yes, I would agree with you, Agent Kang. Xiaolian is essentially a prisoner here, and until her circumstances change, we'll continue on this merry-go-round ride."

"What are you getting at, Dr. Yates?" I asked.

"I now believe in order for us to get to the truth about Xiaolian, we must release her."

My chest rose with excitement. "You're letting me take her home?"

"I wish it were that easy, but that decision is beyond my scope of authority."

"Who around here holds that authority?"

Just then Yates's door opened, and in walked Archer. He was wearing the same hoodie I had seen him in the day I'd first met him. He had a lollipop in his mouth.

"Agents." He leaned against the wall and folded his arms across his chest. "I'll get right to the point. Your progress with extracting information from the girl has been disappointing."

"I would say the same about the facility's efforts, but Dr. Yates has already covered that with us."

A wry smile appeared on Archer's face. "Feisty. I like that about you, Agent Kane."

He bit down on the candy and quickly crunched it into small pieces, his Adam's apple bobbed as he swallowed. He tossed the stick into a nearby trash can.

"Well, now that we've stated the obvious, how about we do something that doesn't waste anymore of our time?" I suggested.

"What are you proposing, Agent? That you take the girl home?"

"I know you think waterboarding her will yield the results you want, but, yes, I am proposing that."

Yates cleared his throat. "If I may speak candidly here. I'm in agreement with Agent Kane. We've hit an impasse. The facility has become a block that, unless removed, will not allow us to move forward."

Archer licked his lips. "All right. Let me see what I can do. But until you hear back from me, she is not to set foot out of this facility. Is that understood?"

I saluted him. "Aye, Captain."

CHAPTER THIRTY

YATES THOUGHT it was better we not meet with Xiaolian that day. He had given her a sedative earlier in the morning to keep her calm.

It surprised me to hear they were drugging her. Of course, I'm sure there were a number of things being done to her that we weren't privy to. Thinking about that really put her situation into perspective for me.

She was a twelve-year-old in a foreign country with no family or friends—with the exception of me, and even that was being generous—being held prisoner by the government so they could perform experiments on her. I thought back to my mindset at that age, and quickly concluded that I would have cracked half a day into my imprisonment.

"Do you still hold the same belief about her?" I asked Kang during our drive back to the offices.

"What? That she's a spy?" He tilted his head from side to side. "You know, sometimes I'm completely convinced, like after watching the video Yates showed us, and at other times, I see an innocent girl having fun at an amusement park. It's weird. You?"

"I've moved into your boat. At first I thought it was really unlikely, but now... I mean forget about her combat training, but a twelve-year-old girl having to endure what she's enduring physically and mentally and not break? I dunno. That seems like training to me, especially after watching those videos."

"Yeah, totally different Xiaolian. It's hard to argue. And it's not like she's just throwing a temper tantrum. It's like there's something going on inside her head."

"You think there's a chance she snapped and has just completely lost it?"

"Maybe." Kang steered the vehicle over to the carpool lane. "I'm a little concerned about you taking her out of the facility and bringing her into your home. You've got the kids and Po Po to think about. Granted, before we didn't know, but now..."

"If I don't do it, Archer will get his way, and she'll be tortured, perhaps even moved to a black site and kept there for Lord knows how long. She'll essentially disappear. I hate to think that harm would come to my family because of her, because deep down inside, I still see Xiaolian and not some Chinese spy."

"Unless that's part of her training. Look, we've got to come at this without bias. If she is a spy, the whole 'innocent girl' is just an act."

I shifted in my seat. "I realize she could be playing us, and that we have to accept the fact she's good enough to counter our actions with changes in her personality."

"It would explain what Yates thinks are mood swings. It's hard to see her that way, but we have to assume she's capable of anything. She's smarter than we realize—that, I believe."

Later that evening, Albert Shi sat in the driver's seat of his vehicle, parked two houses away from Abby's home, while he listened to their dinner conversation through a pair of earbuds attached to a cell phone. Another cell phone sitting on the passenger seat buzzed. He removed an earbud and answered the call.

"Anything to report?" Connie asked.

"Nah. So far it's just normal family talk about everyone's day. Lucy is still pondering joining the Brownies. Is Hailey still interested?"

"She is if Lucy is. Did Ryan mention anything about Colin at the dojo?"

"He talked a little about the dojo, but Colin never came up. We should push him to tighten his friendship with Ryan. It couldn't hurt. You know, I'd hoped she would mention the facility, since they showed up there today, but she remained tight-lipped."

"Maybe she doesn't discuss that with the family."

"Maybe. I've still got the bug in her office and bedroom. So there are opportunities. I wonder if we should put a bug in Agent Kang's home."

"We'll need approval. How much longer are you staying there?"

'They're getting ready to watch an hour of *The Voice*. I think I'll call it a night. I'll see you shortly."

———

Lucy, Po Po, and I retired to the entertainment room to watch TV. Po Po usually doesn't come up to the third floor, but she's addicted to *The Voice*, as we all were, except Ryan. It was the show's semifinals, and we favored the same singer—a girl from San Francisco named Riley.

"I hope Riley has a better song," Lucy said. She plopped down on the sofa with Dim Sum, her stuffed panda, in her arms. She deemed it Riley's good-luck charm. "Last time she almost got told to go home."

"Come on, Riley," I said as I rubbed Dim Sum's belly and then threw the magical luck at the TV screen.

"Maybe I've given away too much of Dim Sum's luck," she said.

"What do you mean, honey?"

"I let Xiaolian have her while she was here, and maybe Dim Sum hasn't fully charged yet."

"Oh, I see. I don't think you have to worry about that. Dim Sum has a big belly. Speaking of, there's a chance Xiaolian might be coming to stay with us again."

Mentioning her name prompted Po Po to sit up and turn to me. "She come again?"

"Yes." Lucy pumped a fist.

"Some details still need to be worked out, but I think it'll happen."

A smile formed on Po Po's face as she leaned back and placed her hands on her lap. That night, we never did bring up the topic of Xiaolian again—the power of *The Voice*.

CHAPTER THIRTY-ONE

THE FOLLOWING MORNING, I arrived at the Bureau and faced two empty desks. Every now and then, I actually beat Kang into the office. I dropped my things off at my desk and made a beeline to the breakroom to fix myself a cup of tea. When I returned, he still hadn't shown up. I glanced at my watch; it was ten after nine. I took a seat, sipped my tea, and turned on my laptop. Kang showed up while I was answering emails.

"Sorry I'm late," he said. "I hit the sack late last night and had a hell of a time getting out of bed this morning."

"What kept you up?" I took a sip of my tea.

Kang slipped his jacket off, swung it over the back of this chair, and sat. "Last night I couldn't shake the thought of what we saw up on Mount Sutro. I decided to dig deeper into this missing-person thing we're looking into, just to see if there were more filings similar to Barnes's and Hammond's. First, I kept it to the Bay Area, but eventually I expanded my search to the state of California." A smile stretched across Kang's face.

"And...?" I let the word trail.

"I found two more filings."

"Yes!" I slammed my palm down on my desk. "Go on."

"Well, until we talk to these people, we can't be sure. But basically these two individuals were reported missing. One report was withdrawn after ten hours, and the other after twelve hours."

"Who were the victims?"

Kang removed his cell phone from his front pants pocket and tapped at the screen briefly. "One is an engineer who lives in Long Beach. The other is an angel investor living in Silicon Valley. We should definitely talk to the investor because, in the report, there's a notation that he insisted he wasn't missing but was abducted."

"What happened?"

"I'm not sure what happened. There wasn't any information noted in the file on whether it was pursued. On my way in this morning, I left a message for the detective assigned to the case. I should hear back from him sometime today."

"Excellent work, Sherlock. Now let's see what talking to this investor does for us."

CHAPTER THIRTY-TWO

Evaristo Damiani was the private investor we wanted to question. He worked out of his home in Atherton, California, probably one of the wealthiest neighborhoods in the Bay Area. When we'd called earlier, asking if we could speak with him, he'd been more than happy to meet with us. In fact, he pleaded that we take on his case.

"Welcome to La Vecchia Dimora," Damiani said with a smile as he opened the door to a home that resembled a villa plucked straight off the rolling hills of Tuscany.

"I'm Agent Kane. This is Agent Kang. We appreciate you taking the time to speak to us."

"Why would I turn down the personal help of the FBI?" He shrugged. "I'm having coffee by the pool out back. Join me."

Damiani wore all white and kept his jet-black hair slicked back. He looked to be in his mid-fifties, was physically fit, and walked a fast pace. He constantly clasped his hands into muffled claps as he spoke.

A rustic stone patio extended to an Olympic-sized pool, surrounded by manicured lawns and potted topiaries.

"I just finished my morning swim. I do fifty laps every day."

He flexed his biceps and raised an eyebrow at me. "Espresso? Cappuccino?" Damiani motioned for a servant who stood nearby.

"I'll have an espresso," Kang replied.

"Just hot water. I have my own tea," I said as I removed my tin from my purse.

Damiani grinned as he shook his index finger at me. "You strike me as someone who is always prepared."

If carrying my own tea around qualifies, then yes. "I'm particular, that's all."

"What have you done so far with my case? Tell me; I'm eager to hear the results."

"I'm sorry to disappoint you, Mr. Damiani—"

"Please, call me Evaristo."

"We haven't been investigating your case, but we are here to learn more about the missing-persons report that was filed on your behalf. Why don't you tell us what happened?"

The servant reappeared with our drinks, and Damiani downed his espresso in one gulp.

"It was about three months ago. I was attending a benefit in the city. I can't remember what it was for. There are so many, and they're all the same. After it finished, I walked back to my car."

"Excuse me, where was the benefit?" I asked.

"The Moscone Center."

"And you were parked in one of the parking lots?"

He nodded.

"Do you remember which one?"

"No. Is that important?"

"I don't know yet. Continue."

"So, I'm walking back to my car. There's no one else around; I was one of the last to leave. Anyway, just as I'm about to open my door, I hear footsteps right behind me."

"And?"

"That's it. From that point on, there's nothing. Poof." Damiani made a gesture with his hand.

"You have no recollection from that moment on?"

"None, and it bothers the hell out of me. The next thing I remember is waking up on a park bench at Fort Mason. A groundsman working there woke me."

"Do you recall the time?"

"Early in the morning, maybe about seven. I still had on the clothes from the night before."

"Did this worker see anyone with you?"

Damiani shook his head. "Didn't think to ask. I told him I couldn't remember anything. You should understand, at the time I was confused and scared."

"We do. That's a natural reaction," Kang said. "You didn't happen to get this worker's name, did you?"

"If I did, I can't remember, but he was a white guy, probably in his forties. He had a mustache."

"After he woke you, what did you do?"

"I checked my pockets and found my cell phone. There were multiple calls from Dino, my butler. When I didn't return home, he became worried."

"You remembered who he was, your butler?" I asked.

"No, at the time I had no idea who he was, but he kept telling me he knew me, so I listened."

"Was he the one who filed the missing-persons report?" Kang asked.

"Yes, bless his heart. He spoke to the groundsman to get my location and then came and picked me up."

"And what about your car?"

"It was still parked at the Moscone Center. I also had my wallet and watch. Nothing was stolen from me."

"According to the missing-persons report, it's been three months since this happened."

"That's correct."

"And what about now? You still have memory problems?"

"My memory has come back, but that night is still foggy. But one thing I remembered early on were three men staring at me."

"In the parking lot of the Moscone Center?"

"No, I think it was indoors somewhere. It's like I was sitting in a chair with a light shining in my face."

"Any chance this imagery could be a dream?" Kang asked.

"That's the same thing the detective who handled my case asked. He didn't believe me. Look, I know the difference between reality and a dream. This happened." Damiani tapped the stone table with his finger. "I'm positive."

CHAPTER THIRTY-THREE

THERE WASN'T MUCH MORE Damiani could tell us. He had problems recalling the events of his mystery night, much like the others we'd spoken with. The difference? Damiani was convinced the men he remembered were real and they had taken him to some location. We emerged from Damiani's home thirty minutes later with more information, but no smoking gun.

"We need more," I said before we got back into the SUV.

"You're right." Kang shut his door and started the engine. "Even though Barnes also mentioned seeing men around him, Hammond didn't."

"We don't have enough to go to Reilly just yet," I said.

"We'll have to figure something out soon if we want to continue to dual-path these investigations." He put the car into gear, and we drove away. "With that said, I do think we're onto something here."

I began a count on one hand. "All three are wealthy... well, Damiani and Barnes more so than Hammond. All were missing for less than twenty-four hours. All have memory problems, even a bit of psychosis."

"Barnes definitely," Kang added.

"The person behind these abductions isn't finished. They aren't harming the victims, aside from memory loss—a great way to stay under the radar. Three victims that we know of so far haven't had their cases investigated. That tells me this individual is calculating and intelligent, and has figured out a way to commit a crime that's invisible."

"We need motive," Kang said. "Money is a common theme. Blackmail is a possibility."

"All three would need to have a secret that is worth covering up, but Damiani wants an investigation, so it seems as though he has nothing to hide. Maybe it's about their stature in the community," I said.

"That's an interesting angle."

"All three are in the Bay Area. Maybe the circles they run in overlap somehow."

"There's a Long Beach victim. So..."

I turned away from him and stared out my window at nothing in particular, the scenery a blur as we sped along the highway. Kang was right; we were lacking the motivation behind these missing-persons events. Without it, we would continue to spin in circles. To complicate matters in my head, I was still searching for a way to connect them to Xiaolian. Was my obsession with her seriously affecting my judgment?

"Earth to Abby," Kang said in a robotic voice. "Come in."

I stretched my arms out in front of me. "Sorry. I was thinking about the victims."

"And?"

"Well, I was thinking it's a lot of work for one person to abduct and hold captive three or more individuals at different times and no one investigates. Even just one victim would be a complicated crime. Is this really the work of one individual?"

"A crew, maybe."

"I think it has to be—a highly trained one, I might add. It's not as if these victims are being snatched off of a dark and deserted highway," I said.

"Okay, so this person has help. We still haven't determined what the motivation would be."

We were stuck in a funk. We needed either fresh thinking or fresh information. I'd held high hopes of learning something crucial from Damiani. While we did get the three-men tidbit, it wasn't enough for us to turn the corner.

I drew a deep breath and then adjusted the seatbelt to relieve the tightness against my chest. *What are you doing, Abby? You're supposed to be focusing on Xiaolian. Why are you wasting time and energy chasing what might very well be nothing?* My inner voice spoke the truth. I had no business exploring this hunch. People were expecting me to flip a Chinese spy. How could I approach Reilly with these cases, when he's expecting an update on Xiaolian?

I had to wonder if this was my attempt to put distance between Xiaolian and myself. Maybe internally, I was against investigating her, against believing what could be the truth about her, so I'd come up with another investigation.

I didn't hear my cell phone ringing. Kang had to nudge my arm.

"Agent Kane speaking... Really? That's good news. We're on our way."

"What?" Kang asked.

"I have approval to take Xiaolian home. We can pick her up now."

CHAPTER THIRTY-FOUR

WE PARKED in the usual spot outside Building D. As we walked to the entrance, Archer appeared out of thin air and intercepted us. *What's with these spooks? Can't they approach us like normal people?*

"Just so you know, I'm against this, even though I made the case for you," he said.

"I appreciate your honesty and your ability to remain unbiased."

Kang and I stopped at reception once we were inside. We figured Yates would meet us as usual, but Archer motioned for us to follow him. "Yates is busy. I'll take you to the girl."

Archer had a security card that gave him access to every door we needed to pass through. He had the run of the place. Seemed he was a bigger deal than I had originally thought.

Still a spook, and I don't trust him.

The CIA was forbidden from carrying out operations inside the country. Utilizing me was their way of circumventing the rules. They had found a loophole to exploit.

We didn't speak another word as we followed him, which

was fine by me. Instead of meeting Xiaolian in the recreation room, Archer took us to her bedroom.

"She's been told you're coming to pick her up. The conditions were not given to her."

"What are they?" I asked.

"You're getting forty-eight hours with her."

"Two days?" I stopped him in the hall. "You might as well make it two hours. Based on my ability to get information from her last time, I'll need more time," I said.

"You'll have to make it work."

"I know all you want is for me to fail so you can have your way with her, but she's just a little girl. Give me four days. If I don't come up with anything worthwhile, I'll support whatever it is you want to whomever needs to hear it from me."

Archer eyed me for a moment. "Done." He turned and continued walking toward Xiaolian's bedroom. "She must never leave your sight. Everywhere you go, she goes. You are not allowed to leave her with your mother-in-law, and you will stay within the city limits."

"Is that it, or shall I start taking notes?"

"It's up to you whether you want to share this information with her." Archer grabbed the door handle to her room but stopped short of sliding his card through the card reader. "I know I shouldn't have to mention it, but I might as well cover everything. No one but Agent Kang, your supervisor, and your family are to know she's there."

"That goes without saying."

Archer slid his card through the reader. It beeped, and the locking mechanism on the door clicked. He pulled it open, gesturing for me to enter first.

Xiaolian was sitting on her bed, with her feet swaying back and forth, inches above the floor. She drew a big breath when she saw me. "Abby, you're here." She scooted off the bed and gave me a big hug. "I missed you."

"And I missed you."

"Hi, Xiaolian," Kang said.

She let go of me and gave Kang the same enthusiastic hug.

"I'm ready to go," she said after releasing her grasp of him.

"Is that all you have?" I asked, pointing at the paper bag on the bed.

"Yup."

She was still smiling from ear to ear. It didn't matter that her only worldly possessions were a few pieces of used clothing and some toiletries. I almost asked if she wanted to bring some of the items in the rec room, like the books and the tablet I had seen, but it quickly dawned on me that she would be back in a few days. It broke my heart. She had no idea.

Albert Shi raced over to Agent Kane's home after a long day at his dental practice. A last-minute root canal for a desperate patient had him running later than usual. By the time he'd parked and turned the scanner on, Abby and her family were just wrapping up dinner.

Shoot! I hope I didn't miss anything.

For the next fifteen minutes or so, broken conversation followed as Kane moved in and out of the dining room. He could pick up only bits and pieces but concluded she wasn't talking about work or the little girl. She and Lucy seemed to be discussing nothing in particular. *How is it women can talk and talk and talk about nothing?*

A little later, Abby went to her bedroom to take a shower. He didn't expect much from that bug, except he figured she might make calls from there. The dining room, entertainment room, and her office would be the fruit-bearing locations.

And he was right about that. While watching television, Abby and Lucy began talking—and so did someone else.

CHAPTER THIRTY-FIVE

ALBERT COULDN'T BELIEVE IT. He turned up the volume and listened closely. There was no mistake. He heard the voice of a young girl, and it wasn't Lucy's. *Xiaolian?*

He pressed the headset harder against his ear, not wanting to miss a single word. A car with a loud muffler drove by just as the other voice, the one that wasn't Lucy's, spoke. He cursed the vehicle.

He leaned over to the right, lowering his head toward the passenger seat, and listened intently. The other voice spoke again, this time longer. Albert was absolutely sure it wasn't Lucy. It had to be Xiaolian. But how? No one had notified him. Had she been snuck out somehow?

Albert needed confirmation. If that other voice he'd heard was indeed the girl, then someone wasn't doing his job very well. According to his contact, they had a person watching the place twenty-four/seven. *Say a name, dammit. Help me out here.*

"What do you think, Xiaolian?" Lucy asked. "I can't believe they don't have this show where you're from."

"I didn't have a TV."

"What? No TV?" Lucy slapped her forehead. "My gosh, how did you live?"

Xiaolian simply shrugged.

"Well, that's okay. You can watch as much TV here as you want. We love TV." Lucy gleamed with delight.

"Good. I love TV too," Xiaolian said joyfully.

"I wish you were staying longer."

Xiaolian's shoulders drooped, along with her smile. "Me too." She turned to me. "What's the reason I can't stay longer?"

I'd told Xiaolian about her short stay. I thought it was best to be straight with her, even if the truth wasn't something she wanted to hear or I wanted to say. I still had an objective to complete. And as it stood, I still felt like I had more trust to earn.

"I don't have a good answer for you, but staying here for four days is a start. Perhaps the next time, we can lengthen your stay."

"Or maybe you should tell those mean people that she will live with us," Lucy said, her voice stern with conviction. "We have the room *and* enough food."

"So I really have to leave after four days?" Xiaolian asked.

"I'm afraid so."

Lucy placed her arm around Xiaolian's shoulders. "That's okay. We'll be thinking of you."

———

A smile formed on Albert's face as he used the other cell phone to send a text message. A few minutes later, he received a reply, giving him a time and location for a meeting. Albert continued listening until the television show ended and they left the entertainment room. Then he dialed the listening device in Abby's home office, but it was quiet. He dialed the bug in her bedroom and the one in the light fixture above the dining room, but both devices delivered nothing but silence. *Where else does Agent Kane spend her time?*

CHAPTER THIRTY-SIX

THAT SAME NIGHT, at the School of Creative Arts, guest speaker Johnny Ellis stood in a packed room, addressing a crowd that clung to every word he said. He was the chief creative officer for Industrial Light and Magic, the visual-effects company created by George Lucas.

Plastic chairs were lined up ten across and seven rows deep, each one filled with an art student listening intently. More students stood huddled together, eliminating any personal space, along the walls and toward the rear of the room. A few were using the flyer for the event to keep cool.

Ellis began his talk that night by playing a show reel of ILM's recent work, which also included a few sneak peeks at what they were currently working on. He went on to discuss the future of VFX—he firmly believed it would play a much larger role, not just in the entertainment industry, but also in all content that was generated. Finally, he talked about what it was like working at ILM, and how they went about hiring talent. Not wanting to miss anything being said, no one dared make a sound, especially those students about to graduate.

After wrapping up his presentation, Ellis hung around to

answer questions from a small group of students. The heat in
the room was unforgiving, though. He suggested they take their
discussion to a nearby bar, where he proceeded to toss back
scotch while pontificating to the eager wannabes. The way they
all looked at him, as if he were immortal, a god amongst gods—it
was a jolt to his ego that never got old.

One drink quickly turned into five. By the time Ellis noticed
the time, it was well past midnight. He had an early morning
meeting the next day, and bid good-bye to the students by
picking up the tab and ordering one more round for the group.

Ellis emerged from the bar and ambled along the sidewalk.
He had parked his vehicle at the school, a few blocks away. The
night air felt cool and refreshing against his face. He took his
time walking. When he reached the end of the block, he waited
patiently at the curb, enjoying the quiet.

He buried his hands in the front pockets of his pants. He
shut his eyes and inhaled slowly and deeply through his nostrils.
His chest expanded, and the air tingled as it entered his lungs.
He exhaled in one long breath. Just as he was about to repeat
the breathing exercise, a hand clamped down around his mouth
and nose. Before Ellis could comprehend what was happening,
someone jerked him backward into a waiting car and whisked
him away from his spot on the curb.

The four men each had a hand on the gurney as they rolled it
quickly through the corridor, and into a room equipped with
medical monitoring devices, and surgical lighting on the ceiling.
They positioned the gurney directly under the bright lights.

One of them applied the brakes on the wheels and started to
strip Ellis's clothes off. Another man attached an oxygen mask
to Ellis's face and began monitoring his vitals. A third man

snapped on a pair of gloves and prepared an injection. Once Ellis's shoes and socks were removed, the gloved man found a suitable vein on Ellis's foot and stuck him with the needle.

The fourth one headed back to the door. "When I return, I expect everything to be finished." He then walked through the doorway and shut the door behind him.

"This was the riskiest grab yet," said the man monitoring vitals. "If we keep at it this way, we're going to get popped. I just know it."

The man giving the injection slowly removed the needle. "Keep quiet and do your job." Then he taped a small piece of gauze over the injection site.

"He's right," said the man who had removed the clothing. "It's insane. It's only a matter of time before someone sees us."

Injection Man cleaned another area on Ellis's leg and then readied another syringe. "Feel free to share your thoughts with the big man. See how far that gets you."

The two complaining men remained quiet. The one who had removed the clothing walked over to a counter along a wall and grabbed an SLS camera that was next to a laptop. He proceeded to photograph every part of Ellis's body.

Injection Man used his needle to draw a full vial of blood, twice. Both samples were then noted in the laptop and put into refrigeration.

"What does this guy do anyway?" asked Vitals Man.

"Didn't you look at the dossier?" Clothing Man asked as he snapped another picture.

"Sort of. I was running late, so I just focused on his physical aspect."

Clothing Man lowered the camera from his face. "He's some bigwig at that company that makes the Star Wars movies."

"It's called ILM... Industrial Light and Magic," said Injection Man. "They're the best in the visual-effects field. They do all the awesome movies." He used a pair of tweezers to pluck individual hairs, with their follicles attached, from Ellis's scalp. He dropped each one into its own container.

"That's pretty cool." Vitals Man turned his head so he could look at Ellis's face straight on. "I bet he's super talented."

"Are you falling in love?" joked Clothing Man.

"Screw you."

"How's the patient?" Injection Man asked.

"He's sleeping like a baby," Vitals Man said. He glanced at a clock on the wall. "We're good on timing too."

"Good. After that mess-up with the tech guy, we can't afford another mishap."

CHAPTER THIRTY-SEVEN

Later that night, after the kids and Po Po had retired to their bedrooms, I sat with Xiaolian in her room. She was tucked under the covers with Dim Sum. Again Lucy had lent her the stuffed panda. I sat near her, on the edge of the bed.

"Comfy?" I asked.

She nodded happily at first, but her smiled disappeared quickly. "Do I really have to go back to that place after four days?"

"I'm afraid so."

"I don't understand why I can't just stay here with you. What's wrong with me?"

"The government is trying to understand where you came from. Right now, you're a mystery."

"Do they do this with everyone who isn't from here?"

"Most people who visit the United States don't come here hidden inside a cargo container. You were part of a group of girls who were trafficked to the States."

"Trafficked?"

"That's what we call it when someone deals or trades in something that is illegal. And because you haven't been able to tell us much about where you came from or who your parents are... well, there are questions. Do you understand?"

"I guess. What will happen when they get their answers? Will they let me come to you then?"

I reached up and brushed a few strands of hair away from her eyes. "Oh, sweetie, I don't know how else to say this, but I believe once they receive their answers, they will most likely send you back to China."

Her eyes locked onto mine as she drew a sharp breath. "Why? Why would they send me there?"

"Right now, the belief is that you're from China or possibly Taiwan... it's one of those two places, but the thinking is China."

"I knew it. You're only being nice to me so you can get your answers, and then after that, you'll throw me out. I thought you liked me." She looked away from me.

"That's not true. I care a lot about you. If I didn't, I wouldn't have invited you into my home. Believe me when I say that. You are part of this family. Ryan, Lucy, and Po Po all think of you as one of us. So I don't want to hear any more talk like that. Understand?"

She nodded but still kept her gaze away from mine.

"The reality is you entered the country illegally, and because you have no blood relatives here, there is no one who can legally take custody of you. That's something I'm unable to do. That's why it's so important to figure out where you are from and how we can contact your family, your real family. I'm sure they miss you."

"I told you before I don't have one."

I placed a hand on her shoulder and gave it a comforting squeeze. "Do you have any family that you know of? A brother? A sister? Or even grandparents or aunts and uncles?"

Xiaolian's gaze fell to the side as she chewed on her bottom lip.

"So all you know are the teachers who raised you?"

She nodded. I lowered my head as I tried to catch her eye. I poked her belly playfully, prompting her to laugh and look at me.

"You know what I think? I think you were at an orphanage. It's a place where children stay when they lose their parents and—"

"I know what that word means. I don't know if it was an orphanage. It's the only place I've ever known. So maybe it was."

"Okay, let's assume it is. Surely they must have rules about leaving the premises?"

"You get punished if you go past the boundary."

"You mean like a gate?"

"There's a gate, but the boundary is really a bunch of bushes and trees."

"I see."

I noodled my inner cheek with my tongue while I watched Xiaolian absentmindedly tug on Dim Sum's ear. She looked so innocent, so child-like, which was a bit insane considering she was twelve, nearly a teenager. But at times, a purity about her came through, something I couldn't quite put into words.

Xiaolian had already revealed a side of herself that contradicted everything I had come to know about her. It was that day she had coldly questioned me in the recreation room. A different person had been sitting in front of me then. I wondered if that person would appear again.

"What else can you tell me about the staff... the people who looked after you at this place?"

She shrugged.

"What do you mean you don't know? You were there, were you not?" My voice grew louder.

"What do you want to know?" She suddenly sounded frustrated.

"We're talking in circles, Xiaolian. I'm asking questions, and you're... well, pretending you don't know the answers, when in fact you do."

"I'm not lying to you." She turned away again and stared at the wall.

"I didn't say you were lying. I just think you're not telling me everything you know. The more you help me to understand, the more I can help you. Your fate is in *your* hands, so don't complain when you find yourself back in China."

She remained silent.

"You know I'm right. I'm done playing games. Are you?"

"They were normal people," she said. "I don't know what else to tell you. I didn't talk with them. We only listened."

"Okay, what about the other children? Were you all the same age? Was there a mix of boys and girls?"

"Some were older, some were younger. And there were boys and girls."

"So it was definitely an institution of some sort."

Xiaolian looked at me with a frown. "What's that supposed to mean?"

"I didn't mean anything by it. The adults who looked after you, were they Chinese?"

"Yes."

"And they were the ones who educated you and trained you?"

"Yes."

"But you weren't the only one learning, right?"

"Everyone had classes, but we weren't all taught the same things."

"Let's talk more about the physical training you received. Do you know why you were taught to fight?"

"No."

How does someone learn that much and not have a clue as to why she's learning it? I watched her chew her bottom lip as she stared into her lap. *Was lying something you were also taught to do?*

"Do you mean to tell me you can't think of a single reason why? No? Any and all reasoning escapes you at the moment?"

She gripped Dim Sum's ear and balled her fist around it. My words seem to be getting through to her. So I pushed.

"I find this laughable that you can't provide an answer. I've seen the reports on the testing Dr. Yates has done. You excel in critical thinking, your ability to problem-solve is exceptional, and yet for some reason, you can't arrive at any sort of logical explanation for why you are here, why you know what you know. Surely you must have an opinion. And don't bother shrugging. That's an answer I've grown tired of. So let's cut the act, okay? Tell me what you really know."

"I am," she said, raising her voice.

"No, you're not."

"Why are you being mean?"

"Why are you playing dumb?"

Xiaolian lifted her head and pursed her lips as her stare drilled into me. Had the cold, calculating side of Xiaolian returned?

A coy smile slowly formed on her face. "It seems I can no longer play this game with you."

"I'm afraid not."

"I know you don't believe me, but I don't have the answers you want. I'm like you; I only have half of the puzzle. This is the way they operate."

"When you say 'they,' you mean the people who watched over you?"

She nodded. "Keeping me and the others in the dark is how they controlled us. They wanted us to fear the unknown."

"But why do this? You're children."

"I don't know. I didn't even think to ask that question back then. It wasn't until I arrived in America that I saw how different the world was from the one I was raised in. Do you believe me when I say I don't have the answers?"

I scratched my forehead. "So you thought your education, your training, your way of living was completely normal?"

"I know now that it's not." She scooted back, so that she sat up straight against the headboard. "I started thinking this after meeting Ryan for the first time. At his age, I was much more advanced."

"You mean in the physical sense? Because I saw the testing. I already know your education is above average."

"Yes, in the physical sense. I peeked inside Ryan's room and saw his training notes. He's good, though. Has real potential."

"How can you be sure of that? You've never sparred with him."

"I've sparred with you. Is he better than you?"

"If I recall, I won."

"Did you really?" Her grin returned.

"You're saying you let me win?"

She said nothing.

I took that as an opportunity to mentally replay everything she had revealed. One thing was clear; she had been playing me, everyone, from the very beginning. Was counter-interrogation also part of her training? As I thought back over our talks, it became ever so apparent. She had exhibited the basics, and I never saw it.

Xiaolian had controlled the conversation from the very start by remaining silent unless prompted, and even then, she related only the bare bones to me. However, when it came to our human-trafficking investigation, she was full of information. She talked a lot. She had deflected. I remembered Agent House mentioning to me that she thought it was odd that Xiaolian could recall information relating only to the investigation but could not remember anything about her personal life. *Dammit, we handed her a neatly wrapped cover story.*

I had provided a way for her to engage and turn over valuable information without so much as revealing a single thing about who she was or where she came from.

At that moment, the question that pressed upon me the most was whether her actions had been a calculated attempt to mask her real identity or, as she'd said, a cautious approach after finding herself thrust into a new world. If it were the latter, it was important that we find out more about this mysterious home of hers.

CHAPTER THIRTY-EIGHT

ALBERT HAD CONTINUED to listen for a few more hours, but heard nothing more during that time. He glanced at his watch; it was time to meet with his contact.

The meeting was to take place at George Sterling Park at the very top of Russian Hill. It was always dead at that time of night. A thick fog on top of the hill was a sure thing.

He drove up Russian Hill, along Chestnut Street, until it intersected with Hyde. There he made a left turn and parked his car against the curb. The park was just past Lombard Street —San Francisco's famous crooked street. He exited the vehicle and walked the rest of the distance.

He climbed a set of concrete steps that led up to a grassy mound. At the top was a pair of tennis courts. They were empty and dark; the park officially closed at nine. Albert had about fifteen feet of visibility in the fog, but he was familiar with the area.

He continued around the courts, following the chain-link fence that contained them, until he reached the far side, where a pathway wound its way through the park toward Larkin Street.

Trees lined the path, and there were benches scattered

throughout. The night was quiet, other than the scuff of his shoes against the concrete, or the occasional crunch of small pebbles under his steps.

The first bench came into view, but Albert walked past it and continued until he reached another one under a tree, where the path turned back and headed in the opposite direction. A person sitting on that bench could see, or on that night hear, anyone approaching from either direction.

Albert didn't notice the shadowy figure as he approached, not until it moved from behind the bench. As he closed the distance, he recognized his contact. A mutual nod was the extent of their greeting.

The man was older than Albert—late fifties to early sixties, he wasn't sure. He wore a black leather bomber jacket and blue jeans. A dark-gray flat cap covered his head.

"Your guy missed her leaving the facility today," Albert said as he took a seat on the bench, leaning slightly forward with both arms resting on his thighs.

The man sat next to him, preferring to lean back against the bench with his hands resting in his lap. "Are you sure it was her in the house? Could it have been a friend of the daughter?"

"They addressed her by name."

The shadowy man nodded. "I'll have to look into how this happened."

"From what I've learned, she's staying with Agent Kane for four days. The timing is tight, but I feel confident we can come up with a plan to grab the girl."

"You have new orders. She is to be eliminated."

Albert tried to grab the man's gaze, but he ignored him, continuing to stare straight ahead. "You can't be serious?"

"This is what needs to be done. We can't risk her returning to the facility, nor can we allow this game of hide-and-seek to continue. She's expendable."

"I can get her out of the house." Albert raised his voice but quickly lowered it and leaned toward the man. "At least give me the opportunity to bring her in, to a safe location. Allow me that much."

For the first time that night, Albert's contact turned toward him. His dark-brown eyes appeared black in the night. "I'm sorry, but she's no longer needed."

"She's a child, for God's sake. How harmful can she really be?"

"Your job is not to question. It's to do what is asked of you. A lot of effort and forward thinking, not to mention a large sum of cash, were invested in you and your wife. Do not forget why you were sent to America in the first place."

"I didn't sign up to kill children."

The man drew a deep breath, as if he were readying himself to say more, but he didn't. He simply stood and walked away.

Albert watched him disappear into the gray thickness. As much as he didn't agree with the order, he had no choice. If he didn't obey, his children would become targets.

CHAPTER THIRTY-NINE

THE FOLLOWING MORNING, Ellis woke to a sharp pain in his arm. He opened his eyes and immediately shut them; it felt like the sunlight had seared his retinas.

"Hey, man. You can't be here," a deep voice said.

Again, Ellis felt a jabbing pain in his arm. He opened his eyes just enough to see a man standing in front of him. Ellis kept blinking, and eventually his eyesight focused.

"What?" he asked, his voice raspy and his throat dry.

"This ain't a motel. You've got to get up and move along."

Ellis realized he was lying on a bench, and the pain he felt came from the rounded end of a rake handle jabbing his arm.

"I ain't playing. Get up and go." The man jabbed the rake handle at him a few more times, each jab harder than the last.

"Ow!" Ellis forced himself upright. "I'm leaving. Just give me a minute and stop poking me with that thing."

The man lowered the rake, his eyes squinty from the sun. He wore jeans and a polo shirt with a logo embroidered on the sleeve. Ellis didn't recognize it.

"You all right?" the man asked.

"Where the hell am I?"

That response triggered the man to laugh. "You don't recognize this place? You're at Pier 39. You know, Fisherman's Wharf? San Francisco?"

Ellis shook his head as none of that sounded familiar to him.

"Man, you must have knocked back a bunch of hooch last night not to recognize this joint." The elderly man extended his hand, and Ellis used it to pull himself to his feet.

"Steady there," the man said, holding on to Ellis's arm. "You got someone you can call to pick you up? Probably not safe for you to drive. I think you're still drunk."

Ellis reached up and gently massaged his forehead. "My head is killing me."

"Sit back down, mister. I can call you an ambulance."

"Where will they take me?"

The man crinkled his brow. "To the hospital. You do know what a hospital is, don't you?"

Ellis shrugged.

"You're worse off than I thought." The man shook his head as he looked around. "I can't have you sitting out here looking like this. This place will be overrun with tourists soon."

Just then a cell phone began ringing. Ellis sat there, ignoring it.

"Hey, aren't you going to answer that?"

"Answer what?"

The man pointed at Ellis's front pants pocket. "Your phone. It's ringing."

Ellis dug his hand into his pocket.

"It might be someone looking for you."

"Hello?" Ellis said. "I'm sorry, who is this? My wife? I don't have a wife."

Ellis disconnected the call and set the phone down next to him.

"Was that someone you know?"

"I don't know."

The phone rang again. This time the old man reached for the phone and answered. "Hello? No, I'm not a friend. I found him sleeping on a bench at Pier 39. He doesn't remember anything. Can you help him? Okay, but you need to hurry. I can't babysit him all day."

The old man handed the phone back to him with a trembling hand. Ellis's eyes focused on it.

"Yeah, I got the shakes," the man said. "You keep on doing what you're doing, and you'll get them too."

Ellis opened his mouth to speak but held his tongue.

"That lady on the phone says she knows you." The old man switched grips on his rake. "She's coming to pick you up."

"But I don't know her."

"She sounds all right to me. You need rest, and you can't do it here." The man licked his lips as he surveyed the area. "Crowds are coming." He motioned for Ellis to stand. "Follow me. There's an area where the workers take their breaks. You can chill there until your ride comes."

"No! I don't know this woman. I don't know you." Ellis stood up and backed away from the man.

"Hey, there. I'm just trying to help you."

"How do I know you're not part of this?" Ellis motioned around him.

"Part of what?"

"Part of whatever caused me to not know anything."

The old man waved off the accusation. "Firewater did that."

"You stay away from me." Ellis took short steps in a number of directions, unsure of where he should go.

"You don't have to worry about me. It's those two officers over there you need to worry about."

Ellis spun around. Two SFPD officers were walking toward them.

"You called the police?" Ellis shouted at the man. "I knew you were lying about that woman."

"I didn't call anybody, but I'm glad they're here. You need help."

CHAPTER FORTY

KANG GOT the call as soon as he arrived at the Phillip Burton Federal Building. Kane wouldn't be in; she had decided to stay at the house with Xiaolian. He sent her a quick text message letting her know where he was heading.

His destination was SFPD's Central Station in North Beach, his old stomping grounds when he had been a detective. He still had a lot of contacts there, including his long-time ex-partner, Detective Pete Sokolov. The drive took a little longer than he'd anticipated—the city was replacing pipes in the sewer system running under the north end of Van Ness Avenue.

Once at the station, Kang decided a quick detour from the business that brought him there wasn't asking much. Sokolov spotted Kang as he walked along a glass divider separating the hall and an open area where the homicide detectives' desks were.

"He returns," Sokolov said in a dramatic tone. A grin stretched across his face. He stood and extended his arm. "Either you can't get enough of this place, or you have a terrible idea that requires our help."

Kang chuckled as he gripped Sokolov's hand and gave it a

firm shake. "It's your lucky day. The answer is no to both assumptions."

Detective Adrian Bennie, Sokolov's current partner, was sitting at the adjacent desk. "Agent Kang, good to see you again. Is this visit strictly personal?"

"I'm afraid not. I'm here to see a man who was picked up this morning."

"A friend?" Bennie crinkled his brow.

"Nah. This guy might have information regarding an investigation I'm involved with."

"Is this something to do with the girl?" Sokolov asked.

"Yes and no. Abby has a hunch, so we're chasing it."

"How is Abby?" Bennie asked.

"She's fine. She's been released and is back with her family and at work."

"That's good to hear. I can't imagine being locked up like that. Any word why they did that?"

"My guess is they were trying to figure out why Abby and Xiaolian have the same DNA, I mean, not in the literal sense. We know *how* the girl was created, but we don't know the *why*."

"That's the three-parent thing, right?"

Kang nodded. "Exactly, but the State Department, they're involved now, are more concerned about the why, not the how."

"They think the girl is a spy, don't they?" Sokolov said bluntly.

His reply caught Kang off guard, but Sokolov had always had good instincts. "You didn't hear this from me."

"Top-secret stuff, huh?" Bennie said. "Don't worry. We won't spill the goods on your *X-Files* investigation." He bounced his eyebrows.

"I'll tell Mulder you said hi. Look, I'd love to chat, but I've got FBI business to handle."

Sokolov pointed at a couple of nearby suits. "Clear the way, people. We have an FBI agent on the hunt."

Kang waved off Sokolov's jab and headed back toward the direction he had come from. Once in receiving, he approached the desk sergeant who sat on the other side of a glass-enclosed area. There was a sliding window for communication.

"Sergeant Becker," Kang called out.

Becker looked up from his paperwork. "You got here fast."

"I wanted to catch this guy before he got released. What's the charge?"

"A patrol car brought him in on public drunkenness, but he ain't drunk. The Breathalyzer has him blowing below .08. He might be mentally unstable, though. Come around." Becker motioned toward a door.

There was a buzzing sound, and the latch on the door unlocked. Kang entered and followed Becker down the hall. They passed three civilian men. Two officers were giving them instructions to face the wall, place their hands against it, and spread their legs. The officers then proceeded to pat them down.

"Is he high?" Kang asked.

"Maybe." Becker tapped his own head. "Something ain't right up here. He can't remember anything. A city worker at Pier 39 found him sleeping on a bench—thought he was a drunk. According to his driver's license, his name is Johnny Ellis, and he lives in Tiburon. He has a wife. She's on her way over."

"So the guy can't remember a thing, not even his name?"

"As far as I know. One of my officers handling intake filled me in."

Becker stopped in front of a metal door with a small window. He found the appropriate key on a large key ring he carried and unlocked it. Inside the small cell were two beds, a sink, and a toilet. Ellis sat hunched over on one of the beds.

"Mr. Ellis, this is Agent Kang. He has a few questions he wants to ask you."

"Are you here to help me? I did nothing wrong." Ellis's voice was shaky.

"I'll leave you two be." Becker exited the room and shut the door behind him.

Ellis was wearing jeans, a white button-down, which was untucked, and a gray sports jacket. He was shoeless and sockless. His eyelids hadn't stopped fluttering since Kang entered the room—he was jumpy.

Kang took a seat on the bed opposite Ellis. "You feel okay?"

"I'm in jail. What do you think?"

"If I understand correctly, you're having trouble remembering things."

"That's right."

"How do you know you haven't done anything wrong if you can't remember anything?"

"I'm not drunk. I know that much. They said so."

"At this exact moment, are you still drawing a blank on anything and everything?"

Ellis took a deep breath and shook his head slowly. "Sort of. I mean there's rapid-fire imagery in my head, but I can't really make any sense of it at the moment. I can recall the basics, like my name, where I live, that I have a wife, and what I do for a living. But last night... it's like someone took what I know, threw it in a blender, hit pulverize, and then poured the contents back into my head. Why are you here anyway?" Ellis scratched the back of his head. "What's the FBI have to do with this? Tell me I didn't do something totally screwed-up."

"No, far from it. But this memory loss you're experiencing... well, we've had other people experience the same symptom."

"Is it something I drank or ate?"

"Mr. Ellis, we believe you were abducted, drugged, and then released."

"Are you serious?"

"I am. You're the first victim we've had a chance to interview right after it happened. There are three others who are from the Bay Area, and those are just the people we know about. All woke up in some random area, and they can't explain why or how they ended up there. Two of them had missing-persons reports filed—they were married. The third person was single. They were all missing for less than twenty-four hours, and they all had a period of time where they couldn't recall anything right away. The good news is your memory will return, mostly."

"What do you mean by *mostly*?"

"We have a victim who was abducted three months ago, and he still can't remember everything that happened during that blackout period."

"Crap!" Ellis ran his hand through his hair. "My work requires that I recall stuff."

"It's just that blackout period that continues to elude the victims. Your memory outside of that should return to normal. Mr. Ellis, I'd like your permission to test your blood. Whatever was given to you might still be in your system."

"Sure, that's fine, but why would anyone want to abduct me? I don't have enemies. If I did, wouldn't they have done something to me? Did anything happen to the others? Like, were there injuries?"

"No, and that's why we're thinking it might not be an enemy in the typical sense. And you might not know this person or persons." Kang paused as a thought popped into his head. "Can I ask what you do for living?"

"I work at Industrial Light and Magic. I'm the chief creative officer."

"Oh, okay. So I'm assuming you're talented and well respected in your field?"

Ellis shrugged. "You could say that."

"The other victims are also well regarded in their fields. They all have money. I'm assuming you make a nice chunk of change."

"So this is about money?"

Kang shook his head. "No financial requests that we know of have been made. In fact, all three victims had their personal belongings on them when they were found. What connects them all, and I believe you as well, is professional status."

"Could it be the competition? We have employees poached all the time. I get calls every month by headhunters. But it's not like we have trade secrets, you know. We make visual effects."

"We don't know the exact reason. Mr. Ellis. Just to confirm —you have only a period of time where you can't remember a single thing. Am I correct?"

"Earlier that answer would have been yes, but now that void is filled with images I don't understand. I know last night I gave a talk at a local art school, and after that, I went to a bar to have drinks with a few of the students. It's from that point on that the fuzziness kicks into play. Next thing I know, a janitor is poking me with his rake handle."

Kang removed a pen and a small notebook from his jacket. "What's the name of the school?"

"Um, it's the one on Van Ness Avenue." Ellis bit down on his lip for a moment before snapping his finger. "School of Creative Arts, that's it. You know it?"

"I do. And the bar you had drinks at?"

Ellis again took to biting his bottom lip. "It's on Polk Street, about a block away. Pay... Paytime, or Pay something, I think."

"Playtime," Kang suggested.

"Yeah, that's the one."

"Any idea what time you left? Did the group you were with leave with you?"

"It was late, I know that much—after midnight—and I think I left by myself. It's a little spotty."

"Okay, so you leave the bar. Are you walking back to your car? Are you hailing a cab?"

"I drive everywhere, so I'm walking back to my car, I'm guessing. I parked at the school or near the school. Again, my memory now is spotty. I have flashes of a sidewalk. I don't see anybody else. A car drives by."

"Do you know the make or model?"

"No, I just see a dark vehicle, a sedan maybe."

"And then what?"

"That's it. I don't know."

"All right, what about the students you had drinks with? Can you elaborate on that?"

"Well, we went out for a few drinks. I knew the name of one of the students because she'd helped set up the talk. Her name was Ashley. She has blond hair."

Kang scribbled the information down. "This is helpful. I understand your wife is coming to pick you up."

Ellis nodded.

"I'll go ahead and make arrangements for someone at our office to look you over, take some blood. I appreciate your cooperation. Do you have a number I can reach you at?"

"If I do, I don't know it, and the cops took my cell phone before they threw me in here."

"Okay, I'll check with them." Kang removed his phone, snapped a picture of Ellis, and handed him his card. "Call me if you remember more."

CHAPTER FORTY-ONE

I WAS curious to see just how advanced Xiaolian's physical training was after her admission about her upbringing. Once the kids were dropped off at school, she and I headed over to a local sporting store, and I bought her workout gear and cross-trainers. First thing on the day's agenda was to test her physical conditioning.

"Did you do much running where you're from?" I asked. We were both on the front porch, stretching our legs.

"We played a lot of games."

"I mean running, not games."

Xiaolian grabbed her foot and pulled it up backward until her heel touched her butt. "Oh, yeah. We ran on a treadmill." She switched to the other leg and stretched it the same way.

"Never outside?"

"No."

I had a couple of routes in my head, three to be exact. Depending on her conditioning, I could always switch it up. We started our run on relatively flat streets, which in San Francisco were either hard to find or didn't last very long. Sooner or later a hill appears. We ran south along Stockton until we hit

Columbus Avenue. I kept a good pace. Xiaolian had no problem keeping up, and she didn't seem to be tiring. *Let's see how she tackles the hills.*

When we reached Washington, we headed west toward Chinatown. The hill wasn't that steep, but it was still a hill. I kept an eye on her, and she seemed fine. Once we hit Powell, we turned right and headed north, back toward the bay.

"How are you feeling?" I asked.

"I feel fine. It's so interesting to see everything. Do we have to go back now?"

"Not yet. Do you feel like tackling a really big hill? At the top, we'll have a nice view of the bay."

"Yeah, let's do it."

We continued north until we reached Union. I stopped, facing west, and pointed at the hill ahead of us. The hill actually consisted of five mini-hills, created by five cross streets, the only flat surfaces on the way up. Each of the mini-hills steepened as they went farther up the big hill.

When we reached the second cross street, I asked her if she was fine.

"Yup," she said, but I could hear that her breathing was labored, the first time since we'd started running.

When we reached the third cross street, I began feeling the burn in my lungs and legs. Usually it happened on the fourth street. It was an indicator for me that I still wasn't at one hundred percent, even though I felt as if I were.

At the fourth street, I didn't bother asking how she felt. I could feel my shirt sticking to my back. Perspiration poured down my face and neck. Xiaolian was just as slick, her black hair pasted against her pale cheeks like spider veins. We were both tired.

"One more hill, and then we're done," I said.

Our pace had slowed by then, and Xiaolian had started to fall behind on that last push.

"Come on, you can do it," I said in between breaths.

I really did want her to do it. She was twelve. At her age, I wasn't sure I could run that hill without resting. I continually glanced at her. She was struggling, but I could clearly see determination in her eyes. She wasn't stopping. She didn't want to.

We were halfway up the last mini-hill. She was doing it. Heck, I was rooting for her. It was then I realized how unnatural this all was. How bragging about this to Yates or Archer would only continue to solidify their thinking—that she was a trained spy. This wasn't a normal game of tag. This wasn't something the average twelve-year-old could do. I was torn. On one hand, I wanted her to stop and throw in the towel. On the other hand, I really wanted to see her power through and conquer the hill.

Xiaolian had slowed considerably, falling twenty feet behind me. I turned around and jogged backward. "Come on, you're almost there. Don't stop."

She kept her head down. Each step looked as if it weighed a ton for her.

Clomp.

Clomp.

Clomp.

She looked up at me. Her mouth hung open as she sucked in air. She cleared her hair from her eyes with her forearm before lowering her head again, most likely concentrating on every step, ignoring the distance separating her from the top.

I continued jogging backward so I could keep an eye on her. When I reached the top, I raised my arms over my head and took deep breaths. It felt like I couldn't get enough air into my lungs. I could only imagine how Xiaolian felt, but pure determination fueled every step she took. She had only ten steps to go, and each step was slower than the last.

Don't stop. You're almost there.

Five.

Four.

Three.

Two.

Yes!

Xiaolian stopped next to me, bent over at the waist, heaving hard.

"Stand up and hold your hands over your head," I said.

She looked at me and opened her mouth to speak but couldn't—she needed air. She straightened up and raised her arms to the sky. Twice more she tried to say something but couldn't. Finally, on her fourth try, she was able to speak.

"You trying to kill me or what?"

I laughed at her remark. "Quite the opposite. I'm really impressed. Your conditioning is incredible."

She tried once more to speak.

"Stop. Catch your breath. We can talk later."

Union intersected with Hyde Street, along which one of the few remaining cable-car routes in the city ran. We walked toward the bay, and as Hyde Street began to dip downward, the view of the bay opened itself up to us. Straight ahead was Alcatraz Island.

It was a magnificent sight, one I never got tired of. The waters surrounding the island were a dark blue and sparkled from the sun beaming upon it.

"Wowww," Xiaolian said when she laid eyes on it. "It's amazing."

"Keep walking. There's another treat up ahead."

A few feet later, San Francisco's best-known landmark came into view: the Golden Gate Bridge.

"Wowww," Xiaolian said again.

"There's something else up here that's pretty incredible

besides the view." We walked farther along Hyde toward where a bunch of tourists had gathered. "That's the top of Lombard Street," I said pointing. "Have you heard of it?"

"No."

"It's the crookedest street in the world."

"Crooked?"

When we reached Lombard, she peered down, and everything I said seemed to fall into place.

"Wowww." Xioalian's eyes nearly popped out of her head as she watched the cars drive slowly down a series of switchbacks, like lumbering caterpillars.

"It's crooked because it's too steep to drive straight down."

"It looks spooky."

We watched the cars for a bit and took in the wonderful view of Coit Tower in the distance before turning back.

"Where to now?" she asked.

"To that small park over there. It has fitness equipment we can play on."

We climbed a set of stairs that led up to George Sterling Park. The fitness equipment was typical of what you find in any park. There were balancing beams, chin-up bars, a sit-up and push-up station, and even a couple of elliptical machines.

"What's first?" she asked.

"Sit-ups." I sat on a low horizontal bench. "This is how I want you to do them." I lay down on my back and kept my legs bent at right angles, feet flat. With my hands resting on my thighs, I raised myself up, sliding my hands along my thighs until I touched my knees, and then returned to my starting position. "You think you got it?"

"Yup." Xiaolian lay on the bench.

"You have one minute to do as many as you can. Ready. Set. Go."

She took off, sliding her hands up her thighs just as I had

showed her, exhaling at the crunch and inhaling as she lay back down. The average male of eighteen to twenty-five could do about thirty-five to forty sit-ups in this time frame. Xiaolian did forty-five.

We moved over to the push-up station. The average young male could do twenty to thirty push-ups. Xiaolian completed forty.

Same deal with the chin-ups. The average for a young man in a minute time frame was about twelve. She did sixteen.

She had an unbelievable amount of upper-body and core strength. "Were these exercises part of your routine?"

She nodded enthusiastically. "Since I was a little girl."

"The other children were just as good?"

"Some were better, but it's because that's all they did."

"What do you mean?"

"Well, I had classes that some other kids didn't have."

"Like what?"

"Solving problems."

"You mean like math?"

"No, more like situations. I had to figure out why something happened. Kind of like what you do. Don't you figure things out?"

"I do."

Xiaolian bit down on her lower lip and dug her heel in the grass.

"What is it?"

"I dunno. I just don't understand."

"Understand what?"

"Why you and I are so much alike."

CHAPTER FORTY-TWO

KANG LEFT Central Station before Ellis's wife showed. He was eager to see if the bar had CCTV coverage. If they did, he might just get lucky with the footage. On the drive there, he realized he hadn't heard from Abby, but he assumed she had gotten his message and that everything was fine at her home.

Playtime was a small bar located on the corner of Polk and Pine, about a fifteen-minute drive from the police station. Kang had passed by it a number of times but had never been inside. At night, young crowds always gathered outside—the smokers. It wasn't until he parked along the curb that it dawned on him it might not be open. He glanced at his watch. Ten a.m.

The windows of the bar were tinted. He pressed his face against the glass, cupping his hands along his cheeks to cut down on the glare. He rapped his knuckles against the door and peered in again. He knocked once more. This time a figure appeared.

The door opened, and a young man dressed in jeans and a T-shirt stood in the entrance. "Sorry, buddy. We don't open for another hour."

Kang produced his identification. "I'm Agent Kang. I'd like to ask you a few questions. May I come inside?"

"Am I in some sort of trouble?"

"I don't think so, but you might hold information that can help me with an investigation. Are you the owner?" Kang walked past the man and into the bar.

"Yes. I'm Owen Townsend."

Kang rested his hands on his waist as he looked around. A wooden counter ran the length of the establishment. Mirrored shelving behind it showcased a myriad of top-shelf liquor. The seating consisted of small, rectangular tables with high chairs. The décor was sleek and modern, with a mixture of earthy shades. He noticed a circular staircase leading to a second floor.

"Mr. Townsend, were you working last night?"

"Yes, I'm here every night."

Kang removed his cell phone and produced the photo of Ellis. "Did you see this man?"

Townsend leaned in for a closer look. "Yeah, of course. He was here with a bunch of students from the art school."

"His name is Johnny Ellis. Did you speak with him?"

"A little. I know the students; they come in here often. He had given a talk at their school that night. Seemed like a cool guy."

Kang removed his notepad and pen. "Could you write down the names of the students for me? I'd appreciate it."

Townsend did as instructed. "Did something happen?"

"We have reason to believe Mr. Ellis was abducted after leaving your bar."

Townsend stopped writing and looked up. "Are you for real?"

"He's fine now. Did you notice anyone else in the group who wasn't from the school? Maybe someone else in the bar who joined their conversation."

Townsend thought for a moment. "I don't think so. I could be wrong, though. It was a busy night." He continued writing the names down.

"Did you see him leave?"

"I didn't, but he definitely left before the students did. They were one of the last to leave."

Kang looked around and spotted the CCTV cameras. "Are the cameras functioning? I'd like to take a look at the footage."

Townsend handed the pen and pad back to Kang and then led him through a door at the end of the bar into the kitchen and eventually into a small office. "It records for forty-eight hours before recording over that footage. It's good you came in right away."

They both watched the video. Ellis stood next to a table. Three students sat in the chairs surrounding it. They appeared to be having an engaging conversation. Ellis did most of the talking. Kang counted the number of drinks Ellis had during the night—five.

"Do you remember what he drank?"

"Scotch."

A little after midnight, Ellis left the group and exited the bar by himself.

"Is there a camera outside?"

"Yeah." Townsend tapped a few keys on his laptop, and the camera view changed to one outside the bar. He then queued the tape to the correct time frame. Ellis could be seen exiting and walking along the sidewalk, away from the bar.

"He's walking in the direction where the school is located. Might have parked his car there," Townsend said.

The camera was angled to view the entire outside length of the bar, so Ellis remained in frame for a while before disappearing.

"Can you download and email me a copy of this footage?"

"No problem."

Kang handed Townsend his card. "If you think of anything else relating to this matter, call me."

Outside, Kang walked to the spot where Ellis had last been seen before exiting the frame. It was a step before Polk intersected with Austin. Kang surveyed the businesses on the corner: a yoga studio, a computer-support store, a Thai restaurant, and a small deli. None appeared to have their own CCTV system. On top of that, Austin was nothing more than a small side street. No traffic lights; therefore, no city-owned cameras. Kang checked his watch. He had been at the bar a little more than thirty minutes. *I'll see if I can track down some of these students and then swing by Abby's home.*

CHAPTER FORTY-THREE

KANG ENTERED the lobby of the School of Creative Arts, and it was abuzz with students chatting in groups, lounging on plush beanbags, or hurrying off to their next class. Student paintings, illustrations, photographs, and advertising pieces graced the walls. On one wall, a large video screen played a short film. Kang walked across the brightly colored, polka-dot carpeting toward a reception desk made of old whiskey barrels. A young girl with a purple Mohawk and more facial piercings than Kang cared to count sat behind the desk.

"Hola," she said in a chipper voice. "How can I help thee?" She winked at Kang. The color black dominated her clothing, hair, nails, and makeup, with the exception of her ruby red lipstick. She chewed gum and made a popping sound on every fourth bite.

"I'm Agent Kang," he said, holding out his identification. "I need to speak to whoever is in charge of this place, the dean perhaps."

"That would be Sammy. Just a minute."

While the young lady made a call, three students carrying a

very large and detailed dragon's head passed by. A serpent's tongue snaked out between the sharp teeth.

"Excuse me, Mr. Agent. Sammy can see you now." She stood and straightened her form-fitting skirt. "Follow me, please."

The girl led Kang down a long hallway lined with classrooms and more artwork on the walls. They made a left and then a right before passing a miniature circus tent with glass walls. Inside was a conference table and chairs. They stopped outside a door made of brushed steel. The girl knocked twice but didn't wait for a reply before pushing the door open.

"Sammy, this is Mr. Agent Kang," the girl said.

"Thank you, Rebecca. Close the door on your way out," Sammy said. "Please have a seat, Agent Kang."

Kang fumbled for his identification, but Sammy quickly waved off his efforts and stood, reaching across the desk.

"Don't bother. I believe you're with the FBI." She winked. "We don't get many visitors dressed in suits."

"Oh, okay," Kang mumbled. They shook hands.

"You were expecting a man, weren't you?" Sammy said. "My real name is Samantha Hill, but everyone calls me Sammy. Have a seat, please."

She sat behind the desk with her legs crossed. She was wearing black leggings, a black top, and a gray blazer. A gold pendant on a gold chain hung down between her breasts. Her bleached-blond hair was straight and cut into a bob that met perfectly with the bottom of her slender jawline. The only makeup Kang noticed was a warm-brown lipstick covering her plump lips.

"Thanks for taking time to speak with me, Ms. Hill."

"Please call me Sammy. Hill is my ex's name, and I detest him, but I'm too lazy to do the necessary paperwork to revert back to my maiden name. So, how can I be of help?"

"I have a few questions for you and for some of your students as well," Kang said.

"Oh, what a letdown. I thought you were here just to see me." She slouched and let out a huff through pouty lips.

"Well, I do need your help," he added.

She sat up straight, clasping her hands together. "I'm happy to help with your investigation. That is why you're here, right?"

"Yes. Last night Johnny Ellis had a speaking engagement here."

"Handsome devil, I must admit."

"We have reason to believe that he was abducted last night and held captive before being released early this morning."

"Oh my. Who on earth would want to hurt a gorgeous man like that?"

"Uh, that's what we're trying to figure out. We know Mr. Ellis left here shortly after his speech and headed over to Playtime to have drinks with a few of your students."

Sammy's eyes shot open. "He did? That son-of-a-bitch told me he had to hurry home—he whined about having an early meeting the next day."

"You do know he's married, right?"

She shrugged. "I heard some rumblings about that."

"Do you know if he arrived here with anyone, or had invited someone to the engagement?"

"Not that I know of, but I suppose he could have."

"What about a parking lot? He said he had driven and that he had parked here."

"We have limited parking behind the building, but we provided him with a parking pass."

"Could you check to see if his car is still parked there?"

Sammy made a quick call. "One of the students will look. Are there any other questions I can answer?"

"That's all I have at the moment. I'd like to speak to these students in particular. He showed her the list. "If that's okay."

The phone rang, and Sammy answered. "I see. Thank you, dear." She returned the handset to its cradle. "His car is still parked back there. So I guess he never made it back... which means if he left the bar alone and never made it back to his car, he was abducted somewhere between the bar and here, unless he made a detour to another bar or met a lady on the way or whatever."

"Do you have cameras in the parking lot behind the building?"

"We don't. I suppose someone could have been waiting for him back there. There's no lighting at night." Sammy looked at the notepad Kang had produced with the three names written on it. "It might take me a while to track them down in their classes. You can wait?"

"It's fine. Why don't you show me the parking lot in the meantime? I'd like to take a look at his vehicle."

Kang exited the building after Sammy and squinted as the sun beat down on them. Sammy hadn't been exaggerating earlier. There was room enough for only eight vehicles in the gravel lot.

"That's his car." She pointed at a black BMW sedan.

Kang grabbed Sammy's arm. "Until I can get a forensic team here, I need to keep everyone away from the car. Is that something you can arrange?"

"Sure." Sammy made a call from her cell phone.

Kang approached the car slowly, carefully scanning the gravel. He walked completely around the vehicle, looking for signs of a scuffle, but the gravel wasn't that forgiving—it barely registered footsteps.

The windows were tinted, and Kang looked for odd prints, like an entire hand, on the window. He didn't notice any. He removed a pair of latex gloves from his jacket, snapped them on, and checked if the car was locked. It was.

"Anything suspicious?" Sammy called out from the spot where she was waiting.

Kang ignored her and peered into the vehicle through the front windshield. The interior was clean. A thermos cup was sitting in the middle console. In the back seat, Kang spotted a shoulder bag. He straightened up and walked back to where Sammy stood.

"Well?" she asked.

"I think I'll hold my observations until after the vehicle is processed."

Upon their return to Sammy's office, they found three students milling about—two young men and a woman. They all looked to be in their early twenties.

"Agent Kang, I'd like you to meet Evan Guzman, Nick Hunter, and Lydia Murphy."

"So you're, like, a real FBI agent?" Guzman asked.

"I am."

"Wow, that's so cool."

"Why don't you four continue this conversation under the circus tent?" Sammy suggested as she pointed to the conference table. "I have calls I need to make."

Guzman led the group over to the tent, his excitement over meeting Kang still obvious.

"Are we in trouble?" Lydia asked as she pulled out a chair and took a seat.

"Not at all, but I'm hoping you can help me."

Kang briefly explained to them what had happened to Ellis without getting into too much detail about the investigation.

"Oh my God." Lydia clasped her hand over her mouth.

"Shit, man, that sucks," Hunter said. "Mr. Ellis is such a cool dude. Why would someone do that?"

"Yeah, man," Guzman followed up. "Everything seemed fine too. We had a great time at the bar with him."

"Did he mention where he was heading?" Kang asked.

"He said he had to go home because he had an early start the next day," Guzman said. "He bought us one last round of drinks and left."

"I feel so guilty," Lydia said. "I thought of asking him if I could help him get back to his car, but I didn't."

"Why? Did he look drunk or incapable of finding it?"

"No, but you know... he was the guest speaker for the evening, plus he paid for all the drinks. We should have walked him back to his car. If we had, he wouldn't have gotten abducted."

"Oh shit. Now I feel guilty," Hunter said.

"Me too," said Guzman.

The three students had all resorted to staring at the conference table.

"Hey, you couldn't have known," Kang said. "This isn't your fault. Put that thought out of your heads. Now, it's my understanding that you three stayed until the bar closed. That was two a.m., right?"

All three nodded.

"And after that, where did you guys go?"

"Well, I went home," Lydia said. "I caught a cab right outside."

"Nick and I live together," Guzman said. "But we walked to a donut shop up the street to get something to eat and then took a cab from there."

"I see," Kang said. It was clear to him the three students were a dead-end. He gave each one a business card. "If you remember anything else, please call me."

CHAPTER FORTY-FOUR

KANG WAITED at the school until CSI arrived and had the car and the area around it secured. He hoped their investigation would shed some light on this. He even briefly wondered if spending all this time on an unofficial investigation was worth it. He hoped so.

By the time he returned to his SUV, he found a parking ticket on his windshield. He shook his head and grabbed the paper before getting into his vehicle. His stomach grumbled as he turned the key in the ignition, reminding him that he hadn't eaten all morning. He glanced at his watch. Lunchtime. He debated stopping off for a bite before meeting up with Abby. Of course, he knew Po Po would be there, and most likely, she would insist that he sit and she feed him. The decision was a no-brainer.

When he reached Abby's home, he parked his vehicle behind her Charger in the driveway. He knocked on the door, and Po Po answered.

"Kyle, come inside. You eat? I fix you something." She closed the door and pointed toward the dining room. "Sit, sit. You look hungry."

Who was he to refuse the sage advice of his elders?

"Where's Abby?" he called out.

"She go out," Po Po shouted back from the kitchen.

This surprised him. "With Xiaolian?"

"Yes."

"But her car is outside."

There was no response from the kitchen. Kang's stomach growled in anticipation—she wasn't one to keep serving the same dishes. It was always a culinary delight every time he stopped by.

As he waited, his thoughts turned from eating back to the abduction investigation. He had spent the entire morning following up on the Ellis lead. There were dots that connected Ellis and the other three men, but nothing substantial. *Am I drinking the Kool-Aid, or is Abby really on to something?*

The roadblock for Kang was Abby's end goal—connecting the abductions to Xiaolian.

He decided then he would not question whether she was right or wrong. He would continue to gather information and let that be the deciding factor. Either there would be enough to support her theory, or there wouldn't be. Worst-case scenario, they would actually discover something criminal about the abductions. *That's not a bad thing.*

Kang was in the middle of demolishing his meal when Abby and Xiaolian returned. Po Po had whipped up fried rice, fried pork with green beans and bitter melon, and a healthy bowl of scallop soup. The soup was left over from the day before.

"So is this what you do when I'm not around?" I asked.

Kang mumbled something, as he had just scooped a large portion of rice into his mouth.

"I'm taking a shower. I'll catch up with you in a bit."

I stopped by the kitchen. Po Po was already preparing plates for me and Xiaolian. "Smells great. We'll be back in a jiffy."

When I returned downstairs, fresh and clean, Xiaolian was sitting at the dining room table, shoveling food into her mouth. Kang had already finished eating. An overly stuffed plate sat waiting for me. I was a little embarrassed, but it was no more or less than the amount Po Po always served me. *I'm such a pig.*

"Xiaolian said you guys went for a run." Kang leaned back in his chair and sipped his tea.

"We did. She's in great physical shape." I filled him in on the route we'd run and her workout at the park.

"Forty-five sit-ups in a minute?" He reached over and poked Xiaolian's belly. "Abs of steel, this one."

She giggled as she chewed her food.

"That's impressive. How many did you do in a minute?" he asked me.

"I wasn't the one being tested," I said in between chews.

After lunch, Xiaolian headed up to the third floor to watch television while Kang and I sat on the back porch so he could fill me in on his day.

"Everything was the same? The memory loss, the waking up in a weird location, a missing-persons report?" I asked.

"No missing-persons report, but everything else matched. What little he could remember was definitely outside of that block of time where he was 'missing,' if we have to call it something."

"If he left the bar after midnight and was discovered the next morning around seven, that's definitely a shorter amount of time than the others," I said.

"Yeah, maybe whatever is happening during this time is taking place faster now."

"CCTV footage wasn't much help?"

Kang pulled up the video on his cell phone and handed it to me. I watched it multiple times. On the last pass, I noticed something just as Ellis apparently disappeared from the frame. "It looks like he doesn't actually leave the frame." I turned the phone around so Kang could see the screen. "Look, you can barely see his feet."

"You're right," he said. "It looks like he stopped."

"Waiting for the light?" I asked.

"I doubt it. There are no streetlights at the next intersection. So if he's waiting at the curb, it's not for a walk signal."

We watched the video over and over.

"What happens at the end? Is that another foot right there?" I asked.

We advanced the footage frame by frame, and it looked like another pair of shoes appeared next to Ellis's. We couldn't be absolute, as the footage had been cut off right at that point.

"It could just be a blip in the video," Kang said.

"See if the owner can send you another video that plays out longer. If that's another foot next to him, then someone was with him that night. What about the students?"

"They were able to confirm that he was at the bar until the time Ellis said he left. That's it."

I glanced at my watch. "You haven't heard back from the lab?"

"Not yet. I'll follow up with them. They should be done processing his vehicle. But this foot seems like something." Kang took his phone back from me. "I should talk to Ellis again, see if his memory has sharpened."

Just then, Kang's phone chimed. "The bloodwork is back from Ellis." He stared at his phone's screen, reading the message. "Propofol was present in his blood." He looked up from his phone.

"This is a connection to Xiaolian," I said.

"She wasn't abducted."

"Maybe not here, but where she came from... she might have been. It can't be coincidental. Xiaolian exhibited the same memory loss as these men. She recovered the same way, and propofol was found in her system."

I filled Kang in on the conversations I'd had with Xiaolian since bringing her home.

"If what she's saying is true, then yes, it sounds like an orphanage, though it's a strange one."

"I don't think it's an orphanage," I said. "It's run like a school, a really organized school."

"So maybe she was sent to a special school—you know, one for gifted children." Just then Kang snapped his fingers. "Wait a minute. You know what this really could be—a sports school, the ones that crank out Olympic athletes. In China, children as young as two are sent to these schools to be raised as Olympic champions. It becomes their life. It's all they know. They live, train, and are educated there at the school. I think they see their parents only once a year, if they're lucky."

"Hmmm, it certainly fits the mold better. And it explains why Xiaolian is so book smart but knows nothing of the real world."

"With her training, maybe she was being groomed to be a wrestler. It would make sense," Kang said.

"You're right. Her grappling skills are highly advanced. Add her top-notch conditioning, considering she probably hasn't had a proper workout for at least a month to a month and a half. Okay, say it is one of those sports schools. Why and how did she end up on the doorsteps of our FBI office? And more importantly, why does she have my DNA?"

"I still don't know the answer to your first question, but the second one might be because someone noticed you at the police academy. You did graduate at age nineteen, right?"

I nodded.

"That's not common for men, let alone a woman. It could also be when you were a child. Were you good at sports?"

I shrugged. "My father taught me everything I know. It's not like I could jump into a boxing ring with one of the boys. And I wasn't into team sports, since I would have to be competing with women. I was a tomboy growing up. Look, I'm not discounting what you're suggesting. It's totally possible."

"Whether you want to believe it or not, you probably impressed some parent or coach, and they stole your DNA. The pressure to have successful children is intense in China. A lot of parents rely on their children to take care of them in their old age."

Kang tilted his head as he looked at me, his brow crinkled.

"What?" I asked.

"You seem disappointed by what I'm saying."

I didn't respond. I thought my connection with Xiaolian was something bigger, but everything Kang said could easily explain a lot about her.

"Did you think it was more than that?" he asked.

I huffed out a breath. "Yeah, I did, but maybe it is what you're saying. It makes complete sense. Some overzealous parent or coach hired a scientist to steal my DNA in hopes of producing offspring that would have my physical abilities."

"Not to mention your problem-solving skills. Not everyone can look at a problem the way you do. It's why you're such a damn good detective. And I mean it when I say that."

"Thanks. I appreciate the pat on the back. But last time I checked, I didn't see detectives competing in the Olympics."

Kang shrugged. "Just saying."

"Maybe it's all in my head," I said. "Hearing the spy angle had me thinking that perhaps our connection was something bigger. I don't know what it could be or why I would wish that—it just seemed like it was possible. You know what I mean?"

"I do." Kang leaned back in his chair and stretched his legs out. "There is something *X-Files*-ish about it."

"Let's talk to Xiaolian," I said.

We both headed up to the third floor. She was on the sofa, lying on her side, watching a program about strangers living together in a house and having their every move and conversation filmed and broadcasted.

"What do you think of that show you're watching?" I asked. "Is it like the place where you lived?"

She shook her head. "These people aren't doing anything except lying around and complaining."

Kang and I both got a laugh out of her response.

"But we had cameras like they do."

Kang and I gave each other a look.

"I want to show you something." I sat next to her on the couch and Googled the Chinese sports schools and found some video footage. "Does this look like the place you grew up in?"

I handed her the phone. She perked up as the video played. After a moment or so, she glanced up at me.

"It reminds me of my home, but I'm not from this place. I don't recognize anyone there."

"We think this place is like the place you are from."

"Oh, okay. The teachers look very serious. Our teachers were serious too. And we all listened to them, just like the kids in the video."

"What about the training?"

"Some of it is the same, some of it isn't. I did a little acrobatic stuff, but not like what those girls are doing."

"I see."

"But the room they are practicing in reminds me of where I practiced."

Xiaolian continued to voice comparisons with her home and what she saw on my phone. The more she spoke, the more convinced I became that we had been wrong about her.

"I can't believe there are other children like me living in another place," she said.

That final acknowledgement sealed the deal for me.

When the video ended, Xiaolian looked up at me. The enthusiasm she'd displayed earlier had vanished.

"Did you find my home? Are you sending me back?"

I motioned between me and Kang. "*We're* not sending you anywhere. But there are others who want to send you back. And there are others who want to keep you at that facility. The good news is I think we might be able to have you released from there, for good."

"And I can stay with you?"

"Perhaps. Let us concentrate on getting you released for now."

She still seemed a little down. I gave her a hug and a peck on the top of her head. "You're a special girl, Xiaolian, and special girls stay strong. Can you do that for me?"

"I can," she said with confidence.

Kang and I left Xiaolian to her television program and headed back downstairs.

"Looks like she was raised in a sports school. That explains her skill set perfectly. No spy mystery there," Kang said as we walked down the stairs.

"It does, but..." I held that last word.

"But what?"

"Xiaolian said something to me last night that doesn't sit right with me, nor does it fit neatly into the sports-school idea."

"What's that?"

"She said she doesn't understand why she was raised to be like me."

"With Xiaolian, there are always unanswered questions. It could be as simple as her not knowing she was artificially created. What would be the advantage of telling her? She's probably just as confused about it as you are."

Kang left shortly after our talk with Xiaolian. He was eager to follow up with the lab to see if they'd discovered anything while processing Ellis's vehicle. He appeared to be making progress with the abduction investigation, but the initial connection I had made with those abducted men and Xiaolian weakened after talking to her about the sports schools. *Is this turning out to be another crime we solve that has nothing to do with Xiaolian?* It wasn't a bad thing; it just wasn't the mystery I wanted most to solve.

Reilly still had no idea we were spending time working on the abductions, or being insubordinate, as he would have called it. Eventually I would have to clue him in on why we had gone rogue. It wasn't a conversation I was eager to have. Putting it off seemed like a good idea.

CHAPTER FORTY-FIVE

Kang was on his way back to the office when he received a call from the lab. There were prints all over the inside of the vehicle belonging to one person: Johnny Ellis. He had showed up to claim his car while it was being processed. The tech on site had him printed. Other than that, their investigation turned up nothing else.

With Ellis's vehicle turning into a dead-end, Kang headed back to Playtime to see more of the CCTV footage. The bar was open for business when he arrived. A bunch of young men were inside drinking draft beer and cheering a San Francisco Giants baseball game airing on the television sets. They looked like students from the art school.

Kang walked over to the bartender. He was busy washing pint glasses. "I'd like to speak to Owen Townsend, please."

"Who's asking?" he asked with a bit of annoyance in his voice.

Kang held out his identification. "The FBI is asking."

The bartender's posturing stopped instantly. He apologized and disappeared behind the double swinging doors leading into the kitchen. It was about a minute before both men appeared.

"Agent Kang, you're back. How can I help you?"

"I'd like to take another look at the footage from outside the bar, if it's all right with you."

Townsend didn't hesitate. "Not a problem."

Kang followed him back to his office and waited for him to cue up the footage.

"Is there something specific you're looking for?" Townsend asked.

"Toward the end, when he walks out of frame, it looks as if he actually didn't. Fast forward a bit, and you'll see what I'm talking about."

Just before Ellis exited the frame, Townsend slowed the video to half speed.

"Right there, pause it." Kang said. "Those are his feet. See it?"

Townsend squinted. "Yeah, it looks like he stopped. Must be at the curb of the next street over."

"Now advance the footage slowly. It looks like someone appears next to him."

Townsend did what Kang asked, and sure enough, a pair of shoes appeared. It was a lot easier to see on the desktop.

"You've got a sharp eye. Don't know why we didn't pick up on it the first time."

"Keep forwarding slowly," Kang said.

Townsend did as instructed, and both pairs of shoes disappeared at the same time.

"Looks like they left together. Maybe another student from the school saw him outside."

"Maybe."

Townsend tapped a few keys. "I'll email you a higher resolution this time."

Kang thanked Townsend and left the bar. As he sat in the

front seat of the SUV, he dialed the number for Ellis's cell phone. A woman answered.

"Hello. This is Agent Kang with the FBI. Am I speaking to Mrs. Ellis?"

"This is she. Is something wrong?"

"I have more questions I'd like to ask Mr. Ellis. I can swing by the house if that's convenient."

"Well, I don't know what help he'll be. His memory hasn't fully returned. He remembers who I am. Can't say the same for the dog."

"Mrs. Ellis, were you at all concerned when your husband didn't return last night?"

"I wasn't. I figured he was with one of those young whores he keeps in the city."

"Oh, I'm sorry. I didn't mean to pry."

"It's not like it's a secret. Johnny's always been a playboy. I knew this before I married him. Sadly, his promise to change his ways lasted a single month, that son-of-a-bitch. You know the reason he won't divorce me is because he's afraid I'll take everything he's got."

"Yes, well, I, ah... I'm heading your way now. I'll see you in about forty-five minutes."

Kang arrived a little later than he'd expected, but Mrs. Ellis didn't seem bothered when she met him at her front door.

"I thought I would be here sooner. I apologize, Mrs. Ellis," Kang said.

She dismissed the formalities with a flick of her wrist. "Please, call me Helen. Come inside."

The couple lived in a large, two-story, colonial-style home, complete with shuttered windows, dormers, columns, and chimneys. Clean, white palettes dominated the décor inside the home. There were pieces of art hanging on the wall, but the spaces weren't overly cluttered. "Pleasantly open" would describe the place.

"He's in his study," Helen said, looking back at Kang as she led him through a sitting room. "He's been in there all day, drawing." She stopped. "I'm sorry. I've forgotten my manners. Would you like something to drink?"

"I'm fine, thank you."

They continued to the rear of the home, down a hallway lined with dark oak flooring. As they approached an open doorway, Helen called out, "Johnny, Agent Kang is here to see you."

Helen stopped at the entranceway and motioned for Kang to go ahead of her. Inside, he saw Ellis sitting at a drafting table with his back to them. He was hunched over a large piece of paper and drawing with charcoal.

"I'll leave you two alone," Helen said before leaving.

Kang nodded as he waited for some acknowledgement from Ellis. There was none.

"Mr. Ellis. It's Agent Kang. We spoke this morning at the station."

Still nothing. Kang walked over to him and tapped his shoulder.

Ellis looked up. "Yes, can I help you?"

"Do you remember me?"

"Yes, of course. What do you want?"

Kang let out a breath as he removed his cell phone from his jacket. He cued up the footage and showed it to Ellis. "This is CCTV video of you leaving the bar last night. Do you remember walking outside?"

He shrugged. "Like I said earlier, I remember random images. A sidewalk was one of them."

Kang paused the video. "You see this? These are your shoes.

You appear to have stopped at the curb of the next street over, only there are no traffic lights there. So, really no reason to stop."

"If you say so."

Kang forwarded the footage a few frames. "Look here, this is another pair of shoes next to you. Someone was with you." He allowed the footage to play on. "It appears you both leave the curb at the same time. Do you remember someone next to you? What he or she looked like? Any distinguishing markings, or something about their clothing come to mind?"

Ellis looked back at the drafting board and fondled the piece of charcoal with his blackened fingers. He had been drawing what looked to be some sort of outer-space mercenary character. It had a face like a bullfrog's, and a bulbous body covered in scaly skin, with muscles rippling underneath. He shook his head in frustration. "I can't make sense of it, man."

"How about making a list of the images you do remember? That might be helpful."

Townsend began scribbling words on the piece of paper he had been sketching on.

Sidewalk
Street
Car
Stop Sign
Moon
Sky
Man/Men

Kang stopped him. "So you remember seeing someone. Was it a man standing next to you?"

"I'm not sure. It's like I can see a face, but when I try to focus on it, I lose the image. I can't even make out where it is. Outdoors or indoors. It's like a void of black all around it."

Kang prompted Ellis to continue with his list.

Mask

Bright Lights
Alcohol

"Wait—when you say 'mask,' do you mean like a Halloween mask?"

"I'm talking about a surgical mask. At least I think that's what it is. I just see an object covering the face. It could be something else."

"And alcohol is liquor? You saw bottles?"

"Actually this is a smell. Rubbing alcohol, I think." Ellis stared at the paper but wrote nothing more. "The rest of the images are too brief for me to make out what they are. I'm sorry; this is all I have. Does it help?"

"All information is relevant until we can rule otherwise. So, yes, it helps. Anything else?"

Ellis shook his head and let out a defeated breath.

"Keep writing the images down as they become clear to you. I'll check back in a few days."

Kang was halfway down the hall when Ellis called out his name. He poked his head back into the room. "Did you remember something else?"

"I did. Cerberus."

CHAPTER FORTY-SIX

LATER THAT EVENING at the Shi household, Connie was busy preparing dinner. It was taco night. Her two boys, Colin and Merrick, were playing video games on their PlayStation. Her daughter, Hailey, was sitting on a stool next to the kitchen island, reading on her Kindle.

"Hailey, will you do Mommy a favor and set the table?"

"What about Colin and Merrick? Why can't they help?"

"They will. They have no idea they have cleanup duties tonight." She winked at Hailey while placing a finger against her lips.

Connie stirred the crumbled hamburger in the skillet for a few more seconds before transferring it to a serving bowl. She had already diced the tomatoes and onions. Hailey had helped earlier by shredding the lettuce. Connie couldn't be bothered with shredding a block of cheddar cheese and always bought the packaged variety.

Normally they ate dinner around six; Albert was usually home in time. He was running late, but so was dinner. By the time the food hit the table and the boys were pulled away from the television set, Albert had parked in the driveway.

"Daddy's home," Hailey sang out.

She rushed toward the front door and escorted him back to the dining room.

"How was your day?" Albert asked her.

"It was fine. We had a test in math class today, but I'm confident I did well because I studied a lot yesterday."

"That's my girl."

"Hi, Dad," Colin and Merrick said in unison.

Albert gave his wife a kiss before sitting at the head of the table. They proceeded to have a stereotypical American dinner. Connie and Albert had long ago learned to play the role perfectly.

After cleanup, the children had homework to finish and retired to their rooms. Connie and Albert sat at the island in the kitchen, opposite each other. They were drinking black coffee.

"I got a good look at the girl today," Connie said. "Abby brought her with her when she dropped Ryan and Lucy off at school—passed her off as a cousin."

"What was she like?"

"Freaky."

Albert scrunched his eyebrows as he sipped his coffee.

Connie added, "She looks exactly like Abby. They even have the same eye color."

"Really?"

"I'm not exaggerating. It's like she could be her daughter, or if she were older, her twin."

"I wonder why that was never mentioned to us."

"I'm sure it has something to do with why so much effort is being invested in retrieving her."

"Maybe they are related."

"Be that as it may, why activate us for something that seems so miniscule? I always thought that, when the time came for us to be involved, it would be for something much greater, much more important."

Albert pushed his empty cup off to the side and rested both forearms on the island countertop. "We're not here to question our orders."

"I realize that, but don't tell me you aren't the least bit curious as to why we were chosen for this low-level snatch-and-grab. Our training is well above this. Anyone, really, could have grabbed the girl." Connie held up a finger, stopping her husband from speaking. "And, no, I don't think Abby is a threat or that her being an FBI agent is cause for concern."

"Are you finished?"

"Sure."

"Has it ever occurred to you that the reasoning could be as simple as the fact that we're Chinese and so is the girl?"

"You don't need to be Chinese to grab the girl."

"We've done more than that; we've earned the agent's trust. You, primarily. Surely, Agent Kane and the US government don't think Xiaolian is just some Chinese girl. They've detained her in a secured, secret facility. Let's not forget that."

Connie hooked a few strands of hair behind her ear. "What is it that makes her so special?"

"I'm not sure. Whatever it is, it seems important."

"I just wish we knew. It's eating at me."

Albert grabbed Connie's hand and squeezed it gently. "Forget about that. Our mission is to grab the girl and deliver her without blowing our cover. All of this," Albert motioned around him, "disappears if we don't accomplish that, so stop minimizing our role here."

"You're right."

"Were you able to catch them talking at home?" Albert asked.

"No. Abby and the girl went for a run, and then they spent

time at that small park on Hyde Street. When they returned to the house, her partner, Agent Kang, was already there. I was able to pick up a conversation with the three of them. Abby questioned the girl about her upbringing. They think she's either an orphan or attended a Chinese sports school."

"Why would they think that?" Albert frowned.

"That girl isn't normal. She kept up with Abby during that entire run. They even ran up Union Street to Hyde. So she's had some sort of training. I think they showed her a video of one of the schools. Xiaolian made a lot of comparisons with the place she is from."

"Hmmm, interesting." Albert scratched his chin. "So it seems as though Abby isn't leaving her alone with Po Po during the day. A day grab won't work. What about the school?"

"She drops both of her kids off but picks up only Lucy in the afternoon. Colin and Ryan go to the dojo together."

"Can you get to Lucy? Does she wait alone?"

"No, she's always with one or two other girls."

"What about the crowd of parents? Can that be used to our advantage?"

Connie thought for a bit. "The problem is separating the girl from Abby. Plus, today is Friday. We'll lose two days waiting for Monday. And isn't that the day she's supposed to take the girl back anyway?"

"You're right." Albert drummed the countertop with his thumb. "I've got it. Tomorrow we'll invite them over, make a day of it. We'll make pizzas, the kids can swim, and we'll have a treasure hunt for the kids. We'll hide fake gold coins around the property, and the kid who finds the most wins a prize. Think about it. The property is big enough, and there are a lot of blind spots. It's an opportunity to get the girl alone."

"Okay, say we do separate her from the others. Then what?

It's not like, if she goes missing, Abby won't be bothered by that."

"No, that's the plan. We want her to freak out about the girl missing. Think about it. This girl is still being held captive by the government. She's on loan to Abby. She's responsible for returning the girl."

"So the girl sees an opportunity," Connie continued Albert's train of thought. "And runs away."

"Exactly. Of course, we really grab her. The shed is the perfect location. We'll knock her out, put her in the large trunk we keep in there. Once Abby is convinced that she's run off, she'll go looking. That's when we move the girl."

At that point, Albert still hadn't told Connie about the change in their orders—that the girl was to be killed. He knew she would fight it, perhaps even jeopardize the mission. After years of being married to her, he knew her weaknesses. She could never harm the girl. It wasn't easy for him either. He was against it. But in the end, he was a loyal soldier. He would do what was asked, even if it meant executing the girl.

CHAPTER FORTY-SEVEN

AFTER MEETING WITH ELLIS, Kang headed back to the office. It was near the end of the day, but he wanted to see if forensics had anything new to report. They didn't. He sat at his desk, removed his cell phone from his pocket, and studied the picture he'd taken of the words Ellis had written down.

The face Ellis had said he saw confirmed someone else was with him, but who? Could it be the owner of the pair of shoes standing next to Ellis at the curb?

Kang rubbed his forehead as he stared at the photo, trying to spin the words into something meaningful. The medical mask was also interesting. Was this person the one who injected Ellis with propofol?

The darkness or void that Ellis spoke of could just be a reference to nighttime. He knew that the location where Ellis had stood was dark at night, so maybe that was why he couldn't place the face. If that was true, did that person lead Ellis down the alley? Why would Ellis go with him unless he knew the person—a student perhaps? Or was that person a complete stranger who convinced Ellis to walk with him?

Ellis didn't strike him as the sort of person to just walk off with a stranger, unless that stranger was female. Mrs. Ellis's revelation about her husband's infidelity opened up some doors. If women were his weakness, perhaps one was used as bait, a way to lead him away, though the pair of feet that stood next to him at the curb definitely belonged to a man.

Kang wrote off inebriation. From his conversation with the students and the bar owner, Ellis seemed to be okay, aware of his actions and surroundings. Was he really planning on driving home, or was he heading to a girlfriend's place? Kang now realized he should have questioned Mrs. Ellis more about those women.

"Cerberus" was the last word to pique his interest. He went online to read up more about the mythological creature—a three-headed dog known as the Hound of Hades, the god of the underworld.

This is so random.

Kang had been unable to draw a connection with Cerberus. Ellis had insisted that the image of he dog he remembered seeing wasn't a tattoo. Kang had then suggested a sticker or a T-Shirt, but Ellis had shaken his head to those suggestions as well.

Kang did an Internet search—aside from all the mythological references, the image of the dog appeared abundantly in digital artwork, paintings, and drawings.

A company that sold antivirus and antitheft software had adopted the word "Cerberus" as the name of their business. The business didn't use the image of the dog, just the name. They claimed to provide triple protection. That was the tie-in to the Cerberus name.

In fact, he soon learned there were a lot of companies utilizing the word "Cerberus." The businesses ranged from an investment firm, to an advertising agency, to a beer microbrewer, to even a maker of headsets. Only the beer company used the imagery of the dog. The others just copped the name. He downloaded the beer logo with the intention of showing it to Ellis. Maybe the person was wearing a T-shirt made by the brewery or was drinking the beer.

Kang continued to investigate the "Cerberus" references that appeared within the Google search. He came across more companies selling services or products using the name. Even a sushi creation had been named after it.

The list was endless. Google had produced more than thirteen million search results, and he had perused only the first twenty pages. *There has to be a way to narrow this down.* He did another search for companies in the Bay Area that used the word "Cerberus" or the image in their name. There were a few, but one stood out. It was called Cerberus Fertility.

Strange that a fertility clinic would choose that as its name.

Kang clicked on the link and was taken to the home page. Right off the bat, it seemed like a normal fertility clinic... well, what he imagined one would look like. It featured pictures of healthy babies, smiling physicians talking to hopeful parents, state-of-the-art laboratories, and a pair of gloved hands handling a tray of test tubes.

The only odd thing was their choice of taking it one step further than the name. They actually used the image of Cerberus. It was a blue-and-white line drawing—sophisticated and with a feminine feel—of a dog with three heads.

Kang nicked the logo from the website and emailed it to himself along with the logo from the beer company. He would show them both to Ellis. The last thing he did was note the location of the clinic, and this made his hair stand on end. It was near Mount Sutro, where Barnes was found running around naked.

CHAPTER FORTY-EIGHT

THAT SAME AFTERNOON, Sid Devlin sat calmly at the table in his office. A video of a cellist performing played on his laptop. He wasn't watching; his eyes were closed, but he did have a pleasant smile on his face. When the cellist completed her performance, he opened his eyes, picked up the phone, and made a call.

"Min, would you come in here, please?"

Five minutes later, Min stood in the doorway to Devlin's office.

"I've made a decision." Devlin said.

"Very good. I'm happy to hear it." Min closed the door behind him and walked over to Devlin. He reached for the stack of folders on the table. "Which one of these people have you chosen?"

"None."

"I'm sorry. I don't understand." Min's voice and expression were laced with confusion. "You said you'd picked someone."

"I have, just not from the pile you're holding."

"Who is this mysterious person you've chosen?"

Devlin turned his laptop around and hit the space bar. The cellist began playing a new arrangement.

"Beautiful, isn't it?" Devlin closed his eyes and retreated back into the lull he was in earlier.

"Tell me you're not suggesting this person?"

"Her name is Nadia Ulrich. She'll be performing in the city three days from now."

"That's not enough time to vet her. We can't begin to—"

"She doesn't need vetting. I'm familiar with her music and her career."

"This is insanity."

Devlin opened his eyes. "You're such a worry wart. The performance will be small, very intimate, only a handful of invited guests. I'm one of them."

"Have you lost your mind?" Min ran his hand through his hair. "You can't be seen around these people. There cannot be any ties to you or this place." He motioned to the general area around him. "Need I remind you that discretion is a key component to this program?"

"I've made my decision. I trust you and your team will figure out the details and ensure that what needs to be done is done."

"I implore you to reconsider. Surely there are others in this pile that are as suitable?" Min opened one of the folders. "Ah, here we are: Camilla Davidson. She's a respected professor at UC Berkeley, one of the top biophysicists in the country. She is also head of the Biochemistry Department and oversees all of the research being done. What's wrong with her?"

"It's not a matter of finding fault; it's about making sure the risk is worth it."

"You're saying Camilla Davidson isn't worth the risk?"

"I'm saying that, at this moment, Nadia is a much worthier one."

Min shook his head. "I simply don't get it."

"Camilla will always be here. She's a tenured professor. Nadia isn't from the Bay Area; in fact, she calls Berlin, Germany, her home."

"But the risks... they are extraordinary."

"No more than any other candidate that we've selected. She'll be staying at the Mark Hopkins Hotel and performing at the rooftop bar. Surely an old institution like that isn't equipped with advanced security measures."

"And how did you come to this knowledge that she'll be staying there?"

"Like I said, it's an intimate performance for a select group of people with more money than they know what to do with." Devlin grinned as he allowed the last of his words to linger.

"Very well." Min closed the file folder holding Davidson's information. He watched as his boss raised the volume on the laptop, leaned back in his chair, and closed his eyes.

Min shook his head as he pursed his lips. He had spent months compiling candidates and then culling that list only to have his efforts discarded like snot on a fingertip. He returned to his office, closed the door, and plopped down in his chair behind his desk. He hadn't stopped grumbling to himself since he'd left Devlin's office.

"That smug bastard. Who the hell does he think he is?" Min said out loud as he slouched down in his chair. "His arrogance will be his downfall. And when that happens, I will take over."

For the first time that day, a smile formed on Min's face. He spun his chair around so that he faced the large, tinted window behind him. His office was on the second floor of the two-story facility. The building was in the shape of an oblong C. Min had a corner office at the very end of the curve. From where he sat, he had a view of the front of the building and the parking lot.

He watched a silver sedan pull into the lot from the street. It parked three spaces from the front of the building, and a man exited the driver's side. He walked around the back of the car to the passenger side, where he greeted a woman. Together they walked hand in hand toward the entrance of the clinic. The man leaned in and whispered into her ear. She acknowledged with quick head nods. *It's always the woman who's nervous.*

The couple stepped up onto a sidewalk that ran the length of the front of the building. It was lined with a low-lying hedge and neatly manicured grass. Near the entrance to the building was the company sign: a large granite block with 3D lettering and a logo made of brushed steel. The name of the clinic was Cerberus Fertility, and the logo was a three-headed dog.

CHAPTER FORTY-NINE

THE KIDS WERE THRILLED to hear that the Shis had invited us over. Connie had called the night before, and I answered for the whole family, except for Po Po. I knew she already had plans—lunch in Chinatown and then an afternoon of Mahjong with a few friends.

Early that morning, I took Xiaolian to buy a swimsuit. It was near eleven when we finally returned to the house. We were getting ready to head over to the Shis' home when I called Connie once more to see if I could bring anything. "Bring appetites and energy," were her words.

Everyone piled into the Charger: me and Ryan in the front, Lucy and Xiaolian in the back. Po Po stood on the porch and waved goodbye.

On the way over to the Shis', I made a quick stop at Fanelli's and picked up a deli platter. They had an amazing tray that consisted of various meats, cheese, stuffed peppers, and a mix of olives. I didn't want to show up empty-handed. Didn't seem right.

We arrived to a warm welcome from Connie and Albert, who met us in their driveway.

"Abby, I told you not to bring anything," Connie said.

"Is that prosciutto?" Albert took the platter from my hand.

"It sure is. And that is Salametti and Calabrese salami."

"I for one am glad you brought this. Cured meat is my weakness."

"He's not kidding. He might eat the whole thing," Connie said as we walked toward the house. She peeked around me. "Hi, Xiaolian. Remember me? I met you at the school."

"Yes," she said softly.

"She's a little shy," I said. "Give her time; she'll warm up."

"I thought it would be fun if everyone made their own personal pizza. We'll give the oven a nice workout today."

The Shis were the only people I knew who had a wood-fired pizza oven in their backyard. Albert had built an impressive outdoor kitchen, complete with a bar and a state-of-the-art grilling station that housed a massive chrome grill.

"The dough is ready. All that's needed are toppings and then into the oven."

Laid out neatly on a long picnic table were individual pizzas, each about eight inches in diameter. In the center of the table were bowls of ingredients: mozzarella and cheddar cheeses, fresh tomatoes, olives, mushrooms, onions, bell peppers, spinach, sliced pepperoni, and a large mixing bowl filled with tomato sauce.

Albert placed the deli platter on the table. "I'm putting this stuff on my pizza."

We spent the next thirty minutes or so customizing our pizzas. As they were completed, Albert slid them into the oven.

"How long does it take to cook them in there?" I asked him.

"The temperature of the oven floor is about seven hundred degrees Fahrenheit. So roughly three minutes."

He wasn't kidding. Within ten minutes, everyone had a piping-hot, personalized pizza. I had followed Albert's lead and loaded my pizza up with the good meat from the deli platter. I also added peppers, olives, and crushed garlic.

Xiaolian had never eaten pizza, and she was utterly confused by the process. Lucy walked her through it. They both did a split pizza—pepperoni and cheese on one side and mushrooms and olives on the other. Ryan put a little of everything on his.

Xiaolian sat next to me. She was still a little shy. Lucy already knew Hailey. Ryan and Colin trained at the same dojo. And Merrick simply followed his older brother around. I could understand if she felt a little left out.

"Are you having fun?" I asked her.

"Pizza is good," she mumbled.

"That's for sure." I took a bite of my slice.

"Who are these people?"

"They're the Shis. That's Connie and Albert. Their kids are Colin, Merrick, and Hailey."

I had introduced Xiaolian earlier, when we'd first arrived. That was one thing we definitely had in common: names went in one ear and out the other. Took a while to stick.

The treasure hunt was the big event. Albert had hidden gold coins around the property. The person who found the most won the prize: a large, gift-wrapped box. The kids, however, couldn't resist the pool, so swimming won out after we finished eating.

While the kids played a game of Marco Polo in the pool, Connie, Albert, and I relaxed on the deck. Albert asked how long Xiaolian would be visiting. I was still playing up the story I had given Connie a few days ago—that Xiaolian was a cousin visiting from New York.

"Just a few more days."

"Her parents send her out here by herself?" He dangled a

piece of prosciutto above his mouth before shoving it inside. "A little young, no?"

"She's twelve, but she looks younger," I said.

Albert nodded his head. "I see. Why didn't they come? The parents."

"Unfortunately, they're having marital problems. They thought it was a good idea if she stayed with us for a little bit while they sorted things out."

"Oh, is it serious?" Connie asked.

"I don't think so. I think they just needed time alone. But enough about them... what about you guys? Any travel plans coming up?" I wanted to change the subject as I had already expanded that fib more than I cared to.

"I wish!" Connie answered, "but with all the kids' activities, it seems like there's never enough time."

"It's been an hour or so. How about we start the treasure hunt?" Albert stood up and whistled. "Everybody out. It's time to hunt for gold coins."

He corralled the kids on the deck while Connie handed each one a towel. "Dry off, because the serious fun is about to start."

I couldn't help but think that the Shis were so nailing the parenting thing. I never would have pulled off something so unique, so grand, at the drop of a hat. We weren't even celebrating a birthday, or a bar mitzvah, or a graduation. It was just a simple if-you're-not-busy-come-on-over sort of gathering.

Albert spent the next few minutes making sure the kids understood the rules.

"It's really simple. We've hidden fifty gold coins around the house. Whoever finds the most gold coins wins the mystery prize. Everybody understand?"

They all answered "yes" in unison.

"Okay, on your mark. Get set. Go!"

The kids took off in all directions. Merrick found the first coin tucked away inside a potted plant.

"How did you guys hide all the coins without your kids finding out?" I asked.

"Albert hid them late last night after they were asleep. Plus they only found out there was a treasure hunt just now."

"You didn't tell them?"

"It was the only way it would work. If they'd known beforehand, they would have started hunting."

"What's in the box?"

"Four movie passes plus a voucher for popcorn and drinks. We felt it best to keep the prize simple."

"Good move. I can't believe you guys pulled all of this off. Where do you find the energy?"

"It ain't easy. Hey, do you drink tea? I picked up some delicious oolong tea in Chinatown the other day. It's called tieguanyin. Heard of it?"

"You're kidding, right?"

"No, why?"

"That's literally all I drink. In fact, I usually carry a tin of it around with me, but I recently ran out."

"Well, you're in luck."

I followed Connie into the house, my mouth watering.

———

Albert played the role of referee, settling any disputes over who spotted a coin first. He also kept an eye on his wife, waiting for her to lead Abby into the house. While listening to the bugs he'd planted in her home, he had heard her mention that she'd run out of her special tea. Buying some had paid off.

Once Connie and Abby were inside the house, Albert headed over to the outdoor kitchen. Under the countertop was a row of built-in cabinets. He reached inside and removed a zippered plastic bag. Inside was a rag he had already soaked in chloroform. He removed it and shoved it into his pants pocket. Then he went looking for Xiaolian.

He found her on the far side of the house, searching under a bush.

"How's the hunt?" he asked as he came up behind her.

"Not too good. I've only found eight."

"Did you check the shed?" Albert smiled and followed with an exaggerated wink.

"Where is that?"

"It's that little house over there."

The shed was on the left side of the house, tucked back into a tall hedge. It was out of sight from the pool and deck, and the only window in the house with a direct view was from his office, which was off limits to the kids.

He had already prepared the trunk that was inside the shed. It was large enough to hold Xiaolian once she was unconscious. Connie had even insisted they put a few bottles of water inside, along with a small flashlight. "She might be in there for a few hours. It wouldn't hurt to give her a little comfort."

Albert also went to the trouble of lining the inside of the trunk with acoustic ceiling panels to absorb any noise she might make. Once Xiaolian was deemed missing, they would do their best to play the role of panicked parents. Abby would immediately jump to the conclusion that Xiaolian had run off, to avoid being returned to the facility. Later that night, Albert would remove the trunk and deliver it to their contact. It was a solid plan, one he and his wife felt good about executing successfully. The only hitch was that Albert had no intention of delivering her alive.

Xiaolian ran up to the shed and tugged on the handle.

"It's locked," she said.

"I'm so stupid." He removed a key from his trousers, unlocked a small padlock, and pulled the door open. "Looks like your lucky day. You'll be the first one to search. Be sure to check the trunk. Hint. Hint."

Xiaolian raced inside.

Albert removed the rag and followed her.

CHAPTER FIFTY

MIN HAD BEEN SITTING SLOUCHED at his desk for almost an hour. He still couldn't move on from what had happened the day before in Devlin's office. *Who the hell does he think he is?* Min was growing tired of Devlin's management style, which consisted entirely of living inside his own bubble, unaware of all the hard work being done by others.

He had long ago accepted that no decision made by Devlin was ever final until it actually happened. He would often make changes to a plan at the last minute, sending Min and his team into a heart-pounding scramble.

And now, picking an entirely new person, one whom no one had heard of before, at the last minute... it was pure Devlin. *He should have run her by me, at the least, allowed me to dig into her background and put her through the rigorous testing the other candidates have been subjected to.*

As Min continued to stew, the grip he held on the pencil in his hand tightened, his thumb pressing harder against the hexagonal shaft until it snapped in half. He flung the piece he still held across his office in disgust. *I am not a low subordinate*

*whose opinion he can dismiss at will. I'm second in command
here. That counts for something.*

He didn't have much time, but Min always prided himself
on getting the job done. It wasn't the logistics of the job that
concerned him. He knew the location; in fact, while inside
Devlin's office, he had already formulated the basis of a plan,
one which he knew could easily achieve the objective. The work
was never the issue. It was Devlin. Something had to be done
about him. Operating the clinic in a reckless fashion...it jeopar-
dized everything they were working toward.

Min hit the space bar on his laptop and woke it up. Then he
located the Mark Hopkins Hotel on Google Maps and worked
on a route. The sooner he fleshed out the details, the sooner he
could brief his team and they could begin putting the plan into
place.

CHAPTER FIFTY-ONE

I FELT my phone buzz in my back pocket. I figured either Po Po or Kang was trying to reach me. Connie and I had been discussing the dojo; she was telling me how happy she was with Master Wen, and Ryan, for making Colin's adjustment easy.

I reached behind and checked the screen on my phone. It was a text message from Kang.

"Do you need to answer that? It's fine if you do," she said.

I shook my head and pocketed the phone. "It can wait until later."

I wasn't sure why I didn't deal with it just then. I never pushed off calls or messages from work, but that day I did. Maybe it was because, at the time, I felt a sense of normalcy, like I was living a stereotypical mom life, drinking tea with another mom as we discussed our kids. For once I wasn't chasing sickos or worrying about the next time one would attack my family. And it made me feel good inside.

Eventually the guilt got to me. Just as I reached back around for my cell phone again, a loud shriek from outside jerked both me and Connie to attention.

"That didn't sound good," she said.

We both hurried out of the kitchen and toward the TV room, where there were doors leading out to the pool. Through the windows, I could see Lucy and Hailey standing on the deck. Connie reached the door before I did.

"What's wrong?" she asked the kids.

"Lucy, is everything okay?" I followed up.

Both girls were smiling.

"We both have six coins," they said together.

"Why are you two screaming?" Connie asked.

"We're not," Hailey answered.

I brushed a few strands of hair out of Lucy's eyes. I felt a little silly. I was still jumpy, after what had happened at our home with Walter Chan.

"Sounded like a scream to me," Connie said. "Where are your brothers?"

"I think they're looking under the house."

"There are no coins under the house." Connie turned to me. "I'm guessing Ryan is under there with them."

She led the way to the opening of a crawlspace leading under the house. A small door was open. She bent down and called all three names.

"We're busy," one of them answered.

It sounded like Ryan, but I couldn't be sure. "Ryan, come out from under there right now."

Colin's head appeared first, then Ryan's, and finally Merrick's.

"Why would you guys look under the house?" Connie asked. "Colin, Merrick, both of you know it's off limits."

"It was Ryan's idea," Merrick quickly blurted.

"I don't care who came up with the idea. You two know better."

"Sorry, Mrs. Shi," Ryan said. He kept his head down, staring at his feet.

"It's okay, Ryan. We don't allow Colin and Merrick under the house because it's dangerous. Now you know too. They should have told you."

"They did, but I didn't listen. I just figured there were more coins there because we couldn't find any more in the yard."

"How many does everyone have?"

"Lucy and Hailey have six apiece," I said.

"I've got eight," Merrick answered.

Ryan and Colin were counting.

"I've got eleven," Ryan said.

Colin laughed. "We're tied. I have eleven."

"There are fifty coins total. So twelve from the girls, plus Merrick's eight makes twenty. Add twenty-two from Ryan and Colin, and that's a grand total of forty-two coins."

At that moment I realized we were missing one child. "Where's Xiaolian?"

CHAPTER FIFTY-TWO

I spun around like a top but didn't see her anywhere. "Who saw Xiaolian last? Lucy? Ryan?"

"The last time I saw her was over by the pool," Lucy said.

Ryan nodded. "Me too."

I hurried back over to the pool. "Xiaolian!" I called out on the way there. Connie and the kids followed.

"Xiaolian!"

There was nobody there.

"Hmm, maybe she's inside the house," Connie suggested. "Bathroom?"

We headed inside. I went directly to the downstairs bathroom.

"I'll check upstairs," Connie said.

"Xiaolian, are you in there?" I asked as I approached the closed bathroom door. I knocked once and then checked the knob. It was open, but the bathroom was empty.

I met up with Connie in the TV room.

"She's not upstairs. I even checked the bedrooms."

"Okay," I said, turning to the kids who were all sitting on the sofa. "I want everyone to split up. Let's look for Xiaolian, but nobody leaves the property. Understood?"

All five heads nodded before they darted off.

"Where do you think she could be?" Connie asked as we exited the front door.

"I don't know. It's not like her to disappear."

As I said those words, an empty feeling erupted in my stomach. The worst possible scenario filled my head—the men who were after her had found her. And this time they had taken her. I didn't want to believe that. I wanted to think she had gotten lost in her search for coins, but as seconds turned into minutes, it became harder to believe that as well.

Connie and I walked down the driveway to the sidewalk and looked up and down the street, thinking maybe she'd wandered off. We both called out her name.

"Do you think she would have left the property?" Connie asked.

"That's the thing that has me confused. None of this seems like something she would do. And I can't really think of a reason for her to leave." I left out the part about her being held at the facility and the dangerous men who'd been hunting her before that. The Shis were unaware of the facility, obviously, and what had happened at our house when Walter Chan had shown up. The FBI, along with other entities in the government, kept a lid on what had taken place. The Shis were aware that I had helped apprehend Alonzo Chan—it had been on the news, but that was where their knowledge ended.

"Where's Albert?" I asked. "Wasn't he overseeing the game?"

"He was. Let's ask the kids."

We headed back inside the house. All five of them were back in the TV room.

"Did you guys look for her?" I asked.

"Yes, we looked all over the house and around the pool," Ryan answered.

"Where's your father?" Connie asked her kids.

All three answered with a shrug.

"Wasn't he playing referee?"

"He was, but I don't know where he is now," Colin answered.

"What about you two?" Connie asked Merrick and Hailey.

They had nothing to add.

I couldn't understand why all five of them seemed a bit indifferent to Xiaolian missing. Maybe it was kids being kids.

I reached for my phone, realizing the worst had possibly happened and I now needed to call it in. Just as I started dialing, the door leading out to the pool opened. It was Xiaolian.

"Xiaolian!" I hurried over to her and gave her a hug. "Where on earth have you been? We've been worried."

"I was hunting coins." In her hand, she held a bunch of them. "Did I do something wrong?"

"For a minute, we didn't know where you were."

"Where were you?" Connie asked.

"On the side of the house, where the tall bushes are. I climbed inside them to look around."

While Abby fussed over Xiaolian, Connie slipped away. There was still one person missing.

What the hell is going on here?

Connie hurried over to the shed wondering why Xiaolian wasn't secured in the trunk as she and Albert had planned.

Did he not have an opportunity?

The door to the shed was closed, but the lock was open and hanging from a metal loop.

"Albert?" she called out softly as she pulled the door open.

She found him sitting on the concrete floor of the shed with his head between his legs.

"Albert! What happened? Are you all right?"

He shook his head slowly, as if he were regaining consciousness.

"Xiaolian is in the house. What happened?"

"I'm not sure. I led her over here. We were alone. She entered the shed. I followed..."

Connie noticed the rag next to him. She picked it up and held it up to her nose. She could smell the chloroform on it.

"Albert, what exactly happened here?"

Before he could answer, voices could be heard growing closer—Abby and the kids. Connie quickly tucked the rag into a box full of outdoor Christmas lights just as they reached the shed.

CHAPTER FIFTY-THREE

WHILE THE DAY AT THE SHIS' had started off great, it ended on a downer. I offered to stick around while Connie tended to Albert, but she insisted that she had everything under control. I waited, at least, until she had Albert upstairs and in bed; he had fought her the whole way. Once he was settled, I rounded up the kids and headed out to the car. Connie walked out with us.

"Not to pry, but did he elaborate on what happened?" I asked.

"He won't admit it, but I think he fainted. It's happened before, but he blew it off. He says it was minor dizziness. This time I hope he takes it much more seriously and visits the doctor for a checkup."

"He should get looked at. Better safe than sorry," I said.

Before Connie had found him, I'd thought it strange and a bit irresponsible for him to have disappeared, especially since he was the referee. Xiaolian had been nowhere to be found, and I had to admit, during that time, I started to blame him.

According to Albert, he had gone inside the shed to get a can of insecticide—he'd noticed a trail of ants on the side of the house. It seemed like a reasonable explanation for his absence.

"I'm surprised none of the kids stumbled upon him, since they were supposedly searching high and low for gold coins," I said.

"Well, my three know the shed is off limits, plus Albert keeps a padlock on the door at all times. He might have gone inside right before we started looking for Xiaolian." She shrugged.

I gave it no more thought and thanked Connie for the wonderful time.

It was four in the afternoon when we returned home. Po Po had just arrived herself. A friend of hers, the youngest and the only one in her group of friends to hold a valid driver's license, had dropped her off.

She headed inside the house and straight for the kitchen, of course. I told her dinner might not be necessary as the kids were still stuffed from their pizzas. She ignored me and said there was leftover rice that she didn't want to go bad, so she would make jook. I let her be.

The kids were beat from the day anyway, and all three were asleep early. I had hoped to talk more with Xiaolian, but that didn't happen. I figured the next day I would have plenty of opportunity, as Ryan had some sort of special training day at the dojo, and Lucy had a Brownie event to attend. She hadn't officially joined. The club allowed potential recruits to test-drive the Brownies for a day, and that was exactly what Lucy had chosen to do.

I was tired and thinking of falling into bed. But I decided I'd better return Kang's call. I got his voicemail and left a message. I called Reilly next.

"Hey, boss. Sorry to disturb you on Saturday. I wanted to check in and give you an update on Xiaolian."

I told Reilly about our talks and that the consensus between Kang and I was she'd most likely been raised in a Chinese sports school and that our best guess as to why she shared the same DNA as me is that someone had thought highly enough of me for being the youngest recruit to graduate from the Hong Kong Police Academy that they wanted a mini-me.

"The reasoning sounds logical," he said. "It certainly begins to explain a lot about her and her background. It's still a mystery as to why she was smuggled into the States and left on our doorstep."

"I agree. It could be a distant relative wanting to get her out of that school and far from it. From what I understand, they're not pleasant places to grow up in. I'll try pressing this point later with her. If this does turn out to be the case, I'm not sure how that information will fare with our CIA counterparts. They're under the impression she's a spy."

"I'm aware of that, but our job is to provide them with the information. What they do with it, and her, is up to them."

"That kind of sucks. She's still just twelve years old. Forget about her training and intelligence. I've spent time with her; she's still a kid at heart. It's like both sides of her personality—the girl from the sports school and the one who plays with my children—are at odds with each other."

"I understand that, Abby, but unless you plan on adopting this child, she's to be returned to the facility on the agreed-upon date. She's not our property. She's a Chinese national who entered this country illegally. You and I both know she'll be deported."

"That I understand. What I'm worried about is that my assessment of her won't fly with them and they'll continue to probe her like she's an experiment. She's not. I'm sure if we visited the school she was raised in, we'd find a whole lot of children exactly like her."

"You're probably right, Abby, but our job is to investigate federal crimes. At best, we can prove she entered the country illegally and nothing more. Return her, enlighten them on what you've learned, and be done with it."

I had no response to his comment. I would do what he had requested and continue to question Xiaolian. And when Monday arrived, I would promptly hand her back over to the facility.

With Abby and her kids gone, Connie hurried back upstairs to speak with Albert. He was out of bed and standing next to the bedroom window. He had watched Abby drive away.

"That didn't go well. We're lucky she bought my story about you fainting. She was starting to suspect that you might have had something to do with Xiaolian's disappearance.

Albert moved his hand away from the curtain, letting it close before turning around to face his wife. "She said that to you?"

"She didn't have to. I could see it in her eyes. With each passing second, she blamed you more and more. You were the referee overseeing everything."

Albert took a seat on the edge of the bed.

"What's the matter? You're acting strange." She sat next to him.

"It's the girl." Albert's gaze fell to the carpet.

"Who? Xiaolian? What about her?"

"She's not normal."

"What do you mean?"

He said nothing.

Connie nudged him in the arm. "Hey, snap out of it. What do you mean she's not normal?"

Albert looked up at Connie. "She attacked me."

CHAPTER FIFTY-FOUR

THE FOLLOWING MORNING, after a late breakfast, the kids and I piled into the car. The dojo was the first stop.

"I'll pick you up at three," I said as Ryan exited the car.

Our next stop was the Marina District, where a troop leader for the Brownies lived. They were having an orientation event. I parked the car, and Xiaolian and I both walked Lucy inside. I stayed a few minutes to chitchat with the troop leader and then left.

"What's a Brownie?" Xiaolian asked as we drove away.

"The Brownies are part of the Girl Scouts. Basically, they're an organization for girls. They learn stuff and have fun. If you're between the ages of seven and nine, you're what they call a Brownie. Does that make sense?"

She nodded. "I like the clothes they wear. It's cool."

"It is, isn't it?"

I know I had given her the overly simplified version, but even I wasn't fully aware of all the activities the Girl Scouts were involved with.

"What would I be called if I were in the Girl Scouts?"

"I believe girls your age are called Cadettes."

"I like that name."

During the drive, Kang pinged me twice on my cell phone. I had totally forgotten to respond to his text message the day before. When we got home, I told Xiaolian I had a phone call to make. She nodded and made a beeline to the downstairs toilet. I headed up to the third floor.

Albert had been sitting in a car outside Abby's home since six that morning. He had gone through the trouble of renting a vehicle from a local car-sharing service. Abby had been over to the house twice, and he hadn't wanted to risk the chance of her recognizing his vehicle. He'd spent a great deal of the morning playing solitaire on his phone, as there hadn't been much to listen to—nobody was awake. It didn't bother Albert. He had the day to pull off his mission, and he wouldn't fail.

Po Po was the first to rise; he assumed it was she, as he heard the clanking of pans in the distance. The bug in the dining room picked up noise from the kitchen. The rest of the family didn't start to stir until later.

Lucy was next. He recognized her voice as she spoke with Po Po in the dining room. She sounded like she was eating something. Xiaolian appeared shortly after, followed by Ryan. Abby was the last to come downstairs. Most of the conversation revolved around Ryan's and Lucy's day. His own son, Colin, was also attending the same training session as Ryan. His daughter, Hailey, would also be in attendance for the Brownie orientation day. Connie had the exact same routine that morning as Abby.

Albert received a call from his wife a few minutes before Abby returned home with Xiaolian.

"I missed her at the dojo but caught up with her at the troop

master's home. We talked a little bit. She said she had no plans
for the day except to relax at home. She looked tired. She might
be heading back to bed."

"She just pulled up to the house. I'll keep listening for that
to happen. I have a bug in her bedroom."

"Today is our last opportunity to grab the girl."

"I know that. Don't worry. I'll get her."

"Anything I can do to help?"

"What about Merrick?"

"That's what the video games are for. I can leave the house
for a few hours, and he won't notice."

"No, stay put. Let me see if I can get her during the day. If
an opportunity doesn't present itself, we'll both try later
tonight."

"What are they doing now?" she asked.

"Hold on."

Albert picked up the other cell and dialed the various
devices until he located Abby. "Okay, it seems like Abby is in
her office on the third floor. She's on a work-related call."

"And the girl?"

"She not in there with her, and I don't hear anything in the
entertainment room."

"Now is the time," Connie quickly replied. "She's probably
in her bedroom. According to Abby, she's staying in the
guestroom on the first floor. I believe she said it's right next to
her mother-in-law's room. Go!"

Albert hung up and pulled his car into Abby's driveway,
behind her vehicle, and exited carrying a clipboard. He wore a
PG&E technician's uniform; it was a local utility company. In
addition, he had applied a fake mustache and was wearing a
wig, not so much to fool Abby as to keep him from being recognized by any neighbors. And if someone did see him leaving

with the girl, Albert figured he would appear to be an employee of the utility company.

He decided against taking the pistol he had in the glove compartment, even after what Xiaolian had done to him in the shed. She had treated him badly, but now wasn't the time to exact his revenge. He needed to extract her quickly and quietly. He pocketed a chloroform-soaked rag.

As a safety precaution, he took a garrote. He figured he would need to use it only if he encountered Abby. As far as he knew, she was busy with work-related matters in her office. His plan was simple.

Get in.

Grab the girl.

Get out.

Albert moved along the side of the house. He had planned on entering through the back porch. Along the way, he peeked into the kitchen window. Po Po had just walked out.

Seems like she's going into her bedroom.

When he reached the back of the house, he peeked around the corner, just in case Po Po had decided to come out to the back porch. Briefly he hoped Xiaolian might be sitting out there. She wasn't.

He entered the screened-in-porch. It hadn't been locked the last time, and it wasn't this time. However, the back door to the house was. He placed his ear against the door and listened. Silence. He removed his lock-picking tools from his back pocket and went to work. Once he had the door unlocked, he slowly turned the knob and pushed the door open.

CHAPTER FIFTY-FIVE

I CALLED Kang again but got voicemail. I left a message that I was home and available to talk. I stood up, ready to head downstairs, when my cell phone rang.

"Hey, partner, what's cooking?" I asked.

"Sorry I missed your call. I was on the treadmill at the gym."

I sat back down in my chair, picked up a pen, and began doodling on a pad of paper. "It's fine. We're talking now."

"How was your day at the Shis' house?"

"It started off fine, but drama ensued."

I gave Kang the lowdown on what had happened.

"Fainted? Maybe he has low blood pressure," Kang mused. "You said his wife found him?"

"Yeah, she slipped out while I was tending to Xiaolian. Why do you ask?"

"Oh, no reason in particular. Just asking." Kang's voice trailed off.

"So fill me in on what you've learned."

Kang started by talking about Ellis and how he had started to recall events or images from that night. I drew stars, a moon, and a cow as he went on about Cerberus.

"A three-headed dog represents a fertility clinic? I wonder who thought that would be a dynamite idea?"

"Not only is that the name, but they actually use the dog in their logo. The other interesting thing about the clinic is that it's near Mount Sutro."

"Our tech guy, Barnes, was picked up near there, wasn't he?"

"He was. I'm thinking it's enough to pay them a visit tomorrow."

"I agree. After, you can introduce me to Ellis. Were you able to run those two images by him?"

"Not yet."

"We can do it when we visit him."

"What time do you have to return Xiaolian to the facility?"

"She's due back before noon."

"You're not supposed to let her out of your sight, right? Are you bringing her with us?"

"Good question."

Albert quietly closed the porch door behind him. The first bedroom belonged to Po Po, and the door was closed. He pressed an ear gently against it and listened for a bit but heard nothing.

She's probably napping.

He continued to the next closed bedroom door, which should be Xiaolian's. He listened but heard no noise on the other side of the door.

She's sleeping as well. Must be my lucky day.

Albert took a few more steps until he was standing at the bottom of the stairs. He could hear the faint sounds of Abby talking on the phone.

This is too easy.

He returned to Xiaolian's bedroom and gripped the brass knob, turning it ever so slowly. Bit by bit, the knob spun until it no longer could. He pressed gently on the door, inching it away from the doorframe. He peeked inside. The room was dark, but he could make out the corner of the bed.

He continued opening the door. As the natural light from the hallway spilled into the room, his view widened. Little by little, the bed was unveiled. It was empty.

"Bringing her with us to the clinic isn't a good idea," I said.

"I agree."

"You know what? I'll just leave her with Po Po while we visit the clinic. We can pick her up after, deliver her to the facility, and then pay Ellis a visit. How much time do we need for the clinic?"

"Not much."

"Exactly. I doubt Archer would discover that I broke his precious rule."

"Unlikely."

"Then it's settled."

"What time should I swing by tomorrow?"

She must be upstairs watching TV. Damn! Albert shut the bedroom door.

He realized his odds of a confrontation with Abby had just multiplied, something he had wanted to avoid. Blowing his cover wasn't an option. His thoughts turned to abandoning the mission and trying later that night, when everyone would be asleep. Surely Xiaolian would be back in her room, and with the exception of Po Po, everyone would be on the second floor.

Albert should have realized that was the smarter move. He should have turned around and exited the home as quietly as he had entered. But he pressed ahead.

Up the stairs he went. He didn't bother stopping on the second floor, and he slowed his pace only as he approached the third floor. He could hear the television in the entertainment room, but he couldn't see inside. He peeked around the corner, and at the end of the hallway, he saw Abby in her home office. She was sitting at her desk, with her back facing him. She appeared to be taking notes while she spoke on the phone.

It was only then that Albert realized she could see the front street from the window.

Did she see me park behind her car?

She needed only to look out the window and she would notice his car behind hers. Surely she would want to find out who had parked their car on her property.

Albert should have left at that moment.

But he didn't.

To Albert's ears, it sounded as if Abby was wrapping up the phone call. He thought about his possible moves at that point. The obvious was to go for the girl and hope Abby remained on the phone a few more minutes. Xiaolian was just a few feet away. A surprise appearance would work in his favor. He'd pounce on her, striking hard with both fists. She deserved it after what she had done to him in the shed. He would not be fooled by her innocent act. The other possible move would be to immobilize Abby first.

Albert didn't need to wrestle over the decision. It was clear to him what course of action was best. He stepped into the hallway, removed the garrote wire, and strode toward Abby's office.

"My plan for the rest of the day is to see if I can pry more information out of Xiaolian," I said.

"Sounds good. We'll talk later."

With the call disconnected, I stopped doodling and looked up at the window. In the reflection, I saw a figure approaching me from behind.

CHAPTER FIFTY-SIX

I T TOOK ONLY a second to determine that the person behind me was a threat. Instinctively, I raised both hands, palms facing outward, and stopped a garrote from slicing into my neck.

Instead, it cut into the fleshy pad of my fingers just below the second knuckle. A searing pain erupted as the wire cut deeply into one of my pinky fingers. I clasped my hands tightly around it and pushed forward.

My attacker grunted as he pulled back. I felt his hot, forceful breaths on the side of my face. It was revolting, violating.

In the reflection, I clearly saw my attacker's face, but I didn't recognize him. He had his jaw clamped tight and a determined look in his eyes. His white-knuckled fists gripped the metal handles at the ends of the wire.

At that point, the only thing preventing decapitation were my hands.

He yanked left and then jerked the wire to the right, working to loosen my grip or slip the wire over my fingers. The wire sliced deeper.

The battle was one of strength. I couldn't win if I fought

that way. I would not be able to push the wire out far enough to slip it over my head. If anything, doing so would only help the wire cut more deeply.

Think, Abby!

Bright red streams snaked their way down my forearms.

Perspiration bubbled on my cheeks and forehead.

I was tiring.

My fingers were numb.

I was losing the fight.

I needed a plan.

I planted my feet firmly against the floor, and when my attacker jerked back again, like he was hauling in a marlin, I kicked off the floor and threw my head back for added momentum.

The front wheels of my chair lifted up, and the rear wheels scooted forward across the wooden floor, flipping the chair backward and crashing to the floor. The garrote slackened, and I slipped it over my head.

My attacker moved quickly to loop the wire back over my head, but I flipped over. I shot my body forward, and my shoulder crashed into his thighs, sending him back onto his butt.

The wounds in my hands were bad. Blood spilled everywhere, covering us both. I moved on top of him and sat on his chest, forcing the air from him. I then worked to pin his arms down with my knees. I was about to ground and pound this son-of-a-bitch.

He bucked hard, sending me airborne. I had no leverage. He freed his arms from beneath my knees and struck the side of my head, near the back, with a balled fist. It stunned me for a second. No way I could resist multiple direct blows.

I released a fury of punches; most of them grazed the sides of his face as he fended off my attack.

He twisted to the side and nearly bucked me off. But I

planted my foot against the wall in the hallway and pushed
back, righting myself back on top of him.

I managed to pin one of his arms under my knee while
striking a blow with my fist. Blood erupted from his nose. But
his defense never let up as he deflected my next two strikes. His
forearms were big. Slipping through them became harder. With
each attempt, I was tiring.

This opened up my defenses.

He landed a solid blow to the side of my head, rocking my
world and causing me to lose consciousness for a second. That
should have scared the hell out of me. Instead it fueled me to
power on.

I could see him slowing. He was forced to breathe through
his mouth as his nose had swollen into a round bulb.

Still, his fist found its mark again.

I fell to the side. My vision blurred. My movements slowed.
I tried striking back, but my arms felt like floppy pieces of
rubber. No matter how hard I worked to clamp my thighs
around his torso, I could feel him scooting out from under me.

And then he flipped me over.

He was on top. He pinned my left arm with a knee first.
Then my right.

I stared at him. He looked different. He no longer had
brown hair. And his mustache dangled from his lip, flapping
from the breaths exiting his mouth. My vision was still working
to right itself, but make no mistake: I knew my attacker.

Before I could begin to make sense of the idea that Albert
Shi was attacking me, let alone figure out what my next move
was, a shadow passed over my face.

Thunk! Albert's head snapped back, and he fell over to the
side.

I still didn't know what had happened, but I quickly moved
to free myself from underneath him.

Again, something moved quickly past my line of vision.
Smack!

A foot had slammed into Albert's face, stunning him
further. I looked up and saw Xiaolian standing over me. She let
out a scream and delivered another kick.

This time, Albert was ready. He caught her foot and
yanked. She lost her footing and fell onto the floor hard. She let
out a tiny cry and rolled over to her side, moaning in pain.

I kicked at Albert, trying to free my leg from beneath his
body. He caught my foot and hung on, immobilizing it from
further strikes.

I glanced over at Xiaolian. She had curled up into a ball. She
was done.

Albert crawled back on top of me. His weight was unbear-
able. I could barely breathe with him on my chest. Out of
nowhere, he threw an elbow into my temple. Pain exploded
throughout my head. I let out a scream.

Xiaolian's kick to Albert's face had given me hope that she
had done enough to turn the tide. I was wrong. Albert had fully
mounted me. Both of my arms were pinned under his knees. I
was unable to defend myself.

Blood stained the areas around his nose and lips. His mouth
hung open, baring his teeth. His pupils were fully dilated,
making his eyes appear darker and bigger than normal. He
looked like a demon, ready to feast on its prey.

He raised both arms high above his head, drew a deep
breath, and let out a roar as both his fists rocketed down
toward me.

I was seconds away from discovering that I was a mere
mortal like everyone else. I was not untouchable. I could be
hurt. I could be killed.

But that day, my life was spared.

CHAPTER FIFTY-SEVEN

ALBERT COLLAPSED onto me like a lifeless rag doll. Dead weight. I tilted my head back and saw a man at the end of the hall. He held a handgun firmly in both hands as he approached me.

"Abby, are you okay?"

It was Archer. He knelt next to me and heaved Albert's lifeless body off of me—he had a bloody hole in his forehead. Archer was the last person I'd ever imagine coming to my rescue.

"How did you know?" I asked.

He was busy looking me over, ensuring I wasn't hurt. I winced when he touched the side of my ribs.

"Might just be bruising," he said. "Your face looks like hell." He gently touched the side of my cheek with the back of his hand. "I don't think your cheek is broken. Ice will help with the swelling. You'll probably need stitches on some of those fingers."

Just then, Xiaolian moaned. Archer left me to attend to her.

"Lie down," he said as he looked her over.

"My back hurts," she groaned.

I flipped over so I could get a better look at Xiaolian. My

entire body ached in the process. I crawled over to her. "Everything will be fine. Don't worry." I brushed her hair out of her eyes.

"Why did he try to hurt us?" Xiaolian asked as her eyes settled on Albert. "I thought he was our friend."

"So did I."

Archer stood a few steps away from us. He was speaking softly into his cell phone.

"Archer. My kids. Someone needs to get to them now." If Albert was a threat, I had to assume Connie was as well.

"Where are they?" he asked.

I told him, and he said not to worry. "I'll send someone to pick them up right away."

"They need to say 'chop suey,'" I said.

"Huh? What are you talking about?"

"My kids won't go with anyone they don't know unless they mention the secret word. It's 'chop suey.'"

"Got it."

"Where's Po Po?

"She's fine. I told her to stay in her bedroom and keep the door locked."

I looked back at Xiaolian. Tears had begun to well in her eyes. I draped an arm around her and pulled her next to me. "You're safe now."

"I don't feel safe," she said.

"You are."

"My team will be here in twenty minutes. We need to keep what happened here quiet. I'll brief your supervisor. Until I do, no one, not even your partner, is to know about what took place here."

"The kids, my mother-in-law..."

"Your kids will be picked up, taken for ice cream, and

brought here after everything is cleaned up. Your mother-in-law will remain in her room until further notice."

"I don't understand. What exactly is happening here?"

"Can you walk?" he asked me.

"Yes."

"You and Xiaolian get cleaned up, and then meet me on the first floor."

No sooner had he said that than he placed another call on his phone and started another quiet conversation.

My head hurt too much to continue trying to pry information out of Archer. I relented and helped Xiaolian to her feet.

"Can you walk?"

"Yes, but my back feels stiff."

"You took a bad fall. A warm shower will help."

We slowly made our way down to the second floor and to my bedroom. Xiaolian showered first while I waited on the bed. Her movements seemed much more fluid after. I gave her some ibuprofen and had her lie down on my bed. Then it was my turn for a shower. My fingers stung like hell when the water hit them, but I still felt a whole lot better with the warmth of the water flowing over my body.

By the time we'd finished cleaning up and headed downstairs, a team of people I didn't recognize were entering my home. They weren't with SFPD or the Bureau. They were all dressed in plain clothes. Archer was talking quietly to two men at the bottom of the steps.

"Can I have a moment?" I asked.

He handed me a zippered plastic bag filled with ice. "Put this on your cheek. I have a medic here who can stitch your fingers." He then placed his hand gently on the small of my back and ushered me and Xiaolian toward the kitchen.

"Your mother-in-law is fine. I told her you and Xiaolian were taking a shower and would be with her shortly."

"How much does she know?" I asked.

"She's a smart woman. She doesn't know the details, but..." Archer let his last word trail.

I nodded. "Xiaolian, I want you to keep Po Po company, okay? And tell her I'll be in shortly."

She nodded.

Archer had the medic tend to my fingers. It took the guy thirty minutes to close and bandage the wounds.

"Let's talk out back," Archer said.

As I reached the back door, I stopped to look at the lock. It didn't look like it had been forced open.

"I came in this way," Archer said, as he stood on the back porch. "So did Albert. I found a lock-picking kit in his shoulder bag. I'll have a guy put a new deadbolt on that door." He opened the screen door and exited into the yard.

I followed him to the middle of the yard, where he stood with his arms folded across his chest.

"I'm assuming you've been keeping tabs on me the entire time I've had Xiaolian in my possession," I said.

"You're right. It's a good thing I was because—"

I spoke over him. "Before you start patting yourself on the back, tell me why you were watching us."

"This has nothing to do with you. My involvement is not meant to be a reflection of your abilities. This has everything to do with that little girl."

"Because she's a spy."

"I know you think we're overreacting, but what happened today should provide you with enough evidence to start supporting our view of things."

"Who is Albert Shi?" I asked.

"We're still working on that. But a few days ago, I spotted him parked outside your home. He's been listening." Archer dug into the front pocket of his jeans and removed a bug. "I have a guy sweeping the rest of your house. I found this one in a lighting fixture above the dining-room table."

I stared at the tiny transmitter in the palm of his hand. All I could hear over and over in my head were his last words about supporting his viewpoint. Had he been right all along about Xiaolian? Were people still after her? It was the only explanation I could think of to explain why my house had been bugged.

"So, is Albert working for the Chinese?"

"We suspect he is, in some sort of capacity. We just took his wife into custody."

"You think she's involved too?" I held my hand against my forehead, struggling to comprehend what Archer was telling me. "We were just at her house the other day; my kids played with her kids..."

"Until I question her, I can't rule it out. Look, I know all of this is hard to grasp, but if what I'm thinking is right, it's okay to feel duped. They're professionals. I believe they're sleeper agents who were recently activated. It would help explain why they weren't on anybody's radar until I spotted the husband camping outside your home."

I buried my head into the palm of my hand and shook my head. "If you hadn't shown up..."

"I did. That's all that matters."

"I feel like an idiot. I was completely fooled by them."

"That's how they operate. You mentioned earlier that your kids and their kids are friends."

"Yes, they attend the same school. Their son Colin also works out at the same dojo as Ryan. And their daughter is applying to be a Brownie with Lucy."

As I said those words, it completely dawned on me that it had all taken place at once: Colin becoming a new student at the dojo, Hailey and Lucy becoming friends at school, and Connie introducing herself to me. It all seemed so clear now, that their involvement with my family's life had happened right after I'd returned home from the facility.

I looked up at Archer. "I want to apologize for dismissing your assumptions about Xiaolian being a spy or connected in some way to the Chinese government. It was unprofessional of me."

He waved it off. "Everyone does. You don't operate in my world, so I don't expect you to get it right away."

"But they're not after me, are they?"

"They're not. They're after the girl. Maybe they had orders to bring her in, or maybe they had orders to make her disappear."

"Well, they came into my life the minute I returned home, probably to see what I knew about Xiaolian."

"That's probably right. So long as she was in the facility, they couldn't get to her."

"And me taking her out gave them an opening."

Archer didn't respond to what I said; instead, he said he'd much rather question Connie and find out the truth than stand around and speculate.

"Is my family safe? Tell me the truth."

Archer let out a breath. "I'm not sugar-coating it. There might be others we don't know about, but regardless, they're after the girl."

"But we are a way to get to the girl."

"Xiaolian will be returning to the facility today. That should help take the attention off your family. We can also place some people with you, just in case. That's your call. But my feeling is we know too much already. The people who control the strings don't want us to know any more than we already do. If they continue to come after you, they open themselves up as well."

I kicked at the grass with the front of my shoe as I processed what Archer was saying. "You know, there *is* one thing that feels off."

"What's that?"

"When Albert was attacking me, Xiaolian kicked him in his face; she nearly took him out. If Albert is also working for the Chinese, it makes sense that he was part of a plan to extract her. And if it's true that Xiaolian is with the Chinese, why would she attack one of her own?"

"I'm not sure, but that tells me there's a lot more we need to learn about her."

CHAPTER FIFTY-EIGHT

AFTER OUR TALK in the yard, we headed back inside the house. Archer went upstairs to check on the cleanup, and I entered Po Po's room.

"Abby, everything okay?" she quickly asked.

She was sitting on her bed, her back against the headboard, watching TV. The volume was turned low, as Xiaolian had fallen asleep next to her.

"Everything is fine," I said in a hushed tone as I sat on the edge of the bed.

She leaned forward and moved the bag of ice away from my face. She *tsk*ed while shaking her head, though I did see some compassion in her eyes.

For a moment or so, I didn't say anything. I didn't know where to start. I wasn't even sure if she knew about the dead body upstairs, but I figured Xiaolian had told her.

"We have people picking up Ryan and Lucy," I eventually managed. "They're safe. They'll be home shortly. The people in the house are taking care of the problem upstairs."

"Xiaolian say a man attack you? He dead?"

"Yes, to both questions. I believe he was after her. What did she tell you?"

"She tell me everything."

"I don't know what to say. I'm sorry this happened. Everything will be back to normal before Ryan and Lucy come back. They don't have to know about anything that took place here."

Po Po nodded. I had to give credit where credit was due. The woman had cast-iron emotions, and she always understood the bigger picture. There wasn't any more to say. I knew she disliked my job, but she also understood it was what I did. It was dangerous. She would blame me, no matter what the situation. I completely understood. I told her I'd check in on them later and left.

I didn't know any of the people Archer had invited into my home, though each had a job and wasted no time getting started.

The atmosphere was somber, like a wake without the crying. No one spoke unless merited, not until my home was completely swept for more bugs and given the "all clear."

Archer and I were talking when a muscular man wearing blue jeans and a black T-shirt approached us. He had an upside-down smile and pockmarked cheeks. Large headsets hung from his neck, and he carried a portable counter-surveillance detector to search for listening devices and wireless hidden cameras.

"Found three more," he said. "One was in her bedroom, another in her office, and the last one in the entertainment room." He held up a plastic baggie containing all three bugs.

"Cameras?" Archer asked.

The guy shook his head. "We're all good."

I walked over to the bay window in the front room and watched a tow truck remove Albert's car. In its place, an unmarked van backed up. The doors opened, and a man exited, holding the doors open. A beat later, three men lugging a black body bag walked down my stairs. They loaded the body into the back of the van, climbed inside, and drove away. The whole thing took forty seconds, tops.

Archer stood next to me.

"What will happen now?" I asked him.

"Forensics will finish their job. We'll clean up and then be out of your hair."

"I meant with the Shis and Xiaolian."

"The investigation will continue. Xiaolian will leave with me." He turned to me. "I still need you to brief me on your conversations."

I nodded.

He pointed to a white utility van across the street. The sign painted on the side read: O'Flanagan's Drywall and Remodeling.

"Those are my guys. They're excellent. They'll hang out here until morning, keep a watch on the house."

Archer handed me a small electronic chip. "Keep this on your body or near you."

I took the bug. I had just traded a Chinese spy for the CIA. I glanced at Archer; he was still staring out the window. The man had saved my life, yet I still found it hard to like him. He came across as so cocky and standoffish. Maybe I was being too sensitive, and I needed to get over it... swallow my pride and accept that I won't always have control of my investigations. That was probably the real reason I resented him. He didn't have to answer to me.

"I never thanked you," I said.

"Huh?"

"I never thanked you for... upstairs. So, thank you."

"You're welcome."

CHAPTER FIFTY-NINE

Archer, Xiaolian, and the rest of his crew left within the hour. I said a quick goodbye to her and promised that I would visit. I wasn't sure if I would be allowed to see her again, but it felt like the right thing to say. She left with a smile.

Ryan and Lucy arrived at the house shortly after, with no clue as to what had happened. According to Archer, the kids had been given a cover story: I had planned an outing but had an accident at the last minute, so I sent a colleague instead.

Meredith was the CIA officer who babysat my children. She dressed casually in jeans and a solid navy-blue top. Her chocolate-brown hair was pulled back into a simple ponytail, and she wore a little bit of pink lipstick. She had kept them occupied with lunch and a shopping trip to the mall.

"Hi, Abby. It's great seeing you again," she said, supporting the story. "Boy, you weren't kidding when you said you had an accident." She eyed the side of my face.

"It's better now that I've put ice on it."

"Mommy, what happened?" Lucy asked. She grabbed hold of my hand and looked at the bandages.

"I was taking a box of files and other stuff off of a tall shelf, and it slipped from my hands. My face broke the fall." I chuckled. "A glass vase in the box broke, and I cut my fingers picking up the pieces."

"Talk about rotten luck. If there's nothing else, I've got another appointment," Meredith said.

"Thank you for looking after them. I appreciate it, really."

She nodded and headed out the front door. I shut and locked it.

"Did you guys have fun?" I asked them.

"I did," Lucy sang out loud. "I'm glad I was picked up early. The Brownies aren't cutting it with me. I gave it all the time I could."

"I see. How was your training session, Ryan?" He still seemed a little irritated that he had to leave the dojo earlier than expected.

"Okay, I guess."

"Just okay? Looks like you got yourself a new pair of shoes."

He had a bag from Footlocker. "Yeah, I got some new cross-trainers, so that was cool. I just don't understand why you planned this today. You knew I had my training session."

"A total mix-up on my end."

A look of confusion appeared on his face. "But you didn't even come. You could have just cancelled it."

"You're right, but I thought I would be able to meet up with you two still. Look, what's done is done." As he aged, it was becoming harder and harder to pull the wool over Ryan's eyes. My BS excuses were barely cutting it with him.

"I wish you had come with us," Lucy said as she appeared from the downstairs bathroom. She had changed into a cute floral romper. "What do you think?" She twirled.

Lucy surprised me. I didn't think she'd go for something like that.

"Meredith helped me pick it out. At first I wanted a black leather skirt, but then she showed me this. It even has pockets." She shoved both hands into them and grinned.

"I think it looks great."

Just then Po Po came out of her room.

"Po Po, look at my new outfit." Lucy skipped over to her, hands still buried in her pockets.

"It look very nice," she said with a smile.

Po Po allowed her eyes to soak in the room... searching for evidence of what had happened earlier. She nodded her approval. Of course, the altercation had taken place on the third floor, which I had yet to check. I trusted that Archer's crew specialized in making it appear as if nothing had taken place.

While Ryan showed Po Po his new shoes, I took the opportunity to duck upstairs and see exactly what had been accomplished.

I walked down the hall slowly, examining the wooden floors and walls for blood splatter or fingerprint-powder residue. The large crimson pool that had accumulated on the floor next to Albert's head was gone. The team had cleaned up well.

I knelt at that location and didn't see any scratches or blemishes in the floorboards. They might have been buffed out. My nose did pick up a faint trace of bleach. I would have expected them to use a stronger cleaning agent.

In my office, my chair was upright and tucked under my desk, and the items on top were arranged neatly. *Not bad.* I grabbed my cell phone off of the desk and looked it over, wondering if it had been tampered with. For all I knew, they might have removed Albert's bugs and replaced them with their own. I looked out the window at the van across the street. *Having fun, boys?*

While it was comforting to some degree to have them sitting outside, I needed one of my own. I dialed Kang's number.

"Hey, what's up?" he answered.

"I need you here. And pack an overnight bag."

CHAPTER SIXTY

DEVLIN'S PENTHOUSE suite was located in the SOMA neighborhood. From his perch on the thirtieth floor, he had striking views of San Francisco Bay that included everything from the Golden Gate Bridge to the Oakland Bay Bridge.

The interior had a clean, modern décor with neutral colors. The walls were covered with painted and photographed works of art. Crown molding and accent lighting appeared throughout the space. The foyer was massive, complete with white marble floors, pillars, wainscoting, and archway entrances to two other rooms. The apartment featured four bedrooms and four bathrooms on two floors. One of the rooms had been converted into a workspace.

Inside the workspace were counters running along two walls with shelving below and cabinets above. One wall had a pegboard with various tools hanging from it: a razor saw, miniature drills, files, a jeweler's saw, a chisel, and a number of craft and carving knives.

In the middle of the room was a rectangular island with a built-in light box and drawers. Devlin stood next to it, hunched over two felt-lined viewing trays. He had a jeweler's loupe

pressed against one eye; it looked like he was wearing a mono-
cle. He was in good spirits as he was humming along to a violin
concerto that played in the background.

Neatly arranged on one tray were detailed dollhouse
furnishings. On the other tray, laid out neatly in two rows, were
dried beetles with colorful patterns on their backs. He was
examining a miniature cast-iron stove.

Shadowbox creations were a personal hobby of Devlin. He
had already completed three and was currently working on the
fourth. Each shadowbox was two feet high, three feet long, and
half a foot deep.

Depicted inside each shadowbox was a cross-section of a
distinct living space: a modern home, an art-deco condominium,
and a houseboat. Imagine a dollhouse opened up.

What made Devlin's art different was that he didn't feature
people in the homes. He used insects. Different varieties were
chosen for each environment. Dragonflies for the boat, cock-
roaches for the modern home, and colorful lizards for the condominium. He posed them so they looked as if they were relaxing
in a recliner with the evening newspaper or enjoying a good
soak in a tub. He titled his work of art "Living Amongst Us."

His favorite was the '80s art-deco condominium. In one of
the bedrooms were two lizards having sex. One was positioned
on its knees taking the other from behind. A mini video camera
on a tripod captured the action. In the kitchen, another lizard
appeared to be snorting cocaine off of a small mirror.

The shadowbox he was currently building would feature
the interior of a rustic cabin with beetles. The structure itself
was made of real wooden branches fashioned to look like logs.
The décor inside featured a large brown-bear hide on the floor, a
stone mantle and fireplace, and a carved totem pole. Other
native Indian artifacts like a tomahawk and a headdress hung
alongside realistic replicas of animal heads: an American

buffalo, a black bear, a moose, bighorn sheep, and other species native to North America.

Devlin built all the furnishings himself. The insects, however, were purchased from a respectable dealer who could obtain any insect in the world. Devlin set the loupe on the table and stood straight, raising both arms over his head and stretching. He glanced at his watch. *Hmmm, four hours passed just like that.*

The only art that hung in his workshop, apart from his own, was a neoclassical painting. The scene was that of a nobleman graciously paying tribute to a king sitting on a throne while a crowd of spectators watched from the sides.

"Dear!" a woman's voice called out. "Where are you?"

A few seconds later, a woman appeared in the doorway. She was tall, slender, and wore a white evening gown. Her chestnut locks were pulled back into an elegant French braid; two spiraled tendrils framed her oval face. Pearl earrings and a matching choker rounded out her jewelry requirements. Her cat eyeliner gave her eyes a sultry and mysterious look.

"Have you been in here all night?" She walked over to the island, where Devlin still had furnishings and insects on display.

"I'm afraid so," he said as he came up behind her and placed a gentle kiss on her neck. "How was the benefit?"

"Dull." She spun around as she let out a defeated breath. She had already kicked off her heels, but at five feet eleven inches, her eyes weren't that far from his.

"I don't know why you torture yourself by attending these functions," he said.

"It would be better if you came along." The woman draped both arms around Devlin's neck.

"Not a chance."

"Kiss me."

Devlin leaned in, but she moved her head back. "Not there."

A coy smile appeared on Devlin's face. "Someone's naughty today. Did the benefit make you horny?" he asked, mimicking the Austin Powers movie character.

"Oh, don't spoil the moment. You know I hate it when you talk that way."

"Really?" he continued with the impression.

As quick as a lightning strike, the woman swung an open palm and connected with the side of Devlin's face.

He gasped as his hand shot up to his cheek. He took a few quick peeks in her direction. The playful curve of her smile had been replaced with an ugly, flat line. Her icy-blue eyes were cold and penetrating.

Unable to hold her gaze, Devlin settled on staring obediently at the floor. One by one, she placed a hand on his shoulders, applied pressure, and forced him to his knees.

"Let's try again," she said. "Kiss me."

CHAPTER SIXTY-ONE

No way I wanted to wait and see if any more attacks were coming without involving my own people. I called Reilly after I had hung up with Kang. I didn't tell them much on the phone, just enough to convey that I needed them to come over. I wanted to speak in person, as I had to assume the men in the van were also listening in on my cell-phone calls.

Kang arrived first with a smile, a small suitcase, and a box of rice cakes.

"Thanks for coming." I closed the door and locked it.

His smile disappeared as he looked at the side of my face. He was about to say something, but I cut him off.

"You can stay in the guestroom since Xiaolian is gone." I pointed down the hall.

"What happened?"

"I was unloading something heavy from the closet and, *bam*, right in the kisser," I said.

Kang's eyes darted back and forth from my face to my bandaged hands. His expression told me he wasn't buying the story, but before he could open his mouth, Lucy and Ryan appeared.

"Uncle Kyle," they both said.

Kang greeted Lucy with a hug and Ryan with a handshake.

"You're staying in Xiaolian's old room," Lucy said.

"Close to Po Po and the kitchen, just the way you like it," Ryan added.

"You got it good." I took the box of rice cakes from him and handed it over to Ryan. "You and Lucy can have one each."

"Abby—"

"Not here. I'll explain later. Let's get you settled in your room."

Kang was prepared to stay at the house as long as I needed. I had told the kids beforehand that his home was being fumigated, so he was bunking with us for a few days.

Ryan was ecstatic about it. All he ever wanted to do with Kang was talk about all things martial arts, which Kang was happy to do; he enjoyed yakking about it just as much.

Lucy followed me and Kang into the guest room. She grabbed Dim Sum from the bed and was about to take him back up to her room when she stopped and turned around. "Uncle Kyle, do you want to keep Dim Sum for company? It's okay. I can lend him to you."

Kang smiled. "That would be awesome. Thanks, Lucy."

"There's a fresh pot of coffee in the kitchen. Help yourself to a cup after you've settled in, and then meet me on the back porch."

Before heading out back, I fixed myself a cup of tea. Next to the kitchen was a small utility room where we kept the washer and dryer. Po Po had just put a load into the washer. I removed the bug from my pocket and placed it on top of the machine. *Enjoy, fellas.*

Kang appeared a little later on the back porch, holding a mug and a plate of rice cakes.

"You read my mind." I reached for a sticky treat and took a large bite.

Kang took a seat next to me and helped himself to a cake. We quietly ate and sipped for the next minute or so, and then I told Kang about everything that had happened. He listened quietly at first. As I continued to debrief him, he began shaking his head.

"Sheesh, Abby. Are you okay? What about the kids, Po Po?"

"Everyone is fine."

"I should have been here," he said.

"How could you know?"

"So, Archer?"

"Yes, Archer. He saved my life."

"I'm sorry if I'm about to come across a little harsh, but I find it all so hard to believe. I mean, I know it happened, but... you know what I'm saying. I thought we had caught everyone who was after her."

"Apparently we didn't, or whoever wants her sent more people. This might not ever be over until they have her or she's dead. What surprised me the most was the attack by Albert Shi."

"Is his wife involved?"

"Archer believes she is. He thinks they were both sent to befriend me in an effort to find out what was happening with Xiaolian. I practically handed her over to them by taking her out of the facility."

Kang raised his eyebrows. "Sleeper agents?"

"That's the assumption. He had a team pick her up. We'll see what his interrogation reveals."

Kang lifted the coffee cup to his lips but stopped short of taking a sip. "You know, for a while, I was becoming convinced that the spooks had it all wrong about Xiaolian, but no one comes after an orphaned kid like this."

"So you're back in the 'spy' camp?" I slouched in my chair, put both hands behind my head, and stretched my legs straight out.

"And you're *not*, after all that's just happened? I think Archer is right about the Shis. They are spies, or at the very least, they work for someone powerful in China."

Just then the back door opened. Reilly had arrived. He took a seat, and I quickly got him up to speed on what had taken place.

Reilly removed his glasses and rubbed his face. "Gee, Abby, I don't know what to say. Had I known the CIA's intentions, I would have never have let you work with them."

"How could you have? How could any of us? This is how they work, in the shadows."

Before Archer left with Xiaolian, I pressed him harder on why he'd kept tabs on me. I couldn't believe he was just making sure I stuck to his rules. After a bit of back and forth, he gave in. A few weeks earlier, he had spotted a surveillance team near the facility. They'd been there every day and were terrible at keeping their position hidden. "Amateurs," he told me. He'd kept an eye on them, but it seemed their only job had been to watch the facility.

"So he had his suspicions weeks ago but said nothing?" Kang asked.

"Yeah, I think we're told only what we need to know, which isn't a lot."

Kang threw his hands up as he looked at Reilly. "We can't work this way. It's clear these people don't give a damn about us."

"I won't fight you on that. It'll be up to us to watch each other's back." Reilly leaned forward, resting his arms on his thighs. "Go on, Abby."

"Archer must have realized letting me take Xiaolian could

provide him with more answers or draw out the people interested in Xiaolian."

"He used you as bait," Reilly said.

"He did. And it worked."

"Was he onto the Shis before the attack?" Kang asked.

"Not initially, but he figured it out. He'd noticed Albert sitting outside my house, sometimes for four or five hours. Then he'd followed him to a late-night meeting. He was unable to identify the man Albert met with."

"That son-of-a-bitch." Kang sat back in his chair, shaking his head. "You could have been killed today, Abby. How do they get away with the stuff they do? I bet Albert's body is in a furnace right now, being turned into ashes. Disappeared for good."

"I'm okay. I made it through."

He shot me a disapproving look. "That's not the point."

"I know it's not, but it is what it is. The question now is: what do we do, if there is something to do?"

We both looked at Reilly. His hand was cupped around his chin, and his brow was wrinkled in thought.

"I'm not sure if there is anything we can do about what happened today. Essentially we gave them the go-ahead weeks ago when we got involved with Xiaolian at the facility."

"Our job was to talk to her, to retrieve information," I said.

"I know. We'll stop all cooperation this instant"

"What about what took place here today?" I asked.

"You were involved in a CIA operation that went sideways, but you came out on the other end. That's how it'll be pitched to whoever needs to know. Nothing will happen to you professionally, though we might rub some people the wrong way for pulling out. It's messed up, I know, but this is over my head. People with much more power and authority are pulling the strings here."

"We don't know if Abby is out of trouble," Kang said. "She could be targeted again."

"These people, whoever they are, want the little girl. She's not here. The best thing is to wash our hands of it. It's not worth the risk. Just let Archer and his team take things from here. It's what they're trained for."

Reilly let out a breath and leaned back into his chair. The three of us sat quietly for a few moments. What he'd said angered me, but what could we do? We'd been brought in to consult for the CIA. This was not a sanctioned operation between the FBI and the CIA. It wasn't anything. But what got me riled up the most was the brazen dismissal of what had happened.

Everything had been quietly swept under the carpet. It left me feeling as if the mission was valued more highly than my life, and the lives of my family. The whole thing was total bullcrap.

As I sat there, letting the reality of the situation soak in, it dawned on me that there *was* one other thing we could do. I cleared my throat, grabbing Reilly's attention. "I have something I need to tell you." I glanced over at Kang, and he nodded. "We've been following up a hunch that has led to an interesting development."

"Does this development lead back to Xiaolian?"

"I'd be surprised if it didn't."

CHAPTER SIXTY-TWO

"DAMMIT, Abby! It's bad enough we got the CIA toying with us. The last thing I need is to have my own people running rogue." His eyes told me he was more than annoyed at my revelation.

"I apologize. It started off as a hunch. If I had brought it to you then, you would have dismissed it. You know I'm right. We had to dig deeper."

I gave Reilly a moment to calm down. I didn't blame him for being angry. He probably felt as if he were losing control of his department. It was bad enough that the CIA had kept him in the dark as much as me and Kang. Hearing I was running an investigation without his knowledge didn't help.

"Regardless, Abby. You should have brought me in on this sooner."

"You're right."

Reilly focused his attention on Kang. "You mentioned a fertility clinic?"

"I did a little digging on the image that Ellis mentioned and discovered Cerberus Fertility. Abby and I were planning on visiting the clinic tomorrow and talking to Ellis to see if the dog he saw matches the one in the clinic's logo."

"The clinic is also near Mount Sutro," I said. "SFPD picked up Geoffrey Barnes in that area."

Kang continued to fill Reilly in on the initial three men he'd singled out from the missing-persons reports and how he'd made connections between the three of them.

Reilly took a minute to take in everything and then nodded. "There's something fishy happening here. It definitely looks like they're targeting intelligent or gifted people in their work fields. You said you found propofol in the latest victim's bloodwork?"

Kang nodded. "Ellis was the first victim we were able to question right after his abduction."

"So we're looking at a series of abductions. Money isn't a motivator, even though it appears each of the victims has plenty of it. How are you connecting this to Xiaolian?" Reilly asked me.

"Propofol was found in her blood. She exhibited memory loss and showed signs of confusion. She was also abducted, not locally, but we believe from China. She didn't volunteer for this."

"I'm not so sure I would say 'abducted.' I think the better word is 'smuggled.'"

"You can phrase it any way you want, but the connection is there."

"In light of what just took place, do you two still think she was raised in a sports school?"

"Well, the kids who are sent to live in these institutions are as young as ages two or three," Kang said. "There they are raised, educated, and trained. It's a plausible explanation for the skills she has, and her sheltered and warped view on life, but what that has to do with Chinese sleeper spies, I don't know."

"Unless they're not really sleeper spies," I said. "They could just be people hired to retrieve Xiaolian."

"Abby, is Archer aware of all of this?"

"I gave him the talking points earlier. He mentioned meeting later for a full debriefing."

"Okay, for now I want you two to continue investigating this series of abductions, but leave Xiaolian out of it."

"But she's connected—"

"Abby, let it go. I don't want either of you contacting her or going anywhere near that facility. Whatever operation the spooks are continuing to run is none of our business. We've fulfilled our obligation. Xiaolian is now their problem."

CHAPTER SIXTY-THREE

CONNIE AWOKE IN A WINDOWLESS ROOM, sitting on a plastic chair. Her hands were secured behind her back with handcuffs, and she had been stripped down to her underwear.

Four rows of fluorescent lights on the ceiling gave the room a sterile atmosphere. The walls were concrete blocks painted the color of putty, and stained tiling covered the floor. Her legs weren't secured. She was free to stand, walk around if she wanted; there were no security cameras in the room monitoring her.

Strange.

Connie remained seated, wondering briefly if her own people had detained her for screwing up. She dismissed the idea as she vividly recalled a tactical unit busting through her front door, shouting and pointing their MP5 submachine guns at her. Her people wouldn't bring her in that way. They hadn't identified themselves, but she figured they had to be connected to some US government agency. It was the only explanation, and that meant Albert could be dead or in a nearby room.

She stretched her legs out in front of her, wondering what would happen next. Her throat felt dry, and every swallow

made it noticeable. She heard footsteps approach the door
before it opened.

A man with boyish looks entered, dressed casually in jeans,
a gray hoodie, and carrying a bottle of water in one hand. He
unscrewed the cap and held it up to Connie's lips. She drank
half of the bottle before pulling her mouth away.

He hadn't said a word since entering the room. He simply
stared into her eyes, as if he were analyzing her.

"Who are you?" Connie asked, breaking the stalemate.

"Your husband is dead," he answered.

The bluntness of the news sparked a heavy feeling in her
stomach, but she did her best not to give him a reaction.

"Of course, we both know he's not really your husband," the
man continued.

Connie kept her mouth shut.

"Why did you want the little girl?"

Connie looked at him with a hardened stare but said
nothing.

"What is it about her that so much effort is being put into
taking her out of our hands? First the Chan brothers, now you
and your husband... she must be something special for you to
risk your life, your freedom... your children perhaps."

"Where are they?" She spat the words out, unable to
continue her silence upon the mention of her children.

"Ah, yes, the children. The oh-so-important children. Are
they really your own, or were they provided to you, much like
the wonderful, upwardly mobile lifestyle you have here in the
home of the brave and land of the free?"

"If you do anything—"

"What? What are you going to do?"

As much as she wanted to continue a verbal assault on her
captor, she refrained. "Who are you? You don't strike me as FBI.

They wear suits and detain people in proper facilities. This grungy room is anything but that."

"Who. Am. I?" The man gripped his chin, mimicking a pondering philosopher. "Why are people always so concerned with who others are?"

"You're CIA, aren't you?"

"Oh, you're so intuitive," he said. "But as much as I love our guessing games, I have pressing needs. Now answer my question. Why did you want the little girl?"

"We were given orders to extract her. Nothing more."

"Who is she? Where is she from?"

"I don't know. We aren't privy to information like that."

The man laughed as he wagged his finger at her. "You know I find that hard to believe."

"It's the truth. We don't question why; we just do as we're told."

"I see. Did your superiors also tell you to try to kill an FBI agent in the process? Certainly makes maintaining your cover difficult. Oh, wait. Maybe you two are those kamikaze types of agents. Activated for one purpose, and that's it."

Connie looked away, and he stepped to the side to catch her eyes again.

"Was this your first mission? Wait. Don't answer. Let me see if I've got a handle on how things played out. You and your husband arrived in the States at a young age, most likely as university students. You graduated, got married, and started a life together. Over time, you became comfortable with your pseudo life here in the Bay Area and forgot your real purpose for being here. What with juggling Colin's judo classes and Hailey's Brownie events, it's hard not to. Hell, I think even I would have fallen into that trap. The problem with that is it makes you rusty."

Connie refused to acknowledge or even let on that she was listening to anything he said.

"Hmmm." The man slowly walked around Connie. "That seems too easy. You know what I think? I think you were inserted into the US not very long ago, maybe eleven or twelve years. That's how old your eldest child is, right? Yeah, this feels right. You weren't sent here by China's Ministry of State Security to engage in espionage. No highly trained MSS would have been caught dead conducting an operation the way you two were. Hmmm, interesting. Perhaps you were hired by a private firm."

Connie coughed.

"Water?" He picked the bottle up off the floor. "No? Okay. I think I'll have some." He drained the rest of the water and then tossed the bottle off to the side, sending it bouncing along the floor. "In case you're wondering, though I assume you've concluded as much, Agent Kane is alive and well. So is the little girl. Your husband failed spectacularly. I'm the one who put a bullet in his head."

Connie swallowed.

"Relax. I'm not here to do the same to you."

"I hate to break it to you, but fear didn't prompt that swallow."

"Good. I don't want you to worry about your safety. You're fine. I promise you that."

"My children... where are they?"

"You care about them, don't you? Of course you do. They're your flesh and blood. You can fake a relationship with your husband but not your offspring."

"Where are they?" she asked once more with a raised voice.

"All three of them are here, in another room, not far. You're wondering what will happen to them, aren't you?"

Connie didn't respond.

"Mothers always have a soft spot for the children. And anyway, what would they know about all of this, right? They're innocent in this matter. What I'm looking for, Connie, is an open dialogue with you—a sharing of information. You help us; we'll help you."

"What will happen to them?"

"That depends on your level of cooperation."

"How do I know you're not lying to me?"

The man nodded. "That's a fair question." He then removed a cell phone from his jeans. "How about proof that your children are alive?"

He turned the phone around and Connie saw that a video call was in progress. Sitting in a chair, breathing heavily and looking back and forth between the person holding the phone and someone else standing out of frame, was her son, Colin. He was still wearing his judogi. Perspiration bubbled on his forehead, and his cheeks were flushed.

A man dressed in black and wearing a balaclava appeared behind Colin. When Colin turned to look at the man standing behind him, Connie saw that her son's hands were secured behind his back.

The man placed a cloth over Colin's face and held it there as he tilted the chair back. Nausea erupted in Connie's stomach. Her eyes welled. Her bottom lip quivered. *They can't be serious?*

Another man dressed similarly appeared, carrying a plastic container filled with water, the ones used for water dispensers in an office. It was filled three quarters of the way.

At this point, Colin's rate of breathing had increased so that Connie could see the cloth bubbling up and down with each inhale and exhale.

Tears streamed down her cheeks, and she started to dry

heave. But try as she might, she couldn't tear her eyes away from the video.

The man lifted the container above Colin's face and tilted it slowly. The water crept toward the opening.

"Like I said earlier, I'm not here to hurt *you*, Connie. I only want to talk."

As those last words passed over the man's lips, a wave of water rushed out of the container, spilling over Colin's face.

CHAPTER SIXTY-FOUR

THE PLAN the following morning was for Kang and me to visit the fertility clinic after we dropped the kids off at school. I wasn't worried about their safety. I agreed with what Archer had said the day before: Xiaolian was the target, always had been.

The van with Archer's men was still parked across the street.

"How long are they supposed to keep watch?" Kang asked.

"A day. They'll be gone by this evening or sooner. Not much going on in the house, unless they're eager to know Po Po's viewing habits on the television."

Cerberus Fertility was located on Locksley Avenue, near the UCSF Medical Center, a solid twenty-five minute drive from where I lived. We arrived there about a quarter to ten. They had a large parking lot, but there weren't many cars, except in a section off to the side. Employee parking.

"They don't look busy. Should be easy to speak to the person in charge," Kang said as he pulled into a spot near the entrance. He turned the ignition off and applied the parking brake. Just off to the side of where we parked was a large granite block with the company name and logo plastered across it.

"It's even uglier in person," I said as I exited the vehicle.

Kang snapped a photo of the sign with his cell phone before we headed inside.

The entrance to the clinic led directly to a large waiting room furnished with leather sofas and small tables with reading material. A middle-aged Asian couple was sitting there, talking quietly.

A young woman entered the waiting room. She wore a crisp, blue dress shirt, a gray skirt, and black heels. She was carrying a silver tray with two coffee cups balanced on top, which she delivered to the couple.

The typical medical advertisements, typed-up procedures for checking in, and other mainstay waiting-room paraphernalia were absent. Instead, there were beautiful paintings on the walls, and classical music playing.

The reception counter was made out of bronzed steel, with a single slab of wood as the countertop. We approached the young woman sitting behind it. She was dressed smartly in a navy-blue pantsuit with a white blouse. She smiled graciously as we approached.

I showed her my identification. "Hello," I said. "I'm Agent Kane. This is Agent Kang. We'd like to speak to the person in charge here."

Her eyes paused briefly on my bruised face. "That would be Mr. Devlin. He's the president. Please have a seat while I check with him. Can I offer you something to drink? A cappuccino or a latte perhaps?"

"No, thank you." I said.

"I'll take coffee, black, if you've got it," Kang said.

"We do. Give us a moment."

Kang and I planted our butts on a nearby loveseat. It was cozy. I noticed all of the sofas were couple friendly.

"Comfy." Kang bounced a bit in his seat.

A few minutes later, the woman we'd seen earlier delivering drinks to the Asian couple appeared from behind a closed door. She placed a cup filled with black coffee on the table in front of us.

"Will there be anything else?" she asked.

"This is fine. Thanks." Kang grabbed his cup and took a sip. "*Mmmm.* They serve the good stuff."

"I'm sure the amount of money this place charges to help couples is outrageous. Good coffee is the least they could do."

"You ever thought of having kids?" Kang asked.

"I have kids."

"I mean, birthing one of your own."

I shrugged. "Sure, I've thought of it. Sort of hard, though—my hand shoots blanks."

"Too much information."

I giggled a bit. "What about you?"

"I got the bun, but I'm missing an oven," he replied, deadpan.

"Touché."

The receptionist came around from the counter. "Mr. Devlin will see you now." The girl who'd delivered Kang's coffee reappeared. "Lacy will show you the way."

"Please follow me," she said.

We followed the girl through a closed door and into a long corridor. We passed an empty, glass-enclosed conference room. We passed a number of offices and closed doors. Nothing on the doors gave an indication of what was on the other side. We took a left at the end of the corridor and then up a flight of stairs to the second floor. We passed another barren glass-enclosed conference room and more closed doors. Along the way, we passed one employee wearing blue scrubs. I thought it was strange. *Seems like a large space for a fertility clinic.*

We stopped outside double doors made of dark wood. Lacy grabbed hold of one of the brass handles, pushed one door open, and led the way inside.

Devlin's office instantly took me by surprise. It had to be at least thirty yards in length and twenty yards in width. Who needs that much office?

"I think he's making up for something that's very tiny," I said to Kang out of the side of my mouth.

The walls were made of the same wood as the door. Large paintings with ornate framing graced one of the walls, framed insects took up another. At the far end of the office were floor-to-ceiling windows running the width of the room. It provided a magnificent view of Mount Sutro. Classical music was playing from hanging speakers.

Sitting behind a circular table, almost in the middle of the room, was an impeccably dressed man with a groomed beard. He kept his eyes closed as he waved a hand around, as if he were directing an orchestra.

"He's expecting you." Before she left the office, Lacy motioned for us to move forward.

We made the long journey toward the table, stepping over an intricately detailed area rug that covered most of the distance. "The Rug of Asia," I mouthed quietly to Kang. When we reached Devlin, he still hadn't acknowledged us, which irritated me slightly.

"Mr. Devlin. I'm Agent Kane, and this is Agent Kang. We'd like to ask you a few questions. Would you mind opening your eyes? And don't make me ask you twice."

Devlin stopped playing conductor. His icy-blue eyes settled

on us, and he smiled. "I'm eager to hear your questions, but first, tell me what happened to your face," he said calmly as he lowered the level of the music.

I ignored his question. "Do the names Johnny and Helen Ellis sound familiar to you?"

"No, should they?"

"They might be clients of the clinic."

"If that were true, I would have recalled their names. I pride myself on developing close relationships with all of our clients. They're very special to us. Of course, I could be mistaken, but I highly doubt it." Devlin tapped a few keys on his laptop and stared at the screen briefly before shaking his head. "It doesn't appear as though the Ellis's are clients or even came in for a consultation. They would be in the system if they had. Are you here to inquire for them?"

"We're investigating a series of abductions in the Bay Area. One of the victims mentioned a three-headed dog."

"That three-headed dog is called Cerberus," Devlin said.

"It's a strange logo for a company specializing in fertility treatments."

"It's certainly out there. But as we say around here, it takes three to make a baby." He steepled his fingers while he grinned. "I think I know why you're here. Your victim mentioned a dog with three heads. Our logo has a dog with three heads. Therefore, we are the abductors. Was that your train of thought? Because I can assure you, we're not in the business of taking. We're givers."

"Mr. Devlin, we're looking for answers, not opinions. So if you wouldn't mind, please keep your flowery commentary out of it."

Devlin doubled down on his smile.

"Who are the people who visit your clinic?" I asked.

"People who want children."

"Humor me, and elaborate beyond the obvious."

"They run the gamut, but if I had to put it into marketing terms, they're older, high-income earners, educated, and we skew Asian. Word-of-mouth inside their community is very positive."

"I take it you have a high success rate?"

"Absolutely."

"Tell me, Mr. Devlin, could you think of any reason why this victim would reference your logo?"

"Well, until you can prove that he mentioned our clinic name and positively identified our logo as the image he supposedly saw while he was abducted, I'll assume what you intended on asking me is why he mentioned a three-headed dog. My answer to that question would be, 'I don't know.' I'm sure there are other places where that image exists."

"Actually," Kang jumped in, "in the Bay Area, your company appears to be the only one."

"Well, then, I take that as a compliment. People must be so pleased with our work that they can't stop talking about us. You mentioned he had a wife. Perhaps they were thinking of using our services. Could that be why he's familiar with our logo, if indeed ours was the one he saw?"

At that moment, I wished we had stopped by Ellis's home first to show him the company logo. It would have felt so good serving Devlin a slice of his BS.

Devlin stood up and buttoned his jacket before coming around to our side of the table. "I think I've answered enough of your questions. Any more, and we'll just be dancing around in a circle. Shall I have Lacy show you the way out, or can you two figure that out on your own?"

"What a son-of-a-bitch," I said as Kang and I walked out of the building.

"It's my fault," Kang said. "I should have run that logo by Ellis before we came out here. Might have saved us a whole lot of time."

"It's fine. This Devlin guy isn't off the hook yet."

CHAPTER SIXTY-FIVE

AFTER LEAVING THE CLINIC, we headed straight for Tiburon, a wealthy neighborhood across the bay. Even though my stomach was grumbling and Kang was itching for another cup of coffee, I wanted nothing more than to return to the clinic with Ellis's positive ID.

We were crossing over the Golden Gate Bridge when I asked Kang the obvious question. "Tell me again why you didn't just email the logo to Ellis?"

"I thought to do that, but I didn't want to miss anything when he viewed it. The answers I got from him the last time didn't come verbally. I had planned to see him yesterday, but you know, the whole Chinese-spy-invading-your-home thing happened."

"Got it. So we're a little backwards this morning. We'll have it straightened out soon."

I stared off into the bay. The skies were clear, and the sun was out in full force. There were sailboats zipping along the waters and ferries shuttling tourists to Alcatraz Island and Sausalito. Crossing the bridge with us were bike tours and walking groups. I turned and looked out Kang's window, at the mouth of the bay. A large container ship was approaching slowly. Seeing it reminded me of Xiaolian. My face must have given something away.

"What's wrong?" He glanced out his window and then back at me.

"That ship made me think of Xiaolian."

"You're still torn?"

"I am. It's weird, after what happened yesterday. I believe Archer is right, in that she is involved with the Chinese government in some capacity. On the other hand, I think about all the time I spent alone with her and how she interacted with the kids and Po Po, well… she seemed like your typical twelve-year-old. A little sheltered but normal."

"I understand where you're coming from. The same thoughts flow in and out of my head, and I haven't spent half the amount of time with her that you have."

"What do you think it is with her?"

"I wish I knew, Abby."

"I even get the feeling Archer is puzzled by her. If the intelligence community can't figure her out, what is that saying?"

Kang shrugged. "Beats me."

We arrived at Ellis's home, and Kang rang the bell. A few moments later, the door opened.

"Agent Kang. You're back." A woman—I assumed it was Mrs. Ellis—peered around him and looked me up and down. "And you've brought a friend, with a black eye."

"This is Agent Kane. She's helping with the investigation."

"Two agents. Is that a good thing or a bad thing?"

"It's not anything," he said. "We're sorry to disturb you, Mrs. Ellis, but we need to speak to your husband again."

"I assumed so. Come inside. Will you be staying long?"

"I don't think so," Kang answered.

"I'm asking because I can fix coffee or tea."

"That's kind of you, but we won't be staying very long."

"Follow me. Johnny is in his workshop. I have no idea when he'll return to the office."

"That must be tough," I said.

"You mean for him or for me?"

"Both," I offered, unsure of what answer I should have given.

"I'm used to having the house to myself during the day. Now, he's here all the time, plus his colleagues from work stop by often. At first the visits were out of concern; now they're all work related."

Ellis was in his study, standing next to a drafting table and drawing on a piece of paper. A Bose speaker system was playing house music, and Ellis's head was bouncing to the beat.

"Johnny, the FBI is back," Helen said. Then she spun on her heel, not waiting for an answer, and left.

"Mr. Ellis," Kang said as he approached him. "It's Agent Kang. Remember me?"

Ellis turned around and looked at Kang. For a brief moment, it seemed as if he didn't remember. "Agent Kang... more questions?"

"I have something to show you."

"Who's the other suit?"

"I'm Agent Kane." I held my hand out.

Ellis took my hand and, instead of shaking it, examined the bandaging. "Why didn't you come for the first visit?"

"How do you know for sure I wasn't here?" I pulled my hand away from his. "You were having a lot of problems with your memory."

"Is that so?" Ellis looked briefly at Kang. "I think I would

have remembered you, darling. So what is it you want to
show me?"

Kang took out his cell phone and pulled up the picture he'd
snapped that morning at Cerberus Fertility. "Is this the three-
headed dog you saw?"

Ellis leaned in for a better look. His eyes darted up toward
Kang and then back to the phone. "I don't believe it." A smile
formed on his face. "Damn, you guys are good."

"Is that a yes?" Kang asked.

He pointed to the screen. "I'm positive that's the dog I saw.
Everything is identical, the brush illustration, the color... though
I don't recognize the name of the company. Stupid name for a
fertility clinic, if you ask me."

Kang cleared his throat. "Mr. Ellis, are you and your wife
thinking about having a baby?"

He laughed out loud. "We are not trying to have a kid. I'm
fifty-five. Helen is forty-nine. Do the math. And if you weren't
aware, we already have a child. His name is Christopher. He's
in his second year at Columbia University."

"We were not aware of that. Understand, we had to rule out
the possibility that you might have seen this image at another
point in your life but somehow connected it with your
abduction."

Ellis nodded. "I see your point."

"Do you have any friends who might have talked to you
about this clinic or in vitro fertilization?"

"Nope."

"What about Mrs. Ellis? Do you remember her mentioning
this company? Perhaps a friend of hers or—"

Ellis waved both hands, cutting Kang off. "We don't know
anybody who needs help having a baby, and we aren't looking to
have another one. I swear I saw this image the night I was

abducted. I can call it that, right? That's what you guys are calling it."

"Is there anything else you can tell us? Was it on a sign like this?"

"No, that granite block, the grass and hedge—none of that is familiar. Not even the name. It's just the drawing of the dog. Does that mean it's not this company?"

"Not necessarily," I said.

"The last time we spoke, you mentioned... well, you wrote down the words 'bright lights.' Can you elaborate on that now?" Kang asked.

Ellis scrunched his eyebrows. "I just keep seeing a bright light, and there's darkness on the sides. Maybe there's movement."

"Mr. Ellis," I said. "Imagine you're sitting in a dentist's chair. There's a bright light shining down on you, and everything around you is slightly darker and maybe out of focus. Does that visual match the flashbacks you're having?"

Ellis started to nod, slowly at first, and then faster. "Now that you mention it, yes. Yes, I think that's pretty close. What does that mean?"

"It could mean someone was examining you, or it could be when they injected propofol into your system."

"So you think this company, this fertility clinic, is involved?"

"We're looking into it. It also could just be an employee acting on his or her own."

"The last time we spoke, you mentioned brief flashes of a man's face, possibly covered with a medical mask. Is that image clearer now?" Kang asked.

"Yes, I'm pretty sure that's what I saw."

Kang and I glanced at each other. "Thanks for speaking with us," I said. "It's been very helpful."

CHAPTER SIXTY-SIX

"WHAT'S OUR NEXT STEP?" Kang asked as he started the ignition of the SUV. "We have Ellis confirming he saw the logo for Cerberus Fertility the night he was abducted. We've also ruled out him, his wife, or people they may know as being patients there or even talking about it."

"I want to confirm one more thing. Do you still have those pictures of that abandoned silo we stumbled across?"

"I do, and before I forget, I did hear back from the city about maintenance. As far as they know, there isn't any ongoing maintenance, and anyone tinkering with the doors or the locks is trespassing."

"Considering Cerberus is near that silo, I want to see if Geoffrey Barnes recognizes the pictures."

———

Min walked down the long corridor, muttering. Lately, he resented being called into Devlin's office. It seemed, with every visit, Devlin had additional or changing thoughts. *I bet the*

*bastard's changed his mind about the cellist. Probably found
someone else who's not on the list.*

Min rapped his knuckles on Devlin's office door twice
before pushing it open and entering.

"Yes, sir. How can I be of help?" Min asked in a pleasant
tone as he approached Devlin.

"I had an unexpected visitor this morning. Do you know
about it?"

"Uh, no."

"The FBI stopped by for a chat."

"The FBI?" Min gasped. "What did they want?"

"Stop playing games. You know damn well why they would
be poking their noses around here. They have a victim who was
abducted, one who apparently recalls seeing the company's
logo."

Min took a seat in a chair opposite Devlin's desk. "Did they
mention the victim's name?"

"They didn't have to. I knew the second they asked if
Johnny or Helen Ellis were clients of the clinic. From what I
can gather, they don't know for sure if the Cerberus image their
victim—Ellis, I presume—is talking about connects to our logo. I
personally think they're on a fishing expedition."

Min ran his hand through his hair. "Is that a risk we want to
take?"

"What are you saying?"

"We need to shut everything down. We need to make sure
no one we've snatched can identify anything here. Do they have
more than one victim claiming this?"

"It sounded like they had just the one. Plus, why would they
think there are others? There's nothing obvious that would
connect them."

"I know, I know. But... are you sure it's Ellis?" Min asked.

"They brought up his name."

"Still, I think we need to cover our tracks. I'll start the protocols we have in place."

"Yes, do that. How are the plans for the cellist? Everything ready to go?"

"You're kidding, right? We can't do that now. That's just inviting trouble. We need to lie low. We need to make sure there's nothing to find if they come back with the intention of searching this place. We have a small window here to cover our tracks."

"And we will, but I want her. Nadia Ulrich will be our final trophy. In the meantime, start doing what you need to do."

Barnes opened his front door before we reached it. He was clean-shaven, dressed in khakis and a white polo shirt, and looked upbeat.

"Hola, amigos. You're back. I've installed a new security system." He pointed past us to the gates at the front of his property. Mounted on top were two security cameras. "I have them all around the property. Those two cameras allow me to see up and down the entire street. Come inside."

"Thank you," I said. "Sorry to show up unannounced."

"I see you've been hard at work fighting crime." Barnes mimicked a boxer throwing a couple of jabs. "Anyway, I don't mind the questions. I want you guys to figure out what happened. People still think I'm a whacko who was high on drugs that day. I need to clear my name."

"I'm glad you have your priorities in order." Kang and I passed through the entranceway and into the foyer.

"Hey, my reputation is everything," Barnes said, closing the door. "There are tons of other people just as smart as I am who can think up the same ideas I do, but what they lack is cachet. That's what allows me to get venture capitalists interested and talent on board. We'll talk on the patio. It's a lovely day, and the bay looks amazing."

We really didn't need to speak on the patio or even enter his home, but he seemed to be in a better place in his life compared to our last visit. No need to spoil his day. Barnes led the way straight through his home and out onto the patio.

"So how can I help catch these bastards?"

Kang removed his cell phone and showed the silo pictures to Barnes. "Recognize this?"

Barnes snatched Kang's phone out of his hand. "Where did you get these pictures?"

"I took them. It's a decommissioned military silo located on the top of Mount Sutro," he answered.

"I take it you recognize it," I said.

"I do. It's weird. I had no recollection until you showed me this. Now it's clear as day. Does this place have something to do with what happened to me?"

"It's possible that you might have been dumped there by your captors. Our thinking is you regained consciousness and eventually made your way down the mountain."

"It totally makes sense. I remember walking down the mountain and not understanding why or how I got there. You said it was decommissioned, so it's abandoned, right?"

"That's correct," Kang said.

"Maybe the military took me? A special program of some sort, and now they're trying to cover it up."

"Mr. Barnes, we have no information that leads us to think the military was involved," I said. "The silo might just be the place where you were released. It's remote for a small city packed with over 850,000 citizens."

"So now what?"

I took the cell phone from Barnes and handed it back to Kang. "Now that we've placed you at this location, we can investigate further. We appreciate your continued cooperation."

CHAPTER SIXTY-SEVEN

As soon as we left Barnes's residence, I put a call in to Reilly to see if he could start expediting a warrant so we could hit the clinic. Not only did I want to search it from top to bottom, I wanted CSI to comb that place for Barnes's or Ellis's DNA.

"Tell me what you've got," he said.

"Ellis confirmed that the image of the three-headed dog he saw the night he was abducted is the same one in the logo for Cerberus Fertility. Also, Barnes recognized the pictures of the silo we stumbled across while we were retracing his steps on Mount Sutro. The clinic is on the other side of the mountain."

"Abby, I know you think the connection is airtight, but I don't see how the clinic being near the silo links Barnes to it, and as for Ellis... well, I question his memory. He might just be projecting, wanting there to be a link, so he has connected what he saw with what you showed him. Plus, where he was abducted and where he was found is nowhere near the clinic."

This wasn't how I had imagined the conversation with Reilly playing out.

"If you're making a judgment based on the vicinity, then the location Barnes was found in should work for you because it's near the clinic," I said. "And I'll add that we also found a hospital gown farther up the mountain, not far from the silo. The lab matched the DNA on it to Barnes. I'm betting the clinic stocks those gowns."

"So might the large hospital next to them. You don't need a warrant to ask the hospital and the clinic to provide you with one of their gowns. I need something stronger if you want to search the clinic. Look, Abby. A Chinese spy was just killed in your home because you insisted that you take Xiaolian out of the facility. Right now, there are a lot of eyes watching. We need to be careful about jumping the gun."

"Jumping the gun?" I asked, annoyed. "What exactly are you trying to say?"

"Don't take this the wrong way. I'm on your side, and I'm looking out for you. But in light of all that's happened—the Walter Chan shooting at your home, the Albert Shi incident—well, there's talk that perhaps you might need some time off. Nothing serious, just a break, some time to clear your head."

"I just had time off while I was sitting in that damn facility."

"You know what I mean."

"Hold on a sec. Am I being suspended?"

The emptiness in my stomach grew with each passing moment of silence. When Reilly did speak, my stomach knotted up as I anticipated hearing him say yes.

"No, you're not, but we need to tread lightly. And when I say we, I'm including myself and Agent Kang."

"Is this coming from Archer? Because that guy—"

"Abby, stop right there. This is coming from way up the chain. Xiaolian, the Chan brothers, and now the Chinese couple turning out to be spies... this has all caught the attention of some very powerful people inside the DOJ and the State Department. We need to make sure everything we do from here on in is by the book and not seen as being reckless in any sort of way."

"Are these people not interested in the truth?"

"I know it makes our jobs tougher to do, but that's the situation we're in right now." Reilly paused for a few moments. "There was talk about removing you from anything having to do with Xiaolian, which includes the hunch you're chasing right now. Now before you give me an earful, know that I've put a stop to any of that sort of talk, but I can only do so much to protect you. I don't want you to be the fall guy in the event this thing blows up and becomes an embarrassment for our superiors."

I was at a loss for words. I'd never thought I would have fingers pointing at me for a job *not* well done. And that was exactly how I took what Reilly had said. I glanced over at Kang. He wasn't paying attention to my end of the conversation; he was talking on his cell phone too, one finger plugging his ear to block out my yammering. He had no idea his name was caught up in this mess... because of me.

My gut told me that everything I had done was right, but in light of Reilly's comments, I needed to come at it from a different angle. No problem. My father had instilled in me the "no closed doors" approach. "It's impossible to shut out a curious person," he had told me. "They can squirm and twist and scrunch their way into anything. Remember that, Abby."

I ended the call. There wasn't much more to discuss. I had my marching orders.

Right about the same time, Kang finished his conversation. "What did he have to say?" he asked as he pocketed his phone. "Is he getting the warrant?"

I spent the next few minutes relaying my phone conversation with Reilly. During my spiel, Kang remained calm. Only when I finished speaking did he say something.

"Abby, we're partners. We win together. We lose together. It's black-and-white for me. Is that clear?"

I nodded. He had no idea how much hearing him say that meant to me. Knowing he had my back, that he didn't question my actions, or tell me I was overreaching—or say anything of that sort—was comforting.

"I appreciate that. I know I've pushed."

Kang held up his hand. "Stop right there. That conversation is over. Understand?"

I nodded.

"Good. With that said, I do have some good news," he said with a smile. "I just got off the phone with my contact at the city. They're sending a guy who's familiar with the silo to meet us there. We still have an investigation to work on, right?"

"Right."

CHAPTER SIXTY-EIGHT

NADIA ULRICH ARRIVED in San Francisco that morning on a chartered jet from San Diego, she had spent the day shopping at the city's famed Union Square. A warm soak was exactly what she needed after all that walking from store to store.

She stepped out of the deep soaking tub inside her suite at the Mark Hopkins Hotel. Her chestnut hair was pinned into a bun on top of her head and soapy bubbles slid down her fair skin. She slipped into a fluffy white bathrobe and tiptoed across the marble floors and out of the bathroom.

Her manager had booked her in the terrace suite: More than one thousand square feet that included a private, glass-enclosed terrace offering views of San Francisco's skyline. She took a seat on a small sofa and stared out across the city. Warm colors filled the sky as the sun slowly disappeared.

The ballroom, and the restaurant on the nineteenth floor affectionately known as the Top of the Mark, had been rented out by a well-to-do couple throwing a fundraiser for a local politician. Nadia was scheduled to attend a cocktail party and dinner in the ballroom before her performance in the restaurant.

Devlin stood inside of the walk-in closet, his arms folded across his bare chest while his eyes scanned the suits hanging on the rack. He had thought of wearing the charcoal-gray suit—it was one of his favorites. The famous Sartoria Caraceni in Milan had tailored it. In the end, however, he chose the black Armani—classic, elegant, and perfect for the evening's events.

As he dressed, he could not remember ever being so excited to attend a fundraiser. But this was no ordinary fundraiser; the one and only Nadia Ulrich would be performing. When he'd learned of it a month ago, he'd known he would have to attend. Not only had he coughed up the ten thousand dollars required for attendance, but he had also made a significant donation to the politician's campaign. This in return secured him a seat at the politician's table for dinner, where he was sure that Nadia would also be sitting.

For Devlin, that was a dream come true. He had been listening to Nadia ever since he'd caught a performance at the Hungarian State Opera House years ago. She had been invited to play with the distinguished Budapest Philharmonic Orchestra. Ever since then, he had been a devoted fan. It would be a special night indeed—Devlin having the pleasure not only of meeting Nadia, but of taking her identity as well.

Min had spent the last few hours finalizing the plans with his team. There were four of them, and they each had a specific job. Min was responsible for overseeing the operation.

According to the schedule, Nadia was to perform for one hour and thirty minutes. Attendees didn't usually loiter at fundraisers. Once the event was over, it was over. Still, he figured she would be obligated to press the flesh and engage in small talk before retiring to her room. With Nadia's performance ending at half past ten, he and his men would need to be on standby from that time onward. They would snatch her from her room.

After a final briefing, Min dismissed his men. He still felt uneasy about the operation. They were taking unnecessary risks, and with the FBI snooping around, they needed to ensure nothing went wrong. He hadn't bothered telling his men about the Bureau's visit—no need to create unnecessary distractions.

Min glanced at his watch. It was time to move into position.

Gordon Cross was the city worker who'd agreed to meet us at Mount Sutro. He arrived in a silver Toyota pickup. He was older, probably late fifties, with a thick, white mustache to match his wavy hair. He was dressed in beige cargo pants and a long-sleeved shirt with large front pockets—one was lined with multiple pens.

"Sorry I'm late. I ran into road construction."

"Mr. Cross, we appreciate you meeting us on short notice. I'm Agent Kane, and this is Agent Kang." I expected a comment from Cross about my face or hands, but none came. I appreciated his professionalism.

"I'm always willing to do my part and help out law enforcement. So you two are interested in the silo, right?"

"We were told you're familiar with it."

"Yes and no. My familiarity comes from my curiosity. I'm a big fan of military history. I've visited a silo similar to this one before but have never been inside of one, so this is pretty exciting stuff for me. This will be a first for me, but do not fear. I've brought the blueprints." He reached back into the cabin of the truck and removed a few pieces of paper. "We have some guidance."

He also removed a large backpack. "My go kit. It's got everything I might need when out and about. We engineers always come prepared." He slipped it over his shoulders. "Shall we?"

Cross led the way up the trail. The sun hadn't yet set, so there was a fair amount of natural light, but the woods still seemed darker. Cross was the first to remove his flashlight; Kang and I did the same. By the time we reached the clearing where the silo was located, the sun had disappeared.

"What part of the silo were you interested in?" Cross asked.

"The last time we were here, we were able to open these two doors." I ran the flashlight beam in that direction. "Below is a second door, but it had a padlock on it. A new padlock, I might add."

"I've got a bolt cutter in the pack. That lock won't be a problem."

I led the way to the doors.

Cross said, "These are the doors used by personnel accessing the silo. The door you're talking about below could lead to a control room or even the chamber where the missiles were housed. We'll know soon enough."

Cross bent down to lift open the doors but stopped. He looked back up at us. "You sure these are the doors?"

"Yes, why?"

He shined his light over the door handles. "There's a padlock securing these doors too."

"That wasn't here the last time."

"Is it possible the city would have padlocked the doors after my initial call a few days ago?" Kang asked.

"I doubt it. We don't move that fast."

Cross slipped his backpack off, removed a compact bolt cutter, and snipped the lock. "Problem solved."

We helped him pull the doors open and then descended the stairs. Right away, I smelled it: the *lack* of anything funky. I looked at Kang. "Does it smell different to you?"

"It smells old, but nice," he replied.

"What did it smell like the last time?" Cross asked.

"Musky, rancid," I said.

Cross inhaled deeply. "I don't smell anything like that. Maybe opening the doors the last time aired the place out."

I thought it strange, but I wasn't about to dwell on it. I moved deeper into the space, to where the other door was. The padlock was still there. "This is the door that was locked the last time."

Cross removed his bolt cutters again and snipped the lock. It fell to the concrete floor with a heavy thunk. He pushed the door open, and it squealed in the process. We were looking at a large, open area.

"This looks much bigger down here than from above," I said.

"That's because this silo housed more than one missile," Cross said. He moved his beam across the area. "Looks like there were three ground-to-air missiles housed here."

"How do you know that?" Kang asked.

"You see these tracks that run the width of the room? On top are three housing units, one for each missile. When the blast doors above open, the missile in the middle is launched and then another missile moves across the track to that middle position."

"You said there's a control room here."

"Yeah, but it wouldn't be here with the missiles. It's usually in a separate area for the protection of the personnel inside. I imagine if we head back up and search some more, we'll find another set of entry doors or another small building, or the remnants of one. Did you want to do that?"

"Maybe later," Kang said.

"So, just missiles here? Nothing else?" I asked.

"Pretty much, though I think that might be another door over there." Cross stepped over one of the tracks. "Watch yourself there."

We followed him across the room, and in the far corner, just as he had suspected, was another door. This one also had a padlock on it, but it didn't look brand new like the one securing the entry doors.

Cross snipped the lock off and pushed the door open. There was nothing but blackness on the other side.

CHAPTER SIXTY-NINE

Devlin arrived at the Mark Hopkins Hotel at the very start of the fundraiser. He was the first to sign in at the reception desk. The night's events were to start with cocktails inside the Peacock Ballroom, where dinner would also be served. It was an opulent room with floor-to-ceiling windows offering cityscape views, and elegant molding complementing gold-and-ivory walls. Devlin wasn't much of a drinker himself and had arrived for cocktail hour only because he'd hoped Nadia would be in attendance.

He located the table he would sit at for the dinner service. There were name settings already in place. Devlin's seat was across the table from Nadia. He glanced around the room, and nobody seemed to be paying him any attention, so he subtly switched his name with another so that he and Nadia would sit next to each other.

An entire hour with Nadia. What more could I ask for?

Devlin began imagining the night ahead. He and Nadia would engage in delightful conversation while enjoying their meals. When the other guests at the table would dare to ask

Nadia a question, she would answer quickly, albeit politely, before returning to him.

As he fantasized, his penis grew erect, pressing against his trousers. He moved over to the windows and stood facing them so he could continue to enjoy the fantasy without drawing attention.

Nadia had spent more time on the terrace than she should have and was running late. She'd already had her makeup and hair done by a stylist provided by the hotel and now just needed to dress.

She stepped into a strapless gown and hiked it up over her breasts. It was a bohemian-style, lavender, lace-and-chiffon number, which complemented the crown of orchids the hair-stylist had given her. She stood in front of the oak-framed standing mirror, her hand resting on a hip as she twisted left and then right. She grabbed her phone and started snapping selfies.

Where on earth is Nadia?

Devlin scanned the room, looking over a sea of heads. His head hadn't stopped swiveling since he'd sat down for dinner.

She should have been here long ago. I hope nothing is wrong. Maybe I should check on her. Oh, don't be silly. She's a woman. She's just making sure she looks her best for the evening. I'm sure she'll be walking through the ballroom doors any second.

Devlin cut into the grilled sea bass and took a small bite. He'd waited as long as possible before eating, not wanting to be a rude dinner guest and start without her—but as the rest of the table had begun to eat, it looked odd with him just sitting there. Instead he chose to take small bites and chew his food slowly.

This is not happening the way I thought.

Devlin had envisioned Nadia walking through the doors hesitantly, unsure of where to go. He would call out her name and wave his arm. "Nadia, over here, darling." She would smile and perk up. Devlin figured he would take a few steps toward her so he could greet her away from the table.

She would have a beaming smile on her face when he offered his hand for a shake, while the other hand would gently pat her on her arm. It would be professional, yet show warmth. He wanted her to know he wasn't a crazy, rabid fan, but *was* interested. "I'm Sid Devlin. It's a pleasure to meet you."

Nadia would be taken in by his generosity and charm. "Don't be silly, darling." She would ignore the handshake and give him a hug followed by a playful tug on his beard.

Devlin would then place a hand on the small of her back and escort her to the table, where he would make the introductions. He would control the dialogue at the table. He wasn't about to let someone else steal his precious moments with Nadia.

Dinner continued without any sign of Nadia. Devlin was nearly finished with his piece of fish and had resorted to chewing with nothing in his mouth.

We should be deep in conversation by now, laughing at each other's stories. Of course, the others at the table would be jealous of the attention she was giving me, especially the all-important politician. What would he care? All he wants is the money. And it wouldn't be my fault, anyway, that Nadia and I hit it off. This is a free country. She can speak to whomever she pleases.

He had a few sips of wine left; most of the table had finished what was in their glasses. The toast he had planned wouldn't happen. Devlin glanced at his watch. Forty minutes had passed.

The servers had begun clearing dinner plates so that they could serve dessert.

There was nothing left on his plate. He had finished every grain of rice, every flake of fish, every slice of carrot. He looked up at the server, who had grabbed the edge of his plate, and nodded. The server then replaced it with a slice of banana cream pie.

It's fine that's she's missed dinner. She can still indulge in dessert, and we can still have our special conversation.

Devlin imagined Nadia taking a bite of her dessert and having cream on the top of her lip. He would reach up with his napkin. "You have a little... There we are, all taken care of." She would giggle like a schoolgirl and thank him for his attentiveness.

It will be perfect. I just need to hold out.

Devlin motioned to the server that he would like coffee.

What's pie without the coffee? I can't very well start eating until I have a cup to cut the sweetness.

After the coffee was poured, he glanced again at the entrance to the ballroom. It was empty. He let out a defeated breath and started eating his pie.

Why me? I don't deserve this. Why can't anything go my way? I put a lot of effort into this evening. Doesn't she realize this?

"Nadia!" A voice called out, pulling Devlin away from his thoughts.

He looked up and saw that the politician was already out of his seat. Devlin turned around and saw Nadia standing at the entranceway, unsure of where to go.

It's just like I imagined. Only the politician is stealing my role.

The politician waved his arm and called her name once more, walking toward her.

You son-of-a-bitch. I was supposed to be the one greeting her. Screw it. I'll call her over too. There can be more than one person informing her where she's sitting.

Devlin pushed his chair back to stand, but the legs dug into the carpet. With barely any room to stand, he bumped the table as he stood, spilling his coffee in the process. He didn't care. He had to be the one to greet Nadia first.

By the time he'd untangled himself from his chair, the politician was giving Nadia a hug. She had a big smile on her face as she whispered into his ear. He placed his hand on the small of her back, but instead of directing her back to the table, to the seat next to Devlin, he ushered her in another direction, to meet someone else.

CHAPTER SEVENTY

THE THREE OF us stood in the doorway, aiming our flashlights into the black void. It was a concrete tunnel a little over six feet tall and maybe five feet wide. The air inside felt much cooler. I didn't notice any odors or wet spots, like I had in the missile room. The structure appeared to have held up fairly well to the elements.

"That's a long tunnel," Cross said. The beams from our flashlights were simply swallowed by the dark. Reaching into one of his shirt pockets, he removed the blueprints for the silo. He tucked his flashlight under his chin, so he could unfold the paper. "Hmmm. This is strange."

"What is?" I asked.

"This tunnel doesn't seem to be on the blueprint. "We're standing here," he said, pointing at the paper.

On it, I could see the line drawings resembling the room.

"But there's no tunnel extending off from here." He tapped his finger on the paper. "There's not even an indication there's a door here."

"Are you sure you have the right blueprint?" I asked as I took a closer look.

"Yup. Here's the registration record and title: SF-89C Mount Sutro. That's the official name for this silo."

"Maybe it's outdated," Kang suggested.

"That's a possibility, but I doubt it." He folded the paper back up and tucked it into his shirt pocket. "Shall we venture forward and find out what's behind door number three?"

———

Min and one of his men, Glen, sat in the front seats of the white delivery truck. The signage on the side was for Young's Laundry —the business didn't exist, of course. The truck was a rental, and the plates were fake.

There were two other men in the back, along with the medical equipment needed for Nadia's arrival. They had a gurney, a portable vital-signs monitor, a CPR kit, syringes, a stethoscope, and other medical devices and medicine that might be needed during transport.

Min uncapped his bottle of water and took a swig, draining the last of it. He crumpled the bottle, screwed the cap back on, and shoved the bottle into a plastic bag.

Authorities had never investigated the reports, because the victims had turned up less than a day later. But with the FBI digging around, Min knew it was important that they plan for the worst. Nadia was a celebrity and her disappearance would prompt an investigation.

He wanted to minimize any traces of DNA. They wore latex gloves and beanies on their head. They were all dressed in black pants, white long-sleeved button-downs, and gray vests— very similar to what the male employees wore in the hotel. They'd also applied facial hair; two of them had mustaches, and the other two had goatees.

It wasn't foolproof. SFPD would easily put two and two together from the hotel's security footage; and eventually they would track down the truck. The license plates and a non-existent company would slow their efforts.

Min assumed Nadia would be their last snatch-and-grab, at least for a while. Any hopes he'd had of succeeding Devlin were quickly fading. And now he had to contend with the possibility of actually being caught.

———

Devlin sat at a table just off to the left of Nadia. He watched the staccato movements of the bow across the cello's strings. Her head was tilted downward and moving in time with the bow. She kept her eyes closed when she played, opening them occasionally, but since she wasn't quite facing Devlin, he was unable to make eye contact.

He tried to take solace in the fact that he was a mere seven feet away from her and watching her perform, but the enthusiasm he'd had earlier in the night had vanished. He never had met Nadia during dinner. She had been whisked away and introduced to one person after another, right up until it was time for her to perform.

Devlin didn't bother to intervene; instead he chose to sit alone at the table and sulk as he stared at Nadia's uneaten pie, the pie that should have left a bit of cream on her upper lip. The cream he would have playfully wiped away.

Why can't you just look to your left? I'm right here. I see you looking straight ahead. I see you looking to the right. How is it that the left side of the audience merits a snub? I don't deserve to be treated this way. I've done nothing but sing praises for you. Why must you return the favor this way?

Devlin's leg bounced faster. His jaw clamped a little tighter. The heat around his collar increased. He no longer viewed Nadia in the same light. She was an ungrateful little bitch.

CHAPTER SEVENTY-ONE

THE TUNNEL WAS EERILY QUIET—JUST the shuffling of our shoes against the floor. I ran my hand along the wall. The previous spaces had all been constructed with blocks of concrete; here, the walls were smooth.

I didn't notice any ventilation shafts or openings, but there still seemed to be a slight breeze. The lack of lighting didn't make any sense. There wasn't a single fixture anywhere. What would be the point of building a tunnel without any access to lights or electricity?

"Where do you think this tunnel leads?" I asked. "The control room perhaps?"

"It's a possibility, but the farther we walk, the less likely that's where it leads," Cross answered.

We would soon learn he was right. The grading in the tunnel angled downward.

"I think it's safe to say we're no longer under the silo and are heading down the mountain." Cross said. He stopped and turned to face us. "Shall we continue or turn around?"

"Let's continue," I said. Kang nodded his agreement.

The grade of the tunnel got a little steeper but not overtly. There were a couple of switchbacks to minimize the steepness.

"Gordon, any idea what this tunnel might have been used for?"

He drew a heavy breath. "Well, considering we've passed no doorways, and the grade is extremely manageable, and the footing is smooth... I'm thinking it was used for transport."

"A missile wouldn't fit in here," Kang said.

"No it wouldn't, but it could be used to covertly transport smaller items from the bottom of the hill to the top."

We continued walking for another thirty minutes or so. It seemed like the tunnel went on forever. We could have literally been walking around in a circle and not known it.

"The grade is starting to level out. We might be nearing the bottom of the mountain," Cross said.

"I wonder what side of the mountain we're on," I said.

Cross slowed as he reached into his pants pocket and removed a compass.

"Right now we're heading west, but that doesn't mean we were heading west the entire time," he said.

We pushed on for another ten minutes or so, until Cross stopped abruptly. "The end is upon us," he said.

"What?" A chill tingled throughout my body.

Cross stepped over to the side of the tunnel so we could see ahead of him. The beam from his flashlight circled around a metal door.

"It doesn't look locked either," he added.

He moved forward, grabbed hold of the door handle, and pulled. The door jerked to a stop.

"My mistake. Looks like the door is secured from the other side."

"That's odd," I said. "All the other doors up until now were locked from our side."

"The other side of this door might be a public area, which could explain why it's locked from the other side."

I pulled out my cell phone. The signal was weak, but I had one. "Let's see what Google Maps tells us."

I opened the app, and after a beat or two, the GPS locator positioned us on the west side of the mountain. Cross was right. "We're clearly off the mountain." I showed the other two the map. I switched it to satellite view, but the signal wasn't strong enough to pull up imagery, so I switched it back to terrain.

"That's the UCSF Hospital right there." Cross pointed to blocks of gray. "We're to the southwest of it. Looks like we're right next to another building, but I don't know what it is."

"I do," Kang piped up. "That's Cerberus Fertility. We're practically right under it."

CHAPTER SEVENTY-TWO

We hurried as fast as we could back through the tunnel. If what I had presented to Reilly earlier wasn't enough to convince him, surely a secret tunnel leading from the clinic to the silo would seal the deal. My bet was that Barnes had been abducted, taken to the clinic, and transported via the tunnel to be released at the silo. And if I was right, our visit earlier in the day would have set off alarm bells.

"They're probably scrambling to cover up," Kang said as he jog-walked ahead of me.

"Exactly. We need to hit that clinic as soon as possible. I also want CSI combing every inch of this tunnel. I'm betting they'll find Barnes's DNA."

Back outside the silo and with stronger cell-phone service, I put a call in to Reilly and told him what we had just discovered.

"We need extra manpower to secure the tunnel and the area around the silo. And I want CSI up here to start their investigation."

The cleanliness at the entrance to the silo now made complete sense. We hadn't air it out on our last visit. Someone had cleaned up.

"You think that's a good idea?" Reilly asked. "They already think we're on to them."

"We're far enough from the clinic that they won't know, and if for some reason they do open that door at the end of the tunnel, then we'll move in. Once the silo is locked down, I think Kyle and I should sit on the clinic. If they are spooked and covering their trail, they'll most likely make a move after hours."

"That sounds like a game plan," Reilly responded. "Once the search warrant is issued, we'll send in the cavalry."

Nadia's jaw had a slight cramp from all the smiling she had done that night, especially after her performance, when it had seemed like everyone in attendance wanted to tell her how much they'd enjoyed it. Of course, she truly was appreciative of their comments, and she loved meeting her fans, but her day had started at five in the morning. The only thing she wanted to see was a bed.

As she rode the elevator to her floor, she thought briefly about taking a shower before bed. She would feel refreshed as she climbed under the covers, but she was so drained; it came across as a daunting task.

She chose the bed. Closing the door to the suite behind her, she left the lights off. Sheer curtains allowed enough moonlight to seep in through the terrace doors.

She kicked off her shoes at the doorway. Flowers from her hair fell to the floor as she crossed the large sitting area. She slipped her gown off her slender frame at the entrance to the suite's bedroom and placed the earrings, choker, and bracelet at the bedside table. Standing in only a pair of white lace panties, she placed a knee on the edge of the bed, pausing briefly.

I should at least wash off my makeup.

Nadia made her way over to the *en suite* bathroom and flicked on the light switch. She stood in front of the double washbasin and stared at herself in the mirror for a moment before turning the chrome faucet handle. She had just begun to splash water over her face when she heard the doorbell. She stopped, thinking she might have imagined it, but it rang again.

Bloody hell.

Nadia grabbed a robe hanging from a hook and pulled it around her, fastening the sash. The knocking continued as she made her way to the door. She peered through the peephole and saw a hotel employee standing outside.

He stood there with a pleasant smile on his face. Off to the side of him she could see a cart with white linen covering it. On top was a sterling silver, dome-shaped cloche with intricate engravings. There was also a champagne bucket, with a bottle protruding from it, and two glass flutes.

"Yes? What is it?" she asked while watching the man through the peephole.

"Sorry to disturb you, Miss Ulrich, but I have been instructed to bring you a midnight snack consisting of chocolate-covered strawberries and champagne."

"I appreciate the gesture, but I'm not hungry."

"I understand but... could I ask a favor?" At this point, he stared directly at the peephole, moving his head forward a bit. For a second, Nadia thought he could see her, but she knew that was ridiculous.

"What is it?"

"My supervisor insisted that I bring this to you. Could I please just bring the cart inside and leave it? I'll be back in the morning to pick it up."

If this will end the conversation and let me be, I'm all for it.

Nadia pushed the door handle down and pulled the door back. Only then did she notice the second hotel employee.

Before she could even consider why two people were needed to push a small cart, the man she had been speaking to rolled the cart through her door and into the suite. The other man stood in the doorway.

"Thank you so much, Miss Ulrich, for understanding our predicament." He set the brakes on the wheels of the cart.

"Do you always send two people to deliver food?"

Oh no," he said as he moved towards her. "Never."

CHAPTER SEVENTY-THREE

"At least their secret backdoor is secured," Kang said.

We parked our SUV a little ways down from the entrance to the clinic's property. It was nearing ten at night, and we hadn't seen any movement in the parking lot. The last employee had cleared out a little after seven.

With regard to the search warrant, things weren't looking very peachy. Reilly had received unexpected pushback from his supervisor, but he also told us he hadn't run out of options and still had some cards he could play.

"You'd think they'd want to get to the bottom of whatever this is," I said.

"Seems like it's turned political. A bunch of administrators are more worried about their precious careers than investigating federal crimes," Kang said.

"This is why I don't want any of their jobs. It clouds your judgment and turns you into a pansy."

Kang chuckled. "How are we doing on pizza?"

I reached behind to the rear seat and opened the pizza box. "There are two pieces left." I handed him one and took the other for myself.

I bit into the cold slice. The cheese had hardened, and the pepperoni had dried around the edges. "Still tasty," I said through a mouthful.

"My stomach will always have room for cold pizza," Kang said. "By the way, have you heard from Archer regarding... what's her name, the wife?"

"Connie Shi. I haven't heard a single word from him since that day. I think the whole family is in custody. I asked Ryan about Colin, and he said he'd stopped coming to school and the dojo. Lucy said she hasn't seen Hailey at school either."

"Rounded up and detained. I bet the kids had no idea."

"Most likely not."

"You think the wife knew?"

I pursed my lips and swished them from side to side as I thought about Kang's question. "I think she did. I think she was in on it. No way he was working alone."

"How does it make you feel? I mean, it seemed like you two really got along."

"It makes me angry. I feel betrayed. I opened up to this woman, talked about my family, even a little about my life back in Hong Kong. To find out she was only fishing for information... well, not only did it hurt, it made me feel a bit foolish."

"Why?"

"Because I got played. And in a major way. I usually can sniff out this sort of bullcrap. Something went awry with my internal antenna."

Kang waved it off. "That's not you. You're not trained in counter-surveillance measures."

"I know, but my gut never tingled at all. She had me completely fooled."

"It's what that woman is trained to do. She was tasked with developing you."

The speaker on the radio crackled. There were a couple of

agents stationed inside the tunnel on the other side of the locked door. We were using high-powered UHF two-way radios to communicate.

"Agent Ross here. It's still quiet on our end."

"How are you guys holding up?" I asked.

"We have sandwiches and water. We'll live."

"Can you hear anything on the other side of that door?"

"Not a thing."

It didn't take much to subdue Nadia. Min had clamped the chloroform rag around her face, and a few moments later, she slumped in his arms. Min removed a leather pouch from his pocket and unzipped it. Inside was a small vial of propofol and a disposable hypodermic syringe.

"Ready the cart," he said as he filled the syringe and then injected Nadia.

The food-service cart had a holding area for trays of food. Two magnetic doors were located on either end. Min loaded Nadia through one side while Glen pulled her through from the other side. It was a tight fit, but they managed to get the doors closed. Not long after the initial knock on the door, they were wheeling the cart back down the hall to the service elevator.

The elevator stopped on the ground floor and opened up into a service hallway with the kitchen at one end and the laundry room/housecleaning at the other end. The exit to the loading dock was straight ahead. They pushed the cart through double doors leading to the dock, where their box truck was waiting. The truck was backed up to the loading dock.

Min knocked on the roll-up door, and it slid halfway up, enough for Glen and the cart to slide underneath. Min then helped pull the door back down before getting into the cab of the truck and driving away. From start to finish, the whole process took no more than fifteen minutes—exactly as planned.

Min drove west on California, toward the Pacific Ocean. The quickest way back to the clinic would have been to turn left onto Masonic Avenue and make their way to 6th and Kirkham, where 6th Avenue turned into Locksley—the street where the clinic was located.

Min knocked on the back of the cab. The small sliding window opened, and Glen's face appeared.

"What is it, boss?"

"How is she?"

"Her vitals are fine, and we've started the process."

"All right, then. Keep moving."

The sliding window closed. The three men in the back would complete a full accounting of Nadia Ulrich. This included collecting hair, skin cells, blood, and saliva, and notating her weight, height, eye and hair color, as well as any noticeable moles, birthmarks, scars, and tattoos.

Min thought of checking in with Devlin but decided against it. Earlier he had pled with Devlin to reconsider attending the performance. It was too risky. The FBI had already spoken to him, and it would seem like more than a coincidence for him to attend a fundraiser where the night's entertainment went missing. Devlin had told Min that if he did his job correctly and kept Nadia no more than ten hours, they would have nothing to worry about. It would look as if she'd wandered off on her own.

Min drove along Irving Street. Coming up shortly was 6th Avenue. From there, the clinic was about half a mile away.

CHAPTER SEVENTY-FOUR

THANKS TO RED TAPE, Reilly wasn't able to prepare the affidavit and warrant until after midnight. Finding a judge to sign it at that time of night would be near impossible. We would have to wait until morning. Kang and I were in it for the long haul, though. We had already figured our surveillance duty would be an all-night affair. Plus, we took some comfort in knowing that we weren't the only ones working around the clock. There was an entire crew at the silo.

At about four in the morning, Leland Miles, the agent leading the forensic investigation, called.

"This is Kane."

"It's Miles."

"Tell me you found something connecting Barnes to the silo."

"Hate to burst your bubble, but so far we haven't found anything. In fact, we didn't find a single trace of DNA in the entranceway space, which made me curious. We should have found something—insect remains or rat droppings or something. What we did find were signs of a cleaning agent."

Miles had confirmed my earlier fears. Someone had cleaned the area.

"It's been wiped, hasn't it?"

"I think so. We're not having much luck with the missile chamber either, and we've gotten about a quarter of the way through the tunnel. I'm doubtful we'll find anything in here. If that tunnel was used to transport things or people from the clinic to the silo, they most likely were on some sort of hand-operated transport, possibly a pushcart or a hand truck or even a wheelbarrow. Odds of finding DNA in that amount of space will be hard. I know this isn't what you wanted to hear."

"It's not. I appreciate the update."

It felt like the pieces of the puzzle were slowly falling away from me. The high I had experienced that afternoon had been squashed into a black piece of nothingness.

"It's not looking good at the silo," I said to Kang.

"There's still the warrant, which we expect to be granted. We're not totally screwed."

A team of fifteen agents, including Kang, Reilly, and me, swooped down on Cerberus Fertility at exactly nine a.m. One by one, the employees were rounded up by agents and corralled into one of the many empty conference rooms. Other agents began the task of confiscating laptops, hard drives, servers, and anything else that might contain information that could help the investigation.

Kang and I headed straight for Devlin's office. We knocked but didn't wait for an answer before pushing the door open. The office was empty. No personal belongings, no briefcase, no cup of coffee, no sports coat. Nothing.

"Looks like he hasn't shown up for work yet," I said.

"Or he's decided not to come in," Kang added.

We made our way back to the area where the staff was being held.

"I'm Agent Kane. I'm looking for Mr. Devlin. Does anybody know where he is?" I asked the group.

The employees turned to each other and whispered amongst themselves.

"Somebody here must know. Does he arrive early, late, or whenever he chooses?"

A woman meekly raised her hand. I recognized her as the young lady at reception.

"Mr. Devlin comes in every day, usually before the start of business hours."

"You're positive of this?"

She nodded. "He always checks in with me."

"Would you mind following me?" I led her down a hallway, away from everyone.

"What's your name?"

"Claudette Lyons." Her voice shook as she folded her arms across her chest, hugging herself. "I remember you two from the other day. Am I in trouble?"

"No you're not, Miss Lyons. I just want to ask you a few questions. That's all."

She looked very young, no more than twenty-five years of age. She was wearing a lavender, long-sleeved blouse and a form-fitting black skirt that came down to just below her knees. Her chocolate-brown hair matched her big doe eyes.

"How long have you been working here?"

"About a year."

"Do you know everyone who works here?"

"Yes, it's part of my job. I know where everyone sits and what their duties are as well. Mr. Devlin wanted me to know all of that."

"Did you report to Mr. Devlin directly?"

"No, well, I mean, I guess everyone here reports to him. I have a direct supervisor, but I think Mr. Devlin took a liking to me and would call me personally whenever he needed something."

"You said earlier that he always checked in with you. Was that only when he arrived, or was it whenever he came *or* left?"

"It's more like I checked in with him in the mornings when I arrived. Because he was already here, like I said. I'd always call his office. He wanted me to. Today, he didn't answer. I can count the number of times I've arrived before him on one hand."

"So Mr. Devlin doesn't have a designated assistant?"

"No, but Min is his second in command. They're always together."

"Is Min his first name or last name?"

"Uh, I don't know. He's just Min. That's what we all call him."

"Can you point him out in that room?"

"He's not there."

"Do you have the same check-in routine with him that you have with Mr. Devlin?"

"No."

"Can you take us to Min's office?"

Claudette nodded.

A few minutes later, Kang, Claudette, and I were standing in an empty office. It seemed Min had skipped work that day as well.

CHAPTER SEVENTY-FIVE

REILLY IMMEDIATELY DISPATCHED two teams—one to Devlin's home, the other to Min's—but we were too late. The agents reported back that both places looked as if the occupants had left in a mad rush: empty drawers in the bedrooms along with missing toiletries. Both had home offices, and it appeared as if both men had rummaged through items in and on their desks, leaving a mess. The agents said they would know more after a thorough search.

"It appears your initial visit to the clinic spooked them," Reilly said.

We were standing in Devlin's office. I had wanted to search it personally, and I had. Kang had taken the task of searching Min's office.

"Clearly. How could we have known?"

"You couldn't have. But we've uncovered something big here. What exactly, I'm not sure." He rested his hands on his waist.

Just then Reilly's radio crackled, and a voice spoke. "We've found a door that's locked. It's different from all the other office doors. It's reinforced."

My eyes popped wide. "I wonder if that's the door that connects to the tunnel."

I texted Kang and told him to meet us where the employees were being held. When he arrived I asked Claudette to escort us to the locked door.

"Are you aware of this room?" I asked her as we walked hurriedly down a corridor.

"I am. As far as I know, it's just used for storage. No one ever goes in there."

Claudette led us to the rear of the building. The door was located on the first floor. It was painted the same off-white color as the walls outside, but the texture of brushed steel was clearly visible beneath the paint. I rapped my knuckles against it. It made a low, dense sound.

Another agent arrived with a bag of tools. He removed a battery-powered drill, inserted a bit, and placed the tip against the keyhole to the deadbolt and started drilling. When he finished, he pushed the door open.

Reilly found the light switch and flicked it on, revealing a room with overhead surgical lights, a multi-functional operating chair/bed, a vital-signs monitor, respiratory ventilators, defibrillators, and even an anesthesia machine. It was a fully equipped examination room.

I turned to Claudette. "Did you know this had been turned into an examination room?"

"I had no idea. Like I said earlier, as far as everyone here knew, it was just an old storage room. No one ever paid it any attention."

"What the hell are these two up to?" I asked no one in particular.

"Good question," Reilly answered.

"There's a door there." Kang pointed to the other side of the room.

It wasn't reinforced, but it was secured with a padlock. A quick snip with the bolt cutter, and we had access. On the other side, we found two agents, sweaty and tired.

"It's about time," one of them said as they both stepped through the doorway.

CHAPTER SEVENTY-SIX

WE HAD TWO SUSPECTS: Sid Devlin and Min. We were pretty sure they were responsible for the abductions. What was missing, besides them? Motive. What was it about Geoffrey Barnes, Johnny Ellis, Lyle Hammond, and Evaristo Damiani that had led to their abductions? And what could Devlin and Min have done with them in such a short time?

"Maybe they're tracking them," Reilly suggested. "They bring them here, insert some sort of tracking device inside them, and then cut them loose."

"Most likely it's something that's embedded under the skin, through a minimally invasive procedure," Kang said.

"All right, let's send some people out to them to conduct a thorough physical examination," Reilly said.

I was still mulling over Reilly's tracking-device theory when I received a call on my cell phone. It was Detective Sokolov.

Strange. He normally contacts Kyle.

I answered, "Agent Kane."

"Hi, Abby. It's Pete. Can you and Kyle come to the Mark Hopkins Hotel now?"

"What's this regarding?"

"Your abductions. I think I've come across another one."

———————

At the hotel, we were directed upstairs to one of the suites. Inside we found Sokolov and his partner Bennie.

"Thanks for coming," Sokolov said, ignoring the bruising on my face. He'd seen me like this before.

"No problem. So, what happened here?"

He quickly brought us up to speed on the missing person, Nadia Ulrich. "A hotel driver should have driven her to the airport this morning, but she never showed up in the lobby."

"So she didn't use the hotel's transportation to the airport. How did you go from this to 'abduction'?" I asked.

"She's a VIP guest. The manager started asking staff if they had seen Miss Ulrich leave the premises. That led him to looking at the security-camera footage on this floor. Two men posing as hotel employees showed up at Miss Ulrich's room with a room-service cart. They enter, and a few minutes later, they leave, *with* the cart. The manager is positive the two men are not employees of the hotel. That confirms abduction. We're here to determine if we're now looking for a body."

"So if it is an abduction, what makes you think it's connected to our investigation?"

"For starters, she's some famous cellist. Kyle, I think you mentioned that all the cases you'd flagged were people who stood out in their field of expertise."

"That's right," Kang said.

"The second thing is this. Bennie, show them the thing you found."

Detective Bennie held up a plastic bag. Inside was a circular piece of foil, about a quarter of the size of a dime.

"What is that?" I asked as I looked closer.

"It's the foil from a medicine vial. You tear it off the cap so you can insert a syringe."

"Are you sure?"

"My grandmother was diabetic. The vials that contained her insulin had aluminum caps with a tear-out center. I'm positive the lab will confirm it."

"Any chance she might be a diabetic?"

"Sure," Bennie said, "but all her belongings are still here, and we didn't find a diabetic kit or an insulin syringe anywhere. Probably be faster to have your guys analyze the foil."

Since we were sharing and cooperating, I told Sokolov and Bennie what we had discovered that morning.

"They built a secret tunnel from the clinic to a military silo? You're kidding, right?" Bennie asked.

"We still need to confirm that the tunnel wasn't military, but from what our guys are saying, the tunnel, the doors... it doesn't look like it's more than five years old. That silo was built more than sixty years ago and decommissioned fifteen years later."

"Did you guys look at the security footage?" I asked.

"We're about to."

The four of us were in the hotel security office, looking at the footage of the two men arriving at, entering, and then leaving Ulrich's room.

"Any of them look like your guy?" Sokolov asked.

I shook my head. "Devlin has a beard. One of them could be Min. We never met him so we can't confirm."

"I have a picture of Devlin," Kane said. "I downloaded it from the website. I'll text it to you just in case."

Do the security cameras pick them up elsewhere?" I asked.

We waited while he searched the video feeds. He found the two men on the loading dock. They were pushing the room-service cart it into the back of a white utility truck with a sign painted on the side: Young's Laundry. Unfortunately, the angle of the camera didn't show the license plate.

Kang did a quick Google search for Young's Laundry. "I'm not finding any business named Young's Laundry."

"Could be a fake," Sokolov said.

"I'll get an APB issued for this vehicle," Bennie said as he dialed a number on his cell phone and exited the office.

"Could you email me a digital copy of the footage?" I asked the head of security. I placed my business card on the desk.

"If Devlin and Min are behind this, they should have brought Ulrich back to the clinic, no?" Sokolov asked.

"We might have spooked them with our earlier visit," I said. "Probably took her to some other location."

"Pretty ballsy of them to abduct this lady, knowing the FBI was already looking at them," Sokolov said. "Maybe they're not that bright."

"Or they think they're smarter than we are," I said.

CHAPTER SEVENTY-SEVEN

WE PARTED with Sokolov and Bennie and headed back to the clinic. They said they would call us if they found Ulrich. If Devlin and Min had abducted her, then we expected her to pop up sometime soon, if she hadn't already. The problem? She wouldn't immediately know where she was or who she was.

We met up with Reilly in the secret examination room. He had been exploring the tunnel and had just returned to the room.

"Abby, Kyle, what did SFPD find?" he asked. He had taken his jacket off, and the sleeves of his dress shirt were cuffed up to his elbows. There was a little wetness on his brow.

"Another person was abducted last night," I said.

We filled Reilly in with the details and showed him the footage of the two men who had entered Ulrich's room. He agreed that it smelled of Devlin and Min.

"They were on to us." Reilly removed his glasses and patted his face with a handkerchief he kept in his pocket. "This place has been cleaned. Forensics is having a hard time finding any evidence to support our claims. Right now, everything we have is circumstantial."

"I want to show this footage to Claudette and see if she can identify these men."

Just then Kang received a call. "You did? Where? Okay, email me that footage." He disconnected the call. "That was Sokolov. They have footage of Devlin at the fundraiser."

"So he attends the fundraiser, probably to keep an eye on Ulrich, and then later, he and Min abduct her from the room."

"You two work on finding Devlin and Min," Reilly said. "I'll stay and oversee the investigation here."

We didn't argue and did an about-face in the examination room. I was eager to see if Claudette—or any of the other employees—recognized the men in the video. Back inside the conference room, we showed the footage to Claudette. She didn't know who the men were. Thus began the painstaking process of showing the footage individually to every person. We got lucky with the tenth person.

"Are you sure this is Min?" I asked. "Take a closer look."

"I don't need to. I know it's him. He dressed this way for a Halloween party I threw - fake mustache, goatee, sideburns. Looked exactly like this."

We had placed both Devlin and Min at the hotel. We needed to find them. Claudette was able to dig up a photo of Min without the disguise. Kang updated Sokolov and texted him the picture. They hadn't found Ulrich yet, but they had issued an APB for her as well.

"It's a matter of time with the truck, unless they dumped it someplace desolate," Kang said.

"While we wait for the truck or Ulrich to show up, let's take a look at Devlin's residence."

Devlin lived in a luxury high-rise in SOMA, south of Market Street. When we arrived, the evidence response team was still conducting their investigation. Agent Oliver Barber, the lead forensic examiner at the scene, met us.

"Agent Kane, Agent Kang. Glad you could stop by. Rough week?" he asked, glancing at my face.

"Long story," I said. "What do you have for us?"

"We found DNA that belongs to a male. It matches the DNA found in Devlin's office. Aside from that, there's nothing in here to identify Devlin. No pictures, no passport or driver's license, no utility bills or paperwork of any kind. It's very strange. We also found two sets of fingerprints. One set belonged to Sheila Davis—she has a couple of priors; misdemeanor drug possession. Her driver's license expired four years ago, and she's no longer associated with her last-known address. The other prints we found we assume belong to Devlin, but somehow he's managed to keep his fingerprints out of any type of government database. Security-cam footage shows him leaving the building yesterday, late afternoon, dressed in a black suit. He never returned. Cerberus Fertility is listed as the owner of this penthouse; I'm assuming Cerberus also pays the utility bills."

"Interesting," Kang said.

"No, it's not. I've got some art that will 'wow' you."

Barber led us through the apartment. Paintings and photographs in frames hung on the walls. There were vases and sculptures on their own stands, but he didn't say anything about these pieces as we passed. I had to wonder what art he was talking about.

We entered a room where the artwork on the wall took a strange turn. Replacing the paintings and photographs were a collection of wood-framed shadowboxes. Inside the glass-encased structures were cut-away scenes of different dwellings, like a diorama. The one nearest to me and Kang depicted life inside a ranch-style home, but instead of miniature human beings, there were bugs cooking, watching television, taking a shower, and so forth. Barber came up behind us.

"Pretty creepy stuff, huh?"

"Yeah, but I'm not seeing the connection to the investigation," I said, unable to tear my gaze away from the little slice of bug life.

"That's not the artwork I'm talking about. One of my guys found a false panel in the wall behind this painting." Barber pulled on the large, gold frame with his latex-covered hand. It opened, revealing a wall safe behind it. "Took us a while to crack the lock. I took a peek inside but left the contents alone once I heard you two were on your way over." He reached inside, removed a large picture album, and set it down on a nearby tabletop. "Are you ready?"

Barber lifted the leather-bound album, and the first page revealed a stark photograph of a woman, bright lights illuminating her face. She was squinting, and her mouth hung half open. Her chin was tucked back and off to the side, as if she were trying to avoid having her photograph taken. Enough of her chest showed to lead me to believe she wasn't wearing a top and might have been completely nude.

He turned the page. The next portrait had been taken under the same conditions. The strained expression captured on the subject's face projected fear, or it could have been pain. I couldn't quite tell. But there was one thing I was sure of: the man in the picture was Lyle Hammond, the abducted brain surgeon. Two pages later, a photograph of Geoffrey Barnes appeared, followed by Johnny Ellis.

I couldn't believe it. Devlin prized his abductions and kept them as pieces of artwork. Opposite each page was a dossier of the person in the photo. It included their name, sex, age, height, weight, noted birthmarks, scars, or tattoos on their body, and their profession. It was a biometric résumé of the person. Oliver continued to flip through the album. Kang and I remained quiet, as victim after victim appeared. The very last picture was of Evaristo Damiani, the angel investor.

Kang and I hadn't even scratched the surface. In all, there were twenty individuals abducted by Devlin and Min. And even then, we couldn't be sure if there were more. Had Min also kept a photo album showcasing their work?

Barber waited until Kang finished snapping photos of each victim and their information before bagging the album as evidence. I asked if there was more to show us. Luckily, there wasn't. I didn't think my brain could take another twisted layer to our investigation.

Helping the CIA to find out what Xiaolian knew had led us to a serial kidnapper operating under the guise of a fertility clinic. And the kicker? I was no closer to figuring out any more about Xiaolian.

CHAPTER SEVENTY-EIGHT

I t had been two days since we'd hit the fertility clinic, and CSI was still on site processing the clinic, tunnel, and silo. Sadly, it wasn't yielding the results we had hoped for. Devlin had been extremely careful and orchestrated a thorough clean up.

We faced the same problem with Min that we had with Devlin. Nothing in his apartment identified him. It made me realize the amount of preparation and planning that had gone into their operation. They had laid the foundation way before the creation of Cerberus Fertility.

We had agents from forensic accounting combing every file in the clinic, looking for any type of money trail, and so far, they were coming up empty. Devlin actually ran the clinic as a business and not a shell company to hide behind. Everything about the place appeared legit. There was nothing fishy about the financial health of the company; they even turned a profit. All required operating licenses and regulations were up to date. The employees were legal and, as far as we could tell, actually did the jobs they were hired for. Cerberus even had a steady stream of customers. They really did help couples get pregnant. Had Devlin created Cerberus to hide the abductions, or had it simply been a convenient place to run his sick operation?

That part of the investigation wasn't amounting to much, but we had our smoking gun: the photo album we'd found at Devlin's penthouse.

Now we needed to find Devlin and Min, who had shot to number-one status on the FBI's most-wanted list. If they hadn't already exited the country, it would now be extremely hard to do. Their pictures would hang in federal buildings, courthouses, and post offices. They could run, but the Bureau would never stop looking.

SFPD found Nadia Ulrich inside Golden Gate Park a few hours after we had met with Sokolov at the hotel. She was delirious and wearing nothing but a hospital gown. Kang questioned her, but we already knew there wouldn't be anything new to gain. We had already cracked open the case.

In the meantime, the investigation into the kidnappings would remain open but inactive. Reilly wanted us to focus our attention elsewhere, on other cases. I really think he wanted to put the whole business of Xiaolian behind us.

We were at the office, sitting at our desks. Kang was busy typing up his report, and I was staring at a piece of paper. In the very center, I had written Xiaolian's name.

She was still a mystery to me. Investigating her had allowed us to break up a human-trafficking and prostitution ring, as well as a scheme to abduct people. I could see her leading us to one, but two? How often does that happen? What are the odds?

I tapped the pencil next to her name. *What is your role? Victim? Spy? Mastermind? Coincidence?*

Above her name, at the twelve o'clock position, I wrote down *Oyster Crew*, the gang that originally smuggled Xiaolian into the country.

Between the twelve and three o'clock positions, I wrote down *Chan brothers*.

At the three o'clock position, I wrote down *Dr. Jian Lee*.

Between the three and six o'clock positions, I wrote down *Three-Parenting*.

At the six o'clock position, I wrote down *Xiaolian's home/Sports school*.

Between the six and nine o'clock positions, I wrote *The Shis*.

At the nine o'clock position, I wrote down *Cerberus Fertility*.

I studied the clock diagram, looking at the connections. I knew Oyster was connected to Xiaolian, as they had smuggled her into the country. I drew a double-headed arrow connecting the two.

I knew the Chan brothers were connected to Xiaolian because they had tried to kill her. I drew a double-headed arrow connecting the two. Oyster was connected to the Chan brothers because Darren and his crew had also been on the hit list. I drew another arrow.

Xiaolian and I shared DNA so she was connected to three-parenting technology .

Dr. Lee had taken Xiaolian from my home to protect her. That connected them. According to Xiaolian, he was aware of my DNA connection with her. That connected him to three-parenting. The place where Xiaolian said she was from was also the place Dr. Lee was from. The three were all connected.

The Shis had been after Xiaolian. They were connected to her. I assumed they might know where she was from or were working for the people responsible for her, so I connected the Shis to the school.

I stared at the diagram. Everything appeared to be connected in some way. The only loose end was Cerberus Fertility. Was there a connection, or was it just a coincidence that we had stumbled across what was happening there? Could Cerberus be connected to Xiaolian? Are they connected to any of the others on the diagram? Those were questions in need of an answer. I continued to doodle.

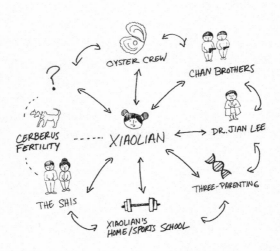

As I stared at the empty space between the nine and twelve o'clock positions, I wondered if there was something else we hadn't discovered. Was there another piece to the puzzle? Should there be?

"What are you working on?" Kang asked. He leaned forward and peered at the piece of paper.

"Connections," I said.

CHAPTER SEVENTY-NINE

TIME IS THE GREAT EQUALIZER. It can bring people and events together, and it can move them apart. In my case, it created distance.

With each passing day, I wondered a little less about Xiaolian and how she was faring at the facility, whether Archer was being nice to her or not. Had she been deported yet? If not, would she ever be? I know it sounds heartless, but I'm being honest. With family life filling my time at home and other investigations occupying my time at the office, there was little room left in my life for Xiaolian.

I never heard from Archer regarding Connie and her children. In fact, the Shis had disappeared from our lives as quickly as they had entered. Ryan and Lucy didn't dwell on it. The BBQs with the Shis had become a distant memory.

I also never spoke to Po Po again about the incident upstairs. She never raised it either. We were meant to move on. Easier said than done for someone like me. I liked resolution, but I wasn't getting answers about Xiaolian, and I needed to accept it.

It was Saturday, almost two weeks after our raid on Cerberus Fertility. Ryan was at the dojo. Lucy was at a friend's house. Po Po was at a luncheon with her friends. And I was home by myself with a bunch of free time and nothing to do.

There was nothing I wanted to watch on television, and there wasn't much to tidy around the house. I settled for cleaning my service weapon. When I finished, I thought about doing yardwork, but Kang was coming over the next day, and he, for some reason, loved taking care of the lawn. Maybe it was because his place didn't have one or that he was a guy.

I sat outside on the front porch. As far as I could see, the sky was blue. The bright sun magnified the greenness of my front yard and the surrounding hedges and trees. With each inhale, the smell of summer filled my nostrils.

I couldn't be sure how long I stared aimlessly at the house across the street from me, but suddenly I noticed a short man standing on the sidewalk in front of my home.

He was wearing slacks, a gray sport coat, and black fedora. His right hand was holding a cane, and he had a leather shoulder bag strapped across his chest. I thought he might be lost, but he started walking along the sidewalk again. Short steps, almost like a shuffle.

Probably had to take a breather.

I leaned back in my chair and kicked my legs out, forgetting him already, but he turned into my driveway and slowly made his way toward me.

I wonder if this is one of Po Po's friends.

He stopped at the foot of my porch. "Abby Kane?" He had a soft, calm voice.

I sat up. "Yes. How can I help you?"

"May I?" He motioned with his cane that he wanted to come up onto the porch.

I nodded, and he climbed the stairs. He was much older than I had originally thought, and he was Chinese. He wore glasses with black frames and had bushy eyebrows. Sunspots marked both of his droopy cheeks. He removed his hat, revealing thinning black hair with tufts of white behind each temple.

"I hope I'm not bothering you," he said.

"You're not. Do I know you?"

He glanced back toward the street for a moment, and then checked the time on a pocket watch he carried inside his jacket. "Do you mind if we talk inside?"

My curiosity got the better of me. "Sure. Would you like a cup of tea?" I asked as I stood.

We sat in the sitting room, a low table between us and tea in hand. I took a sip of mine. He took a sip of his.

"I've been wanting to meet you for a very long time." He placed his mug down on the table. "My name is Dr. Fan Wei. I'm sure you already have many questions about who I am and why I know you. The answers will come in due time."

Wei leaned back into his chair and crossed a leg over the other. He scratched at his chin for a moment or two. "I have thought a lot about this moment, but I've never thought how I would start the conversation." He chuckled.

"Why don't you start with what brought you here today?"

He nodded. "Xiaolian brought me here. I'm the one who sent her to you."

It felt as if his words had slammed into my chest. Just when I thought I had put her behind me and had hushed the nagging voice inside me, the answer to every question I might have ever had about her was sitting across from me.

"Why?" I could barely uttered the word.

"I needed your help. I thought I had the best chance if you knew Xiaolian existed."

"I don't understand what you're saying. I mean, I know she shares DNA with me, and that's why we look the same. It's a technique called three-parenting."

"It's a remarkable technology. I first started experimenting with it in the fifties. Back then, it was only a fantasy I had. But as I continued to tinker, I made progress. I began to see the potential of what my work could lead to."

"You mean cloning people?"

"It's much more than that. A clone is an oddity... a spectacle to gaze at. A circus sideshow. What I wanted to do was take the good within one person and pass it along to another."

I crinkled my brow. "So someone thought giving Xiaolian my looks was a good thing? Did you steal my DNA?"

He shook his head. "I stopped my work long before that, but my partner... he continued with it, against my wishes. I had destroyed my files and forbade him from using any of my findings. But he must have made copies of everything."

"So someone who worked with you stole your research?"

"I'm afraid so. For that, I apologize. After discovering that he was continuing with my work and my ideas, I kept tabs on him, through people loyal to me who were working with him."

"I see. Let's backtrack just a bit to what you said earlier, about taking the good from one person and giving it to another. What did you mean by that?"

"I will try to explain this in a way that is very easy to understand. Michael Jordan is an excellent basketball player. If I were to create a clone of him, and that clone could play basketball just as well as the original Michael, and I put him on my team, do you think people would accept him or reject him?"

"They would reject him."

"You're right, because while everything about him is the same, he's not the original. I wouldn't have an all-star team, nor would I win the NBA championship. I would instead be called a fraud, and laughed out of every basketball arena. But if I could replicate certain traits in Michael Jordan, like his athletic ability, his drive and determination, and put that into another person, I might be able to create a person who plays exactly like Michael but isn't Michael."

"You would have a Michael Jordan without anyone knowing you have one," I said.

Wei nodded.

"So this is the work you were developing but stopped?"

"It is, and the reason I stopped is because I started to see what people really wanted to use my work for."

"They wanted to create an all-star team of all the best players in the NBA and become filthy rich?" I arched an eyebrow.

"Not quite, but you're close. Taking the most talented people you can find and recruiting them to play on your team or work for your company or government is something we do on a daily basis. But my work had the potential to eliminate the wooing. There would be no need to coax or chase; we could simply create."

"I understand what you're saying, but I'm still unsure of where I came into play. I'm no Michael Jordan."

"No, but you are one of the best in your field of work. There are certain traits you have that predispose you to being an excellent detective. Your ability to solve problems is well above average. You're a quick learner, and you have gut feelings that I'm guessing are almost never wrong. You would be an asset to any law-enforcement organization."

"Okay, I'll play along. Say I'm all that. I see your point—more of me means solving more crimes, possibly faster, maybe even preventing them."

"Abby, imagine if someone knew what you were capable of, what you would come to accomplish, and from the age of two, trained you to improve upon those very skills. Do you know how advanced a crime fighter you would be at the age you are now?"

I took that in and then said, "This is the father who trains his son to grow up to be an amazing golfer by putting a club in his hands before he can even speak. Taking him to the course before he can ride a bike, and entering him in competitions instead of taking him camping."

"That's right, except in your example, there is no guarantee the child has a disposition to be a great golfer. We know from what you've become that you did."

"So I was a good bet."

"A guarantee."

Geoffrey Barnes, Johnny Ellis, Evaristo Damiani, Lyle Hammond, and Nadia Ulrich were all proven talents in what they did, some of the best. I could see why someone would want a *version* of them who wasn't *exactly* them.

"Excuse me. I'll be right back." I hurried up the stairs to my office and retrieved the piece of paper where I had listed Xiaolian's many connections.

When I returned, I placed the piece of paper in front of Wei. I didn't say a word. I just let him stare at it. I wanted to see his take on it. He took a pen from his jacket. In the empty spot between nine and twelve o'clock, he wrote his name. He then drew an arrow between him and Oyster, and him and Cerberus, and him and Xiaolian. He had completed the circle.

"You know all about this?"

"More or less. Does this all make sense to you now?"

"I see the whole puzzle. Where I'm still confused is... Why all of this for Xiaolian?"

"It's not just for her. I needed you to see her with your own eyes. Nobody else would have come up with this diagram. Oyster would still be in business, and so would Cerberus Fertility. The Chan brothers would still have been sent to kill Xiaolian. They would have succeeded, thus preventing the Shis from being activated. Dr. Lee would most likely have lived. And my version of three parenting, and the use to which it is now being put, would have remained a secret."

Hearing Wei talk about fate was surreal. Would it have happened that way had he sent Xiaolian to some other person? Would all those innocent people, that the Chan brothers killed, still be alive?

"Is this about revenge? Are you angry that someone stole your work and is now reaping the benefits?"

"I'm afraid you are still confused. Let me show you something."

Wei dug into his shoulder bag and removed a tablet. He tapped at the screen. "Watch carefully," he said.

There was a video playing. It showed a room with a small, round table and a chair accompanying it. The camera filming was set up a few feet away. It looked like an interview might take place. I heard a voice off-camera say they were ready. A few seconds later, a young boy, probably ten years old, walked into the frame. He wore navy-blue shorts and a white, short-sleeved dress shirt tucked neatly inside the shorts. He wore black shoes with white socks. It looked like a school uniform. He sat in the chair and stared directly into the camera without uttering a single word.

The camera zoomed in so that the boy filled the frame, giving me a better look at his face.

I couldn't believe what I was looking at.

Wei cleared his throat. "The DNA for this boy was taken from a man who worked as a foreign intelligence officer for the KGB."

I paused the video just as the boy looked at the camera dead on. I studied his features. He had sandy-blond hair parted on the left side of his head; the edges just barely scraped the top of his right eye. His eyes were light blue and almond shaped, with the eyelids drooping toward the outer edges, as if he were a bit tired. His eye shape signified to me that he was mixed: Chinese/Caucasian. I studied his features for a little longer until I was convinced that I knew who this boy was, or at least where he had come from.

I looked up at Wei in utter disbelief. "Is his name Vladimir?"

CHAPTER EIGHTY

"How?" I asked.

"Vladimir Putin's DNA was taken while he was on assignment in China. He was a young man back then, early in his career, but even then he showed the intellect, the cunning, and the drive to become who he is today. Planning started a long time ago. The program is close to realizing its full potential."

"And what is that? To create your own versions of others?"

"Imagine a China where its citizens, in every professional field, from law enforcement to biochemistry to strategic military planning to government, are all created from the very best the world has to offer. Imagine a China that's creating a society of intellects simply by cherry-picking them from other countries without them knowing. The genius is taking these individuals and recreating them as Chinese citizens. Remember the Michael Jordan analogy?"

"But he looks like Vladimir... well, a Chinese version."

"Yes, well, he's not perfect, and I don't think they care if there are similarities in looks. From what I can tell, every person born of the program resembled the individual they were modeled after. Hand-selected Chinese couples are merely hosts —incubators, if you will—so that the end result is a Chinese version of whoever was recreated."

"But why? Is this about money?"

"The United States has always been the leader of the world. Not a single country could successfully stand up to them. For a long time, China has been a hibernating bear, but it is awakening. It started first by educating its citizens, and then it focused on building a powerful military. Infrastructure was next, then diplomacy, and the ability to develop their own allies and influence other countries by investing in them. You see, the leader of the world will not be the leader because of its military might, a position that the US holds. Warfare with tanks, missiles, troops... that's all a thing of the past. It's ancient. Warfare now is fought through the minds of the people. You can bring down a government by bombing it, or you can bring it down by turning the people against it. This is already being done. The power that social media holds, its ability to spread propaganda and influence the thinking of millions, is already upon us. Russia has had great success with technological warfare, hacking especially. Information is the new bomb. It's much more powerful than any nuclear warhead. It can create chaos, bring about an uprising, and even paralyze a government. Terrorist groups like ISIS have successfully used social media and messaging apps to mobilize their people to fight their war. What China wants to add to their arsenal, on top of everything they have learned from the strategic warfare of Russia and terrorist groups, are the best minds in the world working for them, holding allegiance to them, and ultimately doing whatever is asked of them."

"Is this what they think they will achieve by stealing DNA?"

"It's not what they think. They've already begun. Their

collection of DNA started long ago and is so extensive that they're now lowering the bar. All they needed was the technology of three-parenting to catch up. And they have. There are many others like Xiaolian and Vladimir. I was told they have a ten-year-old Steve Jobs and that he's pinned ideas to the wall that even the late Steve Jobs had not thought of."

I shook my head in disbelief. "This is a wallop to swallow."

"I'll admit it certainly comes across as science fiction, but that's why I needed you to see Xiaolian firsthand, with your own eyes, and experience what she is capable of. I know you saw more of yourself in her than you're letting on. It probably scared you, but you were the right choice. This I believe. If I were to send Vladimir to the real Vladimir, he would either kill the boy or try to figure out the technology that created him. He is not someone you want to possess this ability. I needed someone with a moral compass that was pure. That person was you, Abby."

"Do you believe the Chinese government is actually capable of building an army of imposters?"

"They're not imposters. They're the real thing and will be ten times better because of the specific training they've received since they were born and are *continuing* to receive. The government already knows what they're capable of becoming; the goal is to multiply that ability tenfold, maybe more. Imagine that, and then ask yourself the question: do you really want to see if the Chinese government can pull this off?

"Three-parenting is a technique that scientists are already familiar with, but what they know is so pedestrian. Just last year, the first baby created by three parents was born. They're celebrating bringing a fetus to full term, and all they really did was edit out a rare genetic mutation that the mother had. As I've already shown you, the Chinese are way past that."

I leaned forward, allowing my face to fall into my hands.

"This is too much," I said with a muffled voice. I looked up at Wei. "What are you asking of me?"

"To help, to figure out a way to stop this. It won't be easy, but I didn't know who else I could turn to. I'm a wanted man in my country. Every contact I had who was involved with the program has either been killed or has disappeared. Those loyal to me, many who helped me get Xiaolian out of the country, are all dead. I had to do *something*. I couldn't live with myself if I didn't try."

Wei produced his pocket watch and then glanced over at the front window.

"Are you expecting someone?" I said.

"As a matter of fact, I am."

My hand gripped the arm of my chair as my body tensed.

"Relax." Wei motioned for me to remain seated. "I wasn't followed here. You are not in any danger."

"How can you be sure of that? The others found out Xiaolian was staying with me."

"Yes, I realize your predicament..."

Before Wei could finish speaking, a soft knock on the front door grabbed our attention.

"She's here," he said. "Why don't you answer the door?"

I shook my head as I stood. "It can't be..."

"I assure you, it can. Just look within yourself, and you'll see that I'm right."

I walked over to the door and pulled it open. My jaw fell slack. I simply stared, dumbfounded. Standing before me with that familiar smile was Xiaolian.

"Hello, Abby. There is much to discuss. Shall we get started?"

This concludes book two in the *Suitcase Girl* trilogy. In the third book, *The Hatchery*, Abby must come to grips with the Chinese government's plan to recreate the world's smartest and most talented individuals as Chinese citizens. Can Abby really stop them? Will Xiaolian help her?

Get your copy now.

A NOTE FROM TY HUTCHINSON

Thank you for reading THE CURATOR. If you're a fan of Abby, spread the word to friends, family, book clubs, and reader groups online. You can also help get the word out by leaving a review.

Visit my website to sign up for my Spam-Free Newsletter and receive "First Look" content, and information about future releases, promotions, and giveaways. I promise never to spam. I can't stand receiving it myself. With that said, I've made it really easy to unsubscribe at any time.

I love hearing from readers. Let's connect.
www.tyhutchinson.com
tyhutchinson@tyhutchinson.com

ALSO BY TY HUTCHINSON

Contract: Endgame

Mui Thrillers

A Book of Truths

A Book of Vengeance

A Book of Revelations

A Book of Villains

Mui Action Thrillers

The Monastery

The Blood Grove

The Minotaur

Darby Stansfield Thrillers

The Accidental Criminal

(previously titled Chop Suey)

The Russian Problem

(previously titled Stroganov)

Holiday With A P.I.

(previously titled Loco Moco)

Other Thrilling Reads

The Perfect Plan

The St. Petersburg Confession

Published by Ty Hutchinson

Cover Art: Damonza